To June,

The Gifted One

With a lot of love.

The Gifted One

Eva Fischer-Dixon

Copyright © 2017 by Eva Fischer-Dixon.

ISBN: Softcover   978-1-5245-8033-9
           eBook   978-1-5245-8032-2

All rights reserved. No part of this book may be reproduced or transmitted in any form or by any means, electronic or mechanical, including photocopying, recording, or by any information storage and retrieval system, without permission in writing from the copyright owner.

This is a work of fiction. Names, characters, places and incidents either are the product of the author's imagination or are used fictitiously, and any resemblance to any actual persons, living or dead, events, or locales is entirely coincidental.

Any people depicted in stock imagery provided by Thinkstock are models, and such images are being used for illustrative purposes only.
Certain stock imagery © Thinkstock.

Print information available on the last page.

Rev. date: 02/09/2017

To order additional copies of this book, contact:
Xlibris
1-888-795-4274
www.Xlibris.com
Orders@Xlibris.com
756708

Also available from Eva Fischer-Dixon:

The Third Cloud
A Song for Hannah (Previously titled: Hannah's Song)
For One Last Time (Previously titled: For the Last Time)
A Journey to Destiny (Previously titled: A Journey to Passion)
The Discovery
The Forbidden
Fata Morgana
"Eighteen"
The Chava Diamond Chronicles: The Shades of Love and Hate
The Bestseller
A Town by the River
Five 'til Midnight
Thy Neighbor's Wife
The Roma Chavi (The Gypsy Girl)
My First Son
By the Book
The Angie Chronicles: Six Summers & One Winter
The Angie Chronicles: Angie's Story
The Angie Chronicles: The Resurrection
Five Past Midnight
For Senior Officers Only (Prisoner # 170650)
The Price of the Game
What War May Bring
Dark Storm Rising
On the Midnight Train (My Journey to Freedom)
78 Spring Street (Tavasz Utca 78)
Before …

AUTHOR'S COMMENT

ON NIGHTS LIKE February 13, 1957, when my father, who was a guard at one of the largest pharmaceutical manufacturing companies in Europe, called Chinoin was at work, I slept in the large king size bed that my parents shared. Normally, because our apartment consisted of a small kitchen, a medium size bedroom/living room combination and a tiny pantry, when my father was also home, I slept on the sofa bed that stood by the foot of their bed.

On that particular night, around one o'clock in the morning something woke me. I turned away from my mother, toward the space between the wall and the shrunk (we did not have built in closets), I saw a vision, just as I described it in Maggie's vision in Chapter One. The only difference between what I had seen and what the character saw while she laid in coma was that the white man did not talk to me at all.

I began to scream and my mother turned on the light. I immediately told her what I was seeing; she assured me that I just had a nightmare. The only problem was that while she tried to convince me about the nightmare, even with the light on, I continued seeing the vision. It was still there. My mother, whose profession was registered nurse, checked my forehead but I did not have fever. It was obvious to her that something was upsetting me. She got out of the bed and walked around the bed and the sofa bed that was folded up and stepped to the vision that I was still seeing. I was terrified when in an attempt to calm me down, she reached through the white bars toward the white man with long while hair and long white beard, with the large sheer white dog by his feet. It seemed to her that she was just reaching through air. The man did not move but he looked very sad as I was screaming at my mother not to do it, not to reach in there.

My mother returned to the bed and she told me that my imagination was playing tricks on me, but to this day, I know what I saw that particular night, it was most definitely a vision and I have only seen that once, and never again.

The following day my mother went to work, I went to school. My father returned home after his twelve-hour shift. He was so exhausted that he just laid down on the sofa bed. At work, at the hospital where my mother was a nurse, she told one of her co-workers that I woke her up with my dream, that is the word she used, "dream." Her co-worker asked her details about my dream and she listened carefully until my mother finished. She told my mother that I did not have a dream, what I had was a vision. The white man and the white dog were Messengers; they were there to warn me. My mother wasn't sure what her colleague meant by "Messengers" and by "warn me."

Her colleague pulled her into a storage room and told her that I had the "gift" and that the Messenger was giving me a warning that someone close to me is going to die soon. My mother did not believe her and she thought that her colleague was talking gibberish nonsense.

When I returned from school, which was just across from the apartment building where we lived, I found my father on the sofa bed, gasping for air, he had extreme difficulty breathing. He was suffering from heart and lung asthma and every three months or so, he had to go into the hospital to have the fluid drained from his lungs. I went to our Superintendent, the only one who had a telephone in the entire building and she called my mother at the hospital where she worked. She got home about an hour later and she immediately knew that my father was gravely ill.

In those days, if you dropped off the name and the address of the sick person, the doctor on-call would come out to the apartment or house. It would be lengthy to explain, but a specific doctor's office was to handle so many streets in their districts and home visits only applied only to severe cases and strictly after scheduled daytime hours. It may sound fictional, but it was the way in Hungary back then.

Because it was already after six o'clock in the evening, my mother rushed to drop off my father's name and our address. Luckily the doctor's office was only a couple of blocks away. He arrived three hours later and recognized my father from earlier visits. He checked him over and he told him that there was nothing he could do, but he suggested that if my father was still not feeling well by the morning, then he should go to his office during the following day. His decision not to hospitalize my father immediately was a fatal mistake.

While my mother escorted the doctor out, I climbed to the footboard between their bed where I was sleeping and the sofa bed where my father was. He lifted his tired eyes at me and whispered, *"Csillagom"*, a nickname he always called me, which means "my star" in English, and then he closed his eyes. That word was the last word he ever spoke to me.

My father's condition dramatically deteriorated. When morning arrived; his breathing was shallow and his pulse very weak. My mother knocked on our neighbor's door, he was a Hungarian Army Officer, a very nice man and she asked him if he would not mind to drive my father to the hospital, also a couple of blocks away. Of course, he immediately complied with my mother's request. It was five o'clock in the morning. By six o'clock, my father was dead. He drowned in his own fluid that accumulated in his lungs. The vision's prediction came through, but I do not have the "gift" despite the fact, that sometimes I feel that things are going to happen but I cannot explain how, when, where and to whom. I do not claim to have any supernatural talents.

As I mentioned, I have never seen that vision again, not when my stepfather or before my mother passed away. I have only seen it once and it is just as vivid in my memory today as it was when I actually experienced it.

In this novel, "The Gifted One", all events and characters are completely fictional, with the exception of Maggie's first vision, my vision.

PROLOGUE

SHE WATCHED AS the medication slowly dripped into the IV tube that ran into her vein. It was taking effect quickly, just as the anesthesiologist explained. Her doctor leaned over and she heard his ever pleasant and reassuring voice. "Maggie," he said and it sounded like a whisper. "It will be over before you have a chance to dream."

And then, Margaret Davis-Anderson, Maggie to her friends, fell into a deep sleep.

CHAPTER ONE

"YOU ARE WELCOME here," said the man wearing a white outfit. Maggie wasn't sure if it was a robe, or a suit, but it was sparkling white, as was everything around her. She was amazed that even the trees were white and the animals, too. What amazed Maggie the most is that everything, not only their skin or feathers, but also their entire bodies were white, even the color of their eyes. "Step over here child," she heard the man's voice again.

Surprisingly Maggie did not feel fear, as a matter of fact, she was more curious than afraid. She stepped up to the white throne like chair that had a high backrest and she could not imagine how heavy it was, it did look like a piece of furniture that would have been hard to move. She looked up into the smiling face of the man. He had a long white beard, no surprise to Maggie anymore, and shoulder length white hair, not grey, white again. She had never seen anything like it; the man's eyes were white as freshly washed linen, as was his lips. "Where am I?" Maggie asked the obvious question.

"You are in the house of God," said the bearded man, and just then Maggie noticed the huge dog, yes, he was all white too, which lay by the man's feet. The dog lazily looked up at Maggie and she could have sworn that even the dog was smiling at her. After the initial glance, the dog placed his big head on his front paws and ignored her.

Hearing the man's words, Maggie was neither upset, nor surprised, although she did not fully comprehend the meaning of what he said. The thought that perhaps she died crossed her mind, but she recalled her doctor's words he spoke before she fell asleep. Dr. McFarland had never lied to her, so she obviously was not dead, not just yet.

The white man demanded not only respect with his appearance, but all of her attention as well. Maggie had a difficult time turning her head to look at her surroundings, but when she finally managed, the feeling of disappointment rose inside her head. Other than white trees, white grass and some animals, mostly dogs, cats and birds in her immediate vicinity, there were no other souls around.

She turned to ask the white man some questions, but when she wanted to step closer, out of nowhere, bars, like in prisons separated her from the man. *It was the strangest thing,* she thought about that later, the bars, that were also white, were not ending where they stood, they were just in front of her, there were no bars on either side of the man. "Am I in Heaven?" She asked. The man was no longer smiling back at her.

"As it appears, you are not ready yet to join the house of the Lord," said the man and his voice began to fade as did his entire body. Maggie glanced at the dog and he was fading away as well.

"Please," she yelled out as loud as she dared. "I would like to know who you are."

The white man, who by then stood and was about to disappear actually made an effort to respond to what sounded like a desperate question. "I am what I am," he replied. "But I have also been called the Messenger."

"Why am I here?" Maggie asked quickly. The man by that time was barely visible. He reached through the white bars and Maggie involuntarily touched his out-reached hand. It felt cool and air like.

The man's eyes locked into Maggie wide brown eyes. "You are the one that we call *The Gifted One*." With that said, the man disappeared.

CHAPTER TWO

"MAGGIE, WAKE UP, Maggie," she heard her name called. She tried to open her eyes and when she finally managed, Dr. McFarland came into her sight. He had a concerned look on his face. "Welcome back," he said and turned around to look at Paul, Maggie's husband. "She is going to be fine."

"Hi, love," Paul whispered and Maggie was stunned by Paul's face that showed a great range of emotions. He took her hands and kissed them. He shook his head and shamelessly let his teardrops roll down on his face, leaving Maggie totally confused.

"What is this all about Paul? Did something happen?" She inquired. Paul stared at her and nodded several times. Maggie, already disturbed by her dream, wondered what could have possibly gone wrong during the supposedly brief procedure.

A few weeks earlier when she got out of the shower, Maggie felt that her heart was racing. There was no pain in her chest, arms, neck or shoulder that would have given her a clue that she was having a heart attack. She thought about all of that, but the symptoms were not there, so was not having a cardiac arrest. She got dressed and told Paul that her heart felt as it wanted to jump out of her chest. Paul immediately began to worry and despite her objection, he drove her to the local hospital's emergency room to check out the problem. An EKG was done right away and the attending doctor suggested that she should see a cardiologist to check out her irregular heart beat. Test followed test at the cardiac specialist office as well at University Hospital, located not far from where Maggie and her husband resided.

The Cardiologist concluded after reading all of her test results that Maggie's heart was "only" functioning at 86% normally, but there was that other 14% he felt should be corrected with a relatively common procedure. Dr. McFarland explained the step-by-step procedure, which was accomplished in two phases. During phase one, they had to determine if there was any blockage in her heart's arteries. If they would have found problems, phase two could not have been accomplished.

"Given your young age, thirty-two," he explained. "I don't recommend a pacemaker as 14% is not a high enough number to have you undergo such a procedure, which you would have to deal with for the rest of your life. I am confident that the procedure we have in mind will adjust your heart back into a normal rhythm and with some mild support medication, you are going to be as good as new."

Due to the unpleasant procedure for the artery test, a general anesthetic was administered to Maggie and she was out for the first time within seconds. When she came through, they informed her about the good news, there were no signs of any blocked arteries. Paul, her husband of ten years, who was sitting in the corner of the procedure room, was smiling at her encouragingly when Dr. McFarland arrived to do phase two of the procedure himself. Maggie did not always like him, however, she had great respect for the physician for his honesty and eventually she began to understand his strange sense of humor.

Maggie was somewhat curious as how the second part, what the doctors called phase two was done, but she decided that she would rather not ask about the procedure. It was her and Paul's minimal understanding that they will administer a shock to her heart to get it back into the proper rhythm. According to Dr. McFarland, it was a relatively frequently administered procedure that did not have to be done again if she kept on taking two medication, a beta blocker and the other one to keep her heart from going back to irregular beating. If everything went according to plan in case there was no blockage, she was to be anesthetized once again for a short period of time, not more than ten to fifteen minutes. She remembered looking at the clock when she sleepily closed her eyes for the second time, it was exactly ten o'clock in the morning, but when she came through again, it was eight o'clock in the evening.

Thinking about the day's events, she wondered why they let her be under so long. Maggie looked at her husband's face and she repeated her question. "Did something happen?"

Paul finally gathered himself together to reply to her urging question. "They could not wake you up," he informed her. Maggie took this information in stride as she already suspected that something like that happened. "Dr. McFarland was genuinely concerned, he said that it was a very rare event, especially because they only administered a minimum amount of anesthetics.

"For a while I thought that I had died," she said and stared at the clock across from her bed.

"Why are you saying that?" Paul asked with surprise. "Did you see a tunnel of some sort?" He asked but his voice did not reflect humor or sarcasm.

Maggie shook her head. "No, not a tunnel, but I have met the Messenger." She said almost whispering. Paul did not understand the meaning of her words and he said so. Before Maggie could reply to her husband's inquiry, Dr. McFarland entered accompanied by a nurse. She checked her vitals while the doctor asked her the usual questions, how she was feeling, how was her heart feeling, although he also listen to it, too. All of her vital signs were perfect and Dr. McFarland informed her that they would run one more EKG test before he release her to go home. It was welcoming news to both of them.

Strangely, in general, Maggie liked hospitals, not necessarily as a patient but she liked the complexity of the institution how everything, from the personnel, to the nurses and doctors, the technicians who worked in the labs, to the pharmacists, how everything came together as a whole. Well, except for the lack of rest and the constant disturbance, also known as being taking care of.

The EKG test showed that her heart was beating normally, with the regular rhythm just as before all problem started. After another half an hour, the nurse finally returned with her prescriptions and discharge instructions. Maggie thanked her and her charges for everything and wished them good luck, as they wished her good health in return.

Paul brought their car around and helped her to get in. She was a little bit light headed which was not unusual after being in bed for a whole day. Maggie wanted one thing and one thing only, to be in her perfect bed with her soft comforter while cuddled up to her husband, Paul.

Her husband helped her to undress and covered her with the soft comforter. "Can I get you anything before you go to sleep?" Paul asked.

"No, thank you," Maggie replied and closed her eyes.

CHAPTER THREE

MAGGIE COULD HARDLY control her excitement after hanging up the telephone with her mother. "Paul, honey," she yelled out to her husband from her studio. "It was Mom."

Her husband joined her and she informed him that her parents just revealed that they would be coming from Connecticut to California to visit them. "I guess Mom can't stop worrying about me and couldn't wait until Christmas to see us."

Paul liked his in-laws, they were truly exceptional people and he never appreciated them more than when some of his friends told him horror stories about theirs. "I hope that they stay for a while," he commented and kissed Maggie before he returned to the living room to finish watching his favorite NASA program.

Maggie was way too excited to finish her latest watercolor. She took a liking to painting. She loved to paint buildings, especially landscapes. She never learned the art of painting until one day she watched someone at the market place painting a portrait of a total stranger. She became fascinated how well the young man painted the woman's face so she purchased some videotapes and she self taught herself how to paint.

When it came to art, Maggie was a natural. Within a few years from the first time she painted a landscape, she became a well-known, respected and sought-after artist.

Her husband, Paul was amazed how talented Maggie was despite the lack of training and he proudly called her a natural wonder. All of her paintings shown on exhibits were sold within a couple of hours and Maggie herself could not understand the phenomenon. She only did what she enjoyed doing, painting whatever she thought about or dreamed about.

Maggie turned the light off in her room, which she designated her "studio" in their large home when a thought occurred to her, so she turned it back on. Maggie put on a clear canvas and began to paint a blue sky as a backdrop and an airplane. She painted the plane a bright red color and on its side in dark gold letters the name of the airlines, "CU Airways". On the tail section she painted with small numbers *CU-INH7431*. Maggie took the canvas off from the easel and placed another canvas on it. At that time she painted mountains and valleys and an airplane broken into three parts, that particular airplane was also red and it's side had CU Airways painted in dark gold letters, just as on her other painting. It took her over an hour to compose that painting with all the bodies scattered around the burning plane and she painstakingly painted clothing that littered the place from split open suitcases.

Maggie felt exhausted and after leaving the painting on the easel, she once again turned off the light and went straight to bed. Paul went to check on her in her studio but after seeing that she already turned off the light, he went directly to the bedroom where he found Maggie deep asleep. He was about to leave when he realized that Maggie was moving under the comforter and when he looked at her face closer, he noticed that Maggie's face was covered with perspiration. "No, don't do it," she murmured. "Stay there, don't come here."

"Maggie," Paul said on a soft voice and gently touched Maggie's shoulder. Her entire body was covered with sweat and she was violently shaking. "Maggie, honey, please wake up."

She opened her eyes and looked at Paul. "The plane," she said and covered her mouth in fear.

"What plane Maggie?" asked Paul.

"Mom and Dad's plane," Maggie answered and her breathing became labored.

"Honey, I don't know what you are talking about," Paul said and couldn't figure out what Maggie was getting at. His in-laws always travelled in their RV as they enjoyed the stops along the way, even if they drove a week to get to Los Angeles, California where Paul and Maggie lived.

"Their plane is going to crash," Maggie replied and began to sob. "We have to stop them, please call them and stop them from flying."

CHAPTER FOUR

THEY PICKED UP the phone at the third ring and Paul heard his father-in-law's friendly voice. "Hello."

"Hi, Dad," Paul said recognizing his voice.

"Hello, son," Robert Davis, Maggie's father replied. "Is something wrong?" Paul could almost see Robert's concerned face.

"No, Dad, everything is fine, Maggie is doing real good, she even began to paint again," he explained.

"Okay, so then what's up?" Robert inquired. He knew his son-in-law so well that it was not hard to figure out that the ever so busy physicist was not just making a call to chat.

"Well," Paul hesitated, as it was not an easy thing to explain what he had to say. "The thing is that Maggie had a vision while she was in the coma and now she thinks that she can predict certain things that may take place in the near future."

"So," Robert blurted out. "I heard about things like that. What is she predicting?"

Paul cleared his throat. "She thinks that a CU Airline plane is going to crash and she didn't want you and Mom fly here."

"Who was planning to fly anyway?" Robert laughed. "I would not trade my well broken in RV for a corporate jet." Paul laughed too.

"I know that Dad, but she was so upset that seeing her cry, I could not refuse this phone call to you. She virtually begged me to call you to tell you not to fly here. I need to give you the flight number, too, because I promised."

"Fine," Robert said. "So give it to me."

"It's CU Airlines flight number CU 0617," he read out the numbers from the wrinkled piece of paper that Maggie gave him. "Did you write it down?" He asked.

"No, but I will remember, don't worry. I am not that old yet," Robert answered. "Not that it matters, but which day does she predict that the flight is going to crash?"

"August 11th," Paul informed his father-in-law. "Just for her peace of mind, please don't take that flight, or any flight that day, okay Dad?"

"Son, I told you, Melanie and I are taking the RV and we should be there by that date anyway," he assured his son-in-law.

For whatever reason, when Paul hang up the phone, he also had an odd feeling something may indeed was going to happen. *I need to get back to work,* he thought. *This whole thing is getting to me, too.* He picked up the receiver again and dialed his place of work, New Technology Unlimited, which he actually co-owned.

Few years earlier, he and his friend who also was his colleague shared the Nobel Prize for Physics for their work on quantum physics. They decided that it would be much better if they ventured out on their own and have the freedom to research what they were interested in the most. The money they earned from the Nobel Prize, plus the interest for their work by several major corporations, setting up the research lab was not that complicated. They made a special point to their benefactors that they could not be pressured by deadlines and they would only provide information on any new research at their own discretion. With their prestigious award mentioned after their names, even the US government was interested in their work.

"Hi Chris, it's Paul," he said when he heard the voice of Christopher Collins, his partner and colleague at New Technology Unlimited. "How is everything?"

"Most importantly how is Maggie?" Christopher inquired.

"She is doing better and back to painting, so I am becoming restless myself," Paul informed him. "I am thinking about coming to work on Monday."

"If she is okay, sure, but otherwise take your time," Christopher replied.

"Chris," Paul said stopping his friend from hanging up. "Is everything okay since the break-in?"

"The police have a couple of suspects but they don't think that it's an organized thing," Christopher answered but he didn't sound convincing. Paul was genuinely concerned because there had been two break-ins in less than a month, despite the high security precautions they implemented and which cost them a small fortune. The physical break-ins were only one of their problems; the other was computer hacking, which concerned them the most. The hackers failed, but all of them at New Technology Unlimited knew that it was just a matter of time before they succeed which would be virtually catastrophic for the company. They have been working on some top-secret government projects for close to two years.

When Paul returned to their living room, freshly brewed coffee was waiting for him, along with Maggie.

"How did it go with Mom and Dad?" She asked.

"Robert thought that something was wrong because I called them instead of you," Paul said and questioningly looked at his wife. He still couldn't figure out why Maggie did not want to tell her parents herself why she didn't want them to fly on that particular day.

"They always listened to you more than me," she explained as if she read Paul's thoughts.

"They are driving." Paul announced and he could see an immediate relief on Maggie's face. That felt good to him, too. "By the way, I am going back to work on Monday, but only if that's okay with you."

Maggie knew that Paul had to return to work sooner or later, so she smiled as an agreement that it was all right with her. "I have some painting to do, as usual," she remarked and taking her unfinished cup with her, she headed toward her studio.

The designated room's door, where her studio was located always remained open and Maggie was surprised that she found the door closed. She carefully opened the door and closed it immediately. She thought that she was hallucinating because when the door opened, she almost stepped into Paul's office at New Technology Unlimited. She once again carefully opened the door and it was her wide windowed room with the sun shining right into her face. Maggie could not explain to herself as why did she see her husband's office. *Perhaps,* she thought. *I was just imagining it.*

She placed a fresh canvas on the easel and she sat down to begin to paint, but almost immediately, sleepiness swept over her as she lifted her arm to make the first touch to the canvass. As if she was in a trance, Maggie began to paint fast, mixing and using colors that she normally would only use occasionally. She painted feverishly and when she finished, her entire body gave in and fell off the chair to the floor and into a deep sleep.

Paul was terrified finding Maggie on the floor, but she assured him that she was fine and that she just fell asleep as if she just drank her cup of coffee with some sort of sleeping potion mixed in it. Paul helped her up from the floor and escorted her to their bedroom; eventually helping her to wash her paint stained hands and then get her into bed.

When Maggie fell asleep again, Paul as quietly as he could went back to the studio and looked at the wet painting on the easel. He immediately recognized the location on the painting; it was his place of work. His office and its surroundings looked as if it was hit by a tornado. Desks were turned upside down, computer cables hung from the ceiling while the terminals were all over the place, but the most shocking part on the painting was the dead body of a character lying in a pool of blood with an arm and leg missing. He recognized the person from the precise painting; it was Christopher Collins, his best friend and colleague.

He knew that he could not wake up Maggie to inquire about the subject of the painting but Paul's concern began to grow right away about his wife's well being. He began to wonder how a peace loving person such as Maggie could paint such a horrible scene. Paul began to look at the already finished paintings in Maggie's studio and he came across two paintings that showed the aftermath of the crash of a CU Airlines' plane. On those particular paintings, the tail number was also clearly visible, CU-INH7431.

Dr. Paul Anderson, Nobel Prize winner physicist was sitting in his wife's studio, stunned and unable to understand where all those paintings were coming from. Without a doubt, they were the handiwork of his talented wife, however; that was the point when he, an educated man could not pass. Everyone who knew them was aware of the fact the Dr. Anderson loved his wife Maggie from the moment he first saw her at San Juan University in Puerto Rico, some 10 years earlier and he went through hell seeing her suffer from variety of ailments, but she always bounced back. Physically being ill was one thing, he rationalized, but mental illness is another. *Because,* he thought, *it just had to be something emotionally or mentally wrong with Maggie to paint such horrific pictures and talk about major disasters that not yet happened and probably never will.*

Paul was more than just concerned; he was terrified that he was going to lose Maggie to some mental ailment that would prevent her functioning in their daily life. He knew, and it was never a question that he would stand by her, no matter what, but he would most certainly miss their vibrant conversations and activities. It was then, sitting in Maggie's studio that Paul decided to prove to his wife that her predictions were just products of bad dreams, nothing more. He was going to work on Monday and nothing was going to happen.

The following day was Sunday and the morning offered bright and sunny weather, allowing them to have their breakfast on their backyard patio. Paul as casually as he could, confirmed to Maggie that he was going back to work. She nodded that she understood. Paul explained to her that he believed what she was saying about his place of business, but he also believed that perhaps they were just bad nightmares and that he wanted to prove that to her.

Maggie was not surprised by Paul's response and she stopped her plea in midsentence, she knew that she could not stop destiny and she prayed that God would spare her from becoming a widow. She bitterly thought of what the Messenger said, "You shall be called *The Gifted One*," she murmured. *More like damned,* she thought. First the plane crash and now the explosion at Paul's place appeared to her in nightmares, or were they really nightmares? She could have sworn that she thought about the explosion while she was wide-awake.

CHAPTER FIVE

THE DOOR OPENED effortlessly after Paul punched in the security code and completed his eye and finger bio identification routine. He walked down the long corridor occasionally looking up at the security cameras and waved when he arrived to the last door, where according to Christopher, all the interesting "stuff" was located. The door was operated by two different security systems in two different locations of the building. After the person who wished to enter was verified, both technicians tending the security at that time, must enter a code sequence into their computer to open the door. The codes were changed often and never revealed to more than two people at a time other than Christopher and Paul.

He waved again, thanking the invisible security personnel for letting him enter. Paul wanted to be early on his first day returning after taking an unprecedented two whole weeks off to take care of Maggie. She was his first and most important priority. After her came his work that he loved as well, but of course in a different manner. He was genuinely surprised when he noticed that he was not the first person in the vicinity, Miguel Ponce de Leon, or Ponce as everybody called him was already busy setting up the day's test material.

"Hey, welcome back, Dr. Anderson," the Puerto Rican said with a big smile seeing one of his bosses enter.

"Good Morning Ponce and it's good to be back," he replied and watched as Ponce measured up some distance between the two-laser projectors.

"How is Mrs. Anderson?" Ponce asked as he glanced up at Paul.

"Thank you for asking, she is doing much better," Paul answered and without further delay, he headed toward his office, but then he turned around. "You in early," he remarked as an afterthought.

"Yeah," Ponce replied, and then he added. "I have to leave early today. It was approved by Mr. Collins."

"Oh, that's fine, I was just wondering," Paul commented and entered his office. He felt good at work, not that he was not happy being home with Maggie. The type of work and research his firm was doing created excitement and endless possibilities for future generations.

Paul re-booted his computer and it did not come as a surprise to him that hundreds of emails were waiting to be replied to, although he knew that there was no possible way that he could answer them any time soon. On the left side of the desk, strategically placed in front of Maggie's and his late dogs' picture, in a neat stack stood a pile of telephone messages. *No doubt in chronological order,* thought Paul knowing how Jessica, the firm's secretary, who preferred to be called office manager, operated.

All offices in the firm had glass walls but only Christopher, Paul and Jessica have had it soundproofed. It was necessary as the majority of the test equipment in the larger portion of the test laboratory lay right in front of the five large offices that were occupied by Paul, Christopher, Jessica and two engineer geniuses Richard and Nicholas. They preferred to hear the on-going noises in the testing department.

Shortly before eight o'clock the company was buzzing with activities. Employees from regular workers to engineers would glance up at Paul's office and wave at him. All of them were smiling, Paul noticed. He did not see anything that would give him a hint that there was trouble in the horizon. Not that he didn't believe his wife, Maggie, who predicted a catastrophic event at New Technology Unlimited. Paul told himself, just because she believed that it is going to happen, it did not mean that it would actually take place.

He made it a priority to answer to some of his emails and the more important phone calls that could not be put off any longer. Jessica, his office manager made a point of not contacting anyone at home while on leave, unless it was an emergency and in their line of work, it seldom happened. There was always a back up for Paul if he needed to leave for a business meeting, just as he backed up Christopher if he needed time off for his family.

It was already one o'clock when Christopher knocked on the door and asked him if he wanted to join him for lunch at the Cafe Shop only a block away. "No thanks," Paul replied and put down his reading glasses. "I still haven't called Maggie yet. I just got so wrap up with Eduardo Lugo's proposal that I forgot to call her," Paul explained. Hearing the name, Christopher turned around to see if anyone was in hearing distance, then he stepped into Paul's office and closed the door. Paul looked up at him. "Is something wrong with that proposal? Did you read the whole thing?" He asked.

Christopher sat down in one of the chairs in front of Paul's wide, modern desk. "I have some genuine concerns indeed," he replied and nervously looked at the testing area. "I heard things, some of the them were darn right disturbing."

Paul leaned forward. "Talk to me Chris," he said. "What did you hear?"

Christopher leaned forward too. "I heard that he has a close connection with an organization that is thought to be no longer in existence"

Paul raised his shoulders because he didn't know anything about what his friend just mentioned. "He was born in Puerto Rico, but he was raised in Connecticut," explained Chris. "I always thought that he was Italian, but evidently I was wrong. His father was sent to jail for life for a bombing attack that killed 29 people, including three police officers when they tried to stop their suspicious looking vehicle from leaving the scene."

Paul did not like what he was hearing. "What else do you know?" He asked Christopher.

"His mother committed suicide after Lugo's father was killed in prison by a rival gang," Chris added.

"He offers a lot of money," Paul commented.

"Yeah, he can afford to buy companies ten times the size of ours, easily," Chris confirmed and looked at Paul with questions in his eyes. "It begs the question, why did he choose our company? You are not thinking about accepting his proposal are you?"

Paul shook his head. "No, not really," he replied. "Although I must admit, I do like the sound of the five hundred million dollars," he said with a smile.

"It would be like selling our souls to the devil," Christopher replied. "I just wonder what he would do with our findings?"

"Probably use it against us," Paul commented. "When you came into my office, did you want to talk to me about something?"

"About Lugo," Chris replied and reached into his jacket pocket. He pulled out a folded sheet of paper and handed it over to Paul. He took it and unfolded the printout. It read, *"I highly advise that you talk to Mr. Anderson about giving me a positive response to my proposal to avoid regrettable consequences. Your and your friend's reward would be substantial. E. Lugo."*

"When did you receive this?" Paul asked and tossed the paper on his desk.

"It was waiting for me this morning, according to the date on it, he sent it yesterday," Chris said. "This man has a violent history, we need to be very careful," he suggested and nervously looked through the glass wall. The place was rather empty as most of the employees were taking their hour-long lunch break.

"This particular project is the same what Lugo wants," Paul said pointing a finger at the test area below his office. Why would a private person be interested in laser guided cruise missiles?" Paul asked calmly. "I suggest that we notify the FBI."

"You would unleash some unwanted people around here," Christopher objected. "I suggest that we politely turn his proposal down. Tell him that we talked the proposal over and we are obligated to fulfill our government contracts first."

"My thoughts exactly," Paul agreed. "Who thought that we would become so popular?"

Chris laughed uneasily. They were working on multiple projects; most of them had military themes. They often wondered if it was a mistake to accept government contracts, but at that particular time when they started up their company, they accepted the top five best offers. Chris looked at Paul before he headed to the door and he debated if he should also show him the second message that he received from Lugo, the one that included a physical threat to their company if they failed to comply with his request and his proposal. He decided against it and he left Paul's office.

After the closing the door, he felt a great amount of guilt, but he just couldn't share the information about the threat with Paul because of one part of the message would have given away the secret that only a very few selected people knew. How Lugo found out scared the daylights out of Dr. Christopher Collins, Nobel Prize Winner physicist and confidential CIA informant.

After lunch, Chris returned to his office and stared at his cell phone then dialed. "This is Christopher Collins, ID number 1242312000-TM10."

"Just a moment please," said the operator who did not introduce himself. "I'll connect you, sir." Chris heard three short beeps and a familiar voice came on the line.

"What is going on Collins?" Asked the high ranked CIA officer named George Mallon.

"Lugo made a proposal to us but we are turning it down," Chris informed the man."

"Is he interested in same project as the Air Force?" Mallon asked again.

"Yes," Chris replied.

After a brief silence, the CIA officer gave Christopher his instructions. "I want you and Anderson accept Lugo's proposal and deliver him the prototype."

"What?" Christopher whimpered, unable to believe what he just heard. "Are you sure?"

"Positive, but hold off with your reply to him until I contact you later today. I want to run it again by my contact at the White House." Mallon said and hung up. Chris looked toward the direction of Paul's office next door where his friend was busy working on his computer.

"It just doesn't make any sense," he murmured and wondered how he was going to make Paul change his mind when his cell phone rang. "Hello," Christopher answered into the receiver.

"Lugo is a murderer," said the voice with a Spanish accent.

"Who are you?" Christopher asked although even he knew that it was a stupid question.

"That is not important," the stranger replied. His voice was vaguely familiar to Chris. "If you make a deal with a murderer, you are not much better than him. He must not get the JDAM missile, not now, not ever."

"Where did you get this information?" Chris asked again in vein.

"You have to promise me that you are not going to make a deal with someone who made his money by selling weapons to pirates and mass murderers," requested the man.

"I cannot make such a promise," Chris replied almost angrily.

"Then you are just as guilty as Lugo. You should ask your friend at the CIA what Lugo had done in Rwanda," the stranger suggested.

Chris was becoming deeply troubled and it become quite obvious that someone tapped into his cell phone, how, he could not imagine. "I am going to call the FBI and report this phone call," Chris threatened but he had no intention of doing so.

"My name is El Padre and I am the leader of the *Red December* Organization. We are fighting for Puerto Rico's independence from under CIA control," said the man. "Dr. Collins, I must tell you that this is a warning. I would rather take actions against your company than have a man; such as Lugo get a hold of your JDAM missiles so he could destroy targets in the USA and other cities on this planet. He is just as bad as Al- Quada," the man insisted and Chris knew that he was not bluffing.

"Sounds like you are a terrorist yourself," Chris accused him and he was not happy with himself the way he handled the phone call.

"I am a freedom fighter," the man replied, and then he added. "I am a soldier who is willing to die for my cause. I suggest you call your loved ones and say goodbye to them."

Chris got up when the line went dead. He could see employees returning from their lunch breaks and he glanced over to Paul's office. Paul was putting on his jacket and headed toward the door. Chris caught him just as he was starting down the steps.

"Is everything alright?" Christopher asked from Paul who obviously was in a hurry.

"Maggie had a dizzy spell and fell, she hurt herself," he explained. "I may have to take her to the hospital." Paul explained briefly and ran down the stairs.

Chris yelled after him. "I'll call you later, there is something important I need to discuss with you."

"Okay," Paul yelled back and rushed through the security doors.

"Are you alright Chris?" Jessica asked and handed him a cup of freshly brewed coffee. "You seem awful pale."

Chris brushed his thick blonde hair back. "It's been a tough day."

"It's Monday," Jessica replied cheerfully and left Chris alone in his office.

How did the caller know what we are working on? Chris thought. He reached into the top drawer of his desk and took out a small hand held tape recorder and pushed the record button. "This is Christopher Collins, today is Monday, June 14. This is top secret. I received a phone call from a man who spoke with Spanish accent and he called himself El Padre, the leader of the *Red December* Organization, allegedly from Puerto Rico. He knew about Lugo's proposal and my CIA contact. He also had knowledge that we were working on Joint Direct Attack Munitions, JDAM for short missiles. He basically threatened our company with violence if we sell our technology to Eduardo Lugo, a Puerto Rican businessman whom El Padre called a gun dealer and murderer. Need to take pre-caution. Chris out."

CHAPTER SIX

PAUL PULLED UP into his driveway and he stepped on the brakes so hard that it screeched. Maggie was sitting on the sofa and looked at him questioningly. "I don't really want to go to the hospital again," Maggie said instead of saying "hello".

"I know," Paul replied. "It is just a precaution." He said on an assuring voice. "Let's have you checked out and then we go out for a mocha chip ice cream with lots of whip cream."

Maggie tried to smile but not even hearing the name of her favorite ice cream could take away the knowledge that she would have to sit and wait, and wait some more in the Emergency Room of the hospital, where she spent enough time after each of her surgeries that she never wanted to see the inside of one again. Unfortunately, she knew deep inside that Paul was right, that the dizziness was not normal. One time could be ignored, but three times was three times too many. It may have been something serious, or maybe it was just something minor.

Paul grabbed her light jacket from the coat hanger in the hallway closet and helped her into it. She took her small purse from the entry cabinet and was ready to go. She was no longer dizzy but Paul helped Maggie by her arm anyway as he guided her through the front door to the car that under normal circumstances would have been parked inside their garage.

"I actually feel somewhat better," she replied to Paul's question how she was feeling. "I was just so scared when I became dizzy, and then I tripped on the bathroom rug."

Paul listened to her with concerns of his own. It was the second time since her procedure and subsequent brief coma that she suffered dizziness and he contemplated on asking the doctor to have another round of MRIs completed on her brain. The first MRI results were negative. When she came out of her brief coma after the cardiac arrhythmia procedure, Dr. McFarland ordered the first MRI but it showed normal brain activities and no sign of any irregularities, tumors or trauma.

While Paul suggested that she should wait until he gets a wheelchair, Maggie refused and walked with him into the Emergency Services area. There were not many people around and she was called in shortly after signing the arrivals sheet. Her blood pressure was fine, her pulse was fine and Maggie's temperature was fine as well. She told the Triage nurse the reason of her visit and blamed Paul for it. Once her vital signs and information were taken, she was instructed to wait in the reception area to be seen.

More than anything, Maggie hated waiting, but Paul would not budge, he wanted to have her checked out. After an hour and a half of waiting finally her name was called and Paul accompanied her inside. Yet again, the nurse checked her vitals and put an oxygen mask on Maggie's face despite the fact that her breathing was just fine. She was getting angrier and angrier, and it showed as her blood pressure rose up to 160.

A doctor finally arrived thirty minutes later to her tiny room to check on her and he patiently listened as Paul explained what was done to his wife. The doctor let her explain the symptoms she experienced just hours earlier. Since it was the same hospital where her heart procedure was completed, the doctor told them he was going to cue up her case history on the computer and he would return shortly.

Maggie asked Paul for the time, it was four o'clock in the afternoon. "Eight more hours until midnight," whispered Maggie and Paul squeezed her hand.

"Nothing is going to happen, you'll see," he said encouragingly.

"I want to go home," Maggie said stubbornly and pushed her leg off from the bed where she was laying. Paul looked at her and gently encouraged her to lay back down. Maggie shook her head. "We have to go back to your company and warn anyone who was still working their late shift."

Paul made a promise to himself that no matter what, he was going to be patient with Maggie who went through a lot of health problems in recent years. It was common knowledge among friends that Paul loved Maggie with the deepest depth of his heart and mind. There was no one in the world he would have rather have spent his life with the former Maggie May Davis, now his wife. He smiled at her ever so patiently. "Darling," he said. "Nothing is going to happen."

Maggie looked at him and her eyes were dark, so dark in the bright light of the examination room that Paul took a step back. Her eyes that normally were a light shade of brown was almost black just then. "We must go," she said firmly and reached for her clothing at the foot of her bed. Paul no longer argued and helped his wife out of the hospital gown and into her own clothes.

The doctor appeared in the door way and seeing that she was already dressed, waved at a passing by nurse to join him. "Might as well you go home," he said to Maggie. "All of your medical records and your MRI were clean and clear. The dizziness may be a side effect of the heart medication you are taking. I suggest you talk to your cardiologist to adjust the dosage and you should be alright."

They thanked the doctor who quickly disappeared, possibly to take care other patients. The nurse went through the routine ER discharge instruction and Maggie hurriedly signed her name on the release form. After receiving a copy of the signed form, Maggie grabbed her purse and hanging onto Paul's hand, they quickly made their way into the hospital parking lot.

The New Technology Unlimited was a good thirty-five minutes drive from the hospital and several times during the ride, Maggie urged Paul to driver faster. He obliged but with some limitations, he only increased the speed with two or three miles an hour trying to avoid getting a speeding ticket.

The large three-story building was located just outside the industrial part of the city and was in sight when they excited the freeway. Maggie looked at her watch and Paul noticed that his wife's breathing was becoming labored. Maggie grabbed Paul's hand. "Pull over," she yelled. "Pull over, now."

Paul looked around to make sure that it was safe to stop, he had two options, a gas station on the right corner, or to cross the street where the Café Shop was located. When he put the signal on that he was about to make a right turn to the gas station, Maggie calmly said. "Not here, go across the street."

Paul obliged and parked on the side of the Café Shop, a few steps away from the door. Maggie got out of the car and dashed inside the building. Paul ran after her. Maggie was already talking very loud, telling people to get away from the wide window that faced her husband's company only a short block away. People looked at her wondering if she had a mental problem or something like that. One of the waitresses, a woman in her fifties calmly stepped up to Maggie and looked directly into her eyes. "Tell me what is going to happen?" She asked calmly. Paul turned his head hearing the woman's voice, there was something about that voice…

"There will be an explosion within minutes and the glass will shatter into millions of little pieces. Those who would not move will either die or be seriously injured and even blinded."

Paul noticed that the waitress had tears shining in her eyes. "Are you *The Gifted One?*" She asked. Maggie slowly nodded. The woman lifted Maggie's hands to her lips and kissed them. She let them go and quickly turned around. "Everyone, move away from those windows, toward the back. There are vacant tables, you are welcome to sit where ever you like."

A big guy and his buddy, both already finished with their meals and were having apple pie a la mode, just laughed and continued to eat and drink their steaming cup of coffee. "We can only do so much," the waitress said to Maggie and both of them helped couple of families with children to move to the backside of the establishment.

Paul stood there, away from the window and watched his wife. Her eyes were still very dark but not as dark as they were in the hospital. Maggie looked at him and smiled with a smile that would freeze water over. Since they left the hospital and in those moments at the restaurant, she seemed very different to him, she was colder and more direct.

"Everyone," Maggie looked at her watch and yelled. "Cover your ears."

Two seconds after her instruction, a series of violent explosions rocked the entire area. The restaurant shook for several minutes, and yet another sound of a second explosion was heard. The glass windows where the booths were located at the side of the Café Shop that faced the industrial section were shattered, just as Maggie predicted. When the sound quieted down, the multiple sounds of sirens became audible in the distance and closer as they approached the sight of the company that once stood at the place of New Technology Unlimited.

Paul straightened out and dusted off his clothes from the fine powder like plaster. He turned to the right where the gas station was on fire; the latest explosion they heard was the sound of the exploding underground gas tanks. The waitress who spoke to Maggie earlier, told the parents of the children, there were three and two to each family, not to let them see what was by the window where they previously sat.

The two large men, who refused to move when they were asked, were dead. Both of them were wearing leather jackets with Harvey Davidson logos printed on their backs were killed by large pieces of shattered glass, it was most certainly a gruesome sight.

Maggie stood up from the table where she was sitting and reached out to Paul who took her into his arms. Her eyes returned to their normal warm brown color. "I am sorry," she whispered.

"So am I," he replied. "What happened, do you know?" He asked. The explosions were obvious, but who and why would do such a thing was not.

Unless, it was Lugo, Paul thought but he hushed that thought away. He didn't even give the man an answer to his proposal yet.

"I am not sure," Maggie replied. "All I felt was that something was going to happen."

"You painted a picture of the event," Paul remarked as they stepped carefully over the many of small pieces of glass.

"I just saw the outcome, I do not know any details," Maggie explained and walked outside through the shattered door. Their car's body was badly dented all over and the front window was cracked in every direction. However, the engine came alive right away when Paul turned the key in the ignition. They were about to leave the parking lot when the waitress who was talking to Maggie prior to the explosion dashed toward their car. Paul stopped the car so the woman could reach them.

"God bless you Ma'am," the waitress said. "You are indeed the Gifted One."

"You take good care of yourself and your daughter, she will be fine in a year or two," Maggie said and they drove off. The waitress looked after the disappearing car in stunned silence. She never mentioned to anyone that her twenty-five year old daughter was gravely ill, and the reason why she was doing double shifts every day because they needed all the money she could make. Moreover, nobody even knew that she had a daughter, only the stranger, whom she thought, was *The Gifted One*, did.

CHAPTER SEVEN

IT WAS A nightmare Paul wanted to wake up from but he could not. The following two and a half months were spent with arguments, questioning and endless interrogations from all sides. As if they were the bad people and not the victims. Their house was searched first by the police, then the FBI and later on, ATF along with an anti-terrorist branch of Homeland Security.

Maggie's paintings were confiscated and while most of them were eventually returned, her painting predicting the explosion and the airplane crash were not. She and Paul were asked to take lie detector tests on three different occasions and they agreed, both of them passed all three of them with flying colors. Maggie was asked the same questions as Paul and vice versa.

Maggie, of course was not aware of the details of Paul's work or his business dealings, other than that she knew what Paul was doing, testing missiles, as of what kind, or for what reason, she did not know and she was never interested in physics. She knew that Paul and Christopher had government contracts, but Paul never discussed business details with her, on purpose to have less liability.

Paul explained to the very much concerned Air Force officials and some of the CIA agents that there was no compromise of the Top Secret materials, and that no test results were lost as they had secured backup systems at a different location, on a nearby military installation.

He told all of the interrogators about Eduardo Lugo's proposal due to the threatening emails that Christopher received. Just thinking of his college friend, co-winner of the Nobel Prize for physics and his business partner made him very sad. It was very difficult for Paul to accept the fact that Chris was dead, his body was found just as it was predicted on Maggie's painting. They found altogether seven employees, including Ponce's body, badly burned in the fire that followed the explosion.

Maggie's interrogation was a lot less stressful although she had to endure distrusting stares of her interrogators who refused to believe anything she said. She told all of them about her experience while she was in coma, but she could tell from the looks on the faces of those who were present that her story sounded more like fiction, than the truth. As a matter of fact, one of the female police detectives tossed a Stephen King book in front of her, a copy of the Dead Zone. She shrugged and told them that she had never read the book and she was telling the truth.

There were questions raised to her about the pictures she painted about the airplane crash, but she was unable to give more details other than what she already disclosed, the name of the airline, the flight number and the number on the plane's tail section. She repeatedly told them that she was concerned about that plane because in her dream, her parents also perished on that particular flight.

Eventually things quieted down and Paul and Maggie's life returned to semi normal. It was clear to them that they had been followed from time to time, at least when it was too obvious not to notice the women or men tailing them, or having a dark government car parked 24/7 across their house. It was also obvious to both of them that whichever agency was involved in their surveillance, they were not making a secret of it. Maggie thought about filing a complaint, but Paul explained to her that in a way it was for their own protection as well.

Because of all the activities, Maggie's parents delayed their travel from June to August; it was the month when Maggie and Paul's celebrated their wedding anniversary. Maggie repeatedly told her parents that she did not want them to fly and her father repeatedly told her that they were going to drive. It went back and forth almost each time they talked on the phone.

Paul needed to reorganize his entire company and finding a place was not a problem as they had plenty of buildings to chose in the old companies vicinity where used to have factories that failed in the desperate economic situation that cast shadows over a great many American companies in that time frame. Once his realtor located a building that was to Paul's specification, the surviving employees regrouped and under military and police protection, any salvageable machinery and equipment were relocated into the new building after the accelerated renovations were completed.

Before the highly sensitive testing equipment and computers were set up, a security firm that Paul hired upon the recommendation of his military liaison, implemented security sensors all over the building and their location was only known to Paul and the security firm that installed them. At least, that is what he was told. Paul was fairly certain that the military was also aware of that information as well but he refused to dwell on that subject.

There was one subject that Paul was not pleased to discuss and he argued with high ranked Air Force officials, was the subject of hiring of employees. One of the meetings went particularly bad for Paul and it haunted him for days and he lost many nights' sleep over what he found out. When he walked into the large meeting room, he immediately noticed that he was not the only person, as usual, who was wearing civilian attire. There were two other civilians in the meeting room and they both took place on the opposite side of the long oval dark wood table from him.

General Evans whom Paul genuinely liked opened the meeting by welcoming Paul and the representatives of the other branch of the Department of Defense, the Coast Guard Colonel from the Homeland Security and two gentlemen from the FBI. Paul looked at them and smiled but he did not receive the same reception. General Evans informed everyone about the conclusion of what the FBI, the CIA, the ATF, along with Homeland Security, and of course the local police investigators drew after a combined investigation.

Paul suspected that Eduardo Lugo had something to do with the explosion that caused the death of seven innocent people and the almost total destruction of his research lab. The real culprit of the threats was Miguel Ponce de Leon, also suspected to be El Padre, a Puerto Rico native who was the leader of the *Red December* terrorist organization. Evidently the CIA intercepted a telephone call between Ponce de Leon and Christopher Collins on the day of explosion. In that phone call El Padre threatened Christopher about going into business with Eduardo Lugo whom he called during his call a *murderer*. Without a doubt, and all of the organizations that were involved with the investigation of the explosion agreed, that the pattern of the explosions and the explosives used was identical to two other explosions at other companies, one in Michigan and one in Texas, that conducted similar research as Paul's company was working on, and who also had military affiliations.

Paul was troubled for more than one reason about that announcement. A few days earlier when he went through Chris' belongings, he found a small recorder with a tape that was damaged but was still usable. He was shocked to learn from Christopher's taped notes, that Chris had a CIA connection. In his head, Paul replayed years of conversations between himself and Chris about politics in general, and it made him wonder if his friend ever talked about him to the CIA and if so, what did he say.

As Paul was listening to the second speaker at the meeting about various security measures, he couldn't help thinking about all the people whom he trusted, such as Chris and even Ponce who had betrayed him in many different levels. He had to force himself to concentrate on the meeting and when he was addressed with the question about future employees, Paul sat up straight in the leather chair where he was sitting.

"We will assist you with the selection," said the man who was supposed to represent the FBI. "We can do pre-selection interviews, background checks and such," said the older of the two. "Of course," he added. "Only with your approval."

"And there won't be such approval," Paul said calmly. "No matter what contract you may have with my company," Paul replied and turned toward General Evans. "The company is still my company and I will make sure this time that all employees meet up with my standards, including security, and not yours."

"Mr. Anderson," said the second FBI officer. Paul interrupted him.

"Agent Perkins," said Paul. "It is Dr. Anderson."

General Evans tried to hide his smile but Paul noticed it in a nick of time. "Dr. Anderson, we are not your enemy and any suggestion we may have is an attempt to secure your company and protect our government's investments," the senior FBI officer explained.

Paul smiled but it was a sarcastic smile. "With all respect, Special Agent Muller, evidently it did not work the first time. I will make sure that the additional people my company needs to hire will pass proper background checks."

The FBI agents turned toward General Evans. He nodded to Paul. "Dr. Anderson's company is a private company that happened to have a contract with the government. I know that the next subject you are going to say is that it is a matter of national security and I cannot agree with you more. However; I have full trust in Dr. Anderson that he and his team will work out all the details of whatever is necessary to be done," said the General and after another half an hour of discussion about the re-opening progress of Paul's company and some minor issues, the meeting ended and Paul could hardly wait to get home.

He called Maggie's favorite restaurant on his cell phone and picked up some dinner for that evening. Maggie was a good cook but ever since she was experiencing restless and sleepless nights, especially her latest and newest urge to paint, cooking was no longer a priority. Paul never complained as he also worked long hours and it would not have been feasible for Maggie to cook only for herself.

He got home just pass five in the afternoon and he found Maggie in her studio. She had paint all over her face and when she looked up as he entered, for a moment Paul was concerned that she had another vision, another nightmare. He carefully walked around some paint droppings on the floor and after taking a deep breath; he looked at Maggie's latest painting. It was breathtaking. Maggie painted the picture of a beautiful white cottage that even had a small bell tower with a splendid garden and trees surrounding the cottage with lush hedges as fences around the yard.

"It's beautiful," Paul commented and kissed the top of her head. She looked up and Paul was shocked to realize that Maggie's face was covered with tears. "What is it darling?" He asked with genuine concern. "Why are you crying? This painting is absolutely beautiful."

"There are children buried in that garden," Maggie said and put the paintbrush down.

"Where is this cottage?" Paul asked holding onto her paint stained hand. She shook her head.

"I am not sure," she whispered. "I took a nap this afternoon and I saw this garden. I got up and begin to paint it before I forgot all the details."

Paul sighed. It happened again, Maggie obviously had another vision. He didn't take her words lightly, not ever again since the explosion, but how could he tell the police that there were murdered children somewhere in the city, the state or it could be anywhere in the country.

"Let's clean you up and have dinner," Paul suggested. "We will talk about this later." Maggie listened to her husband's words and she allowed him to lead her into the bathroom down the hallway.

CHAPTER EIGHT

PRESSURE WAS BUILDING from all directions and Paul tried very hard to divide his attention on re-starting a once successful and advancing business, fulfilling a government contract, but most of all, he was stressed because of his wife's condition. That is how he began to call when Maggie talked about her visions, although she had not done that often, as she didn't want to upset her husband. There was just one problem with Maggie's latest vision and her painting, Paul could not get it out of his head that perhaps somewhere out there people were missing their children and worried about them endlessly.

Two detectives stopped by in the afternoon of Maggie's call to the Los Angeles Police Department. Detective Matthews was a seasoned professional with twenty years of experience in homicide under his belt, his partner of five years, Detective Calhoun, seemed like an intelligent woman with bright eyes.

"Please, have a seat," Paul offered as they identified themselves upon entering the house. "Just one moment, I'll get my wife, she is in her studio."

When he left the living room, the two detectives glanced around in the modestly but stylishly decorated living room and they both shrugged. They had enough nut cases to solve, but their Captain was persistent because his wife liked Maggie Davis-Anderson's paintings and he told them that if they would not look into the painter's claim, he would never hear the end of it. Matthews told him that maybe he should not be taking his work home, to which the Captain replied to him that Mrs. Anderson was all over the news about her prediction of an explosion at her husband's company.

They immediately realized that they were wrong about Maggie Davis-Anderson because when she entered, she had a sweet, self-assured smile on her face. The detectives talked about her during their drive to the Anderson household. They looked on the Internet for newspaper articles and interviews with the painter, but there was hardly anything to find, there was not much information on Wikipedia either. Evidently Maggie Davis-Anderson was not a partygoer, as they were unable to find anything in any of the many social columns, she seldom ever gave interviews, she didn't even attend her own gallery shows. The word "hermit" came to their minds and they simply could not imagine what she was all about.

When Maggie entered the room, she reached out to shake hands with both of them and asked her husband if he had a chance to offer any coffee or tea to the detectives yet. Paul asked them what would they like, and the agreement was on coffee. While Paul disappeared into the kitchen to prepare coffee, Detective Calhoun complimented Maggie on her home.

"Being such a successful painter I expected more luxury," she said to Maggie with honesty.

"Paul and I don't believe in wasting money on large homes where rooms would go unused. We do not have any children and having four large bedrooms is more than plenty for the two of us. If we have visitors, we have a guest room, but you know what? Why don't I give you the grand tour," she offered.

Matthews whispered to Calhoun. "You are good."

The tour did not last long as the house was not large in size; they spent most of their time in Maggie's studio where she showed them the paintings of her vision. Matthews looked surprised seeing the detailed painting but did not say anything until later. Finished with the "tour", which included the fair sized backyard, they returned to the living room where Paul already set the tray with coffee mugs, sugar and cream on the coffee table.

"Mrs. Anderson," Detective Matthews turned to Maggie. "Have you ever seen the television show titled "Fantasy Island?" He asked.

Maggie thought about it and then she shook her head. "No, I don't believe that I have."

"That building in your painting, that white cottage reminded me of that television show. However, I must tell you that I know exactly where that cottage is," he announced. Even Calhoun looked at him with surprise. "I have taken my wife and children to the Los Angeles County Arboretum and Botanical gardens many times, that cottage in your painting with the trees and the hedges, with the garden, that is exactly how it looks in real life."

"Have you ever been there?" Detective Calhoun asked. Maggie shook her head.

"My wife has severe allergies for certain types of trees and some of the flowers, that is the reason why we don't venture outdoors a lot," Paul explained.

Detective Kathy Calhoun, KC to everyone who knew her, watched Maggie very closely, tried to figure out what was so special about the painter if there was anything special at all, other than that she was good at what she was doing. KC glanced up to Dr. Anderson who sat there next to his wife, looking straightforward, being a thousand miles away. Not that KC blamed him, knowing what she found out about his company, the government contracts that were sealed from the public and his wife who may or may not be going insane. Paul looked at his wife and he smiled at her with a smile that was rare. Strangely enough, KC became unconvinced at that moment that Dr. Paul Anderson, the Nobel Price winner physicist truly and deeply loved and cared about his wife.

"Mrs. Anderson," KC refocused on Maggie. "Do you or your husband belong to any religious organization?" She asked the question based on the fact that the Anderson's home lacked any religion symbols.

Maggie smiled as she replied. "We do not, but if you ask me if I believe in God, speaking only for myself, I do. Strongly and without doubting his existence."

Detective Matthews asked Maggie when did she have her first "vision" and Maggie, ever so patiently told them what happened to her in the hospital. Paul looked at her with admiration as she was asked the same question for about the hundredth time, and yet she remained calm as she repeated her story again.

"Have you seen the "Messenger" again?" KC asked.

Maggie shook her head. "I hope that I never will. Detectives," she continued after a brief moment of hesitation. "It was a very strange experience, a frightening one for that matter. I was certain that I was dead and I did not know where I was. It was a colorless and sad environment where I would never want to go."

"My apologies," KC said. "I didn't mean to upset you."

"You did not upset me, you just made me recall something that I would rather not think about," Maggie replied.

"May I ask you about the vision of the cottage?" Matthews asked.

"Of course, that is what you are here for," Maggie answered and without waiting for the question, she began to explain what she had seen. "In my vision, I saw this beautiful white building with a small bell tower, surrounded by tall trees and a flower bed that were fenced in with neatly trimmed hedges. As I was walking up to the front porch I heard sounds coming from the left side. I walked to the edge of the porch and looked down and just before the tree line, I saw small arms sticking out from the ground but they disappeared when I yelled out, *what are you doing there.* That is why I didn't paint the arms. I believe there were four sets of arms, eight all together, they looked like children's arms, different ages." She explained and took a deep breath. "It was a horrifying scene.

I woke up crying and I immediately went to paint the scene so I wouldn't forget the details."

KC and Matthews noticed right away that Maggie had tears shining in her eyes and Paul protectively put his arms around his wife.

"I suppose," KC said in a quiet tone of voice. "Seeing visions would make you the *Gifted One*? I read on the Internet that several people claimed that title. I suppose it is good to have that kind of gift."

Maggie looked up at KC with a tear soaked face. "Detective Calhoun, do you think I want this "gift" to see visions of dead children, my husband company's explosion and airplane crash? Do you think that it is a gift? No, Detective Calhoun, it is not a gift, it is a curse and it is eating my heart and soul. There are many times that I wish that I had died."

Matthews got up and KC followed his example. "We are going to get a court order to dig up the area that you saw in your dream, or vision," he said to them as they said their goodbyes. "Would you be willing to accompany us to the scene?" He asked.

"I will have to wear a protective mask for my allergies, but yes, Detective Matthews, I'll going to join you and the search team to assist you any way possible," Maggie said and they shook hands again with the departing officers.

Two days later Maggie received a phone call from the LAPD that they obtained a court order to search around the cottage on the property of the Los Angeles County Arboretum, and for her convenience, so they told her, they would send an unmarked police car to pick her up. Needless to say, Paul would not hear about her going by herself to participate such a traumatic event, and since the police detectives did not have any problem with him joining them, he, too got into the Crown Victoria.

It was evident that the Director of the Arboretum and Botanical Garden was not happy but he had no choice other than to comply with the search warrant issued by a local judge. The Director shook his head expressing his strong dislike for the bulldozer or any heavy machinery that the police intended to bring in for their search, but he stepped aside to let them do their jobs.

Maggie took an anti-histamine before she left the house and just for the safe side, she wore a mask when she boarded the golf cart that was provided for her convenience. She just sat there when several police officers cordoned off the area and the machine began to remove soil from the area that she pointed out. The digging went on for a couple of hours without much success and the detectives without speaking out loud, began to question her claim that the place where four small children's bodies were buried was the very same cottage that she had seen in her vision.

The diggers wanted to take a break but Matthews asked them to do another half an hour before they stopped for lunch. They did not argue, the digging continued until unexpectedly Maggie got up, stepped off from the golf cart and walked up to the disturbed earth on the ground. She looked down into the hole and waved KC over. "I have made a big mistake," she said to her with apology in her voice.

KC began to visualize all the hassle they will have to endure from the press, the Director of the place and by their Captain once they find out that they spent thousands of dollars out of the tight budget for the heavy equipment and manpower to find absolutely nothing because the painter retracted her vision. "What do you mean by you made big mistake?" She asked Maggie while trying to sound understanding.

"They are digging on the wrong side," Maggie said. "I painted the cottage as I saw it in my vision, but I just realized that in real life, the front door up on the porch is to the right and so is the bell tower, while in my vision and on the painting is on the left," she explained.

KC shouted to Matthews who in turn stopped all the equipment from digging further down on the right side. The Director of the Arboretum and Botanical Garden was outraged when they began to move their digging equipment to the left. KC showed him the court order which said the "cottage and its surroundings", which meant both sides and behind the building.

Paul couldn't help but to notice the looks Maggie was getting from the policemen and policewomen present, but he also noticed that Maggie ignored them. Twenty minutes later, the machines were shut down because one of the policemen yelled that they found the first remains. Shortly after, to everyone's heartache, the second, the third and the fourth remains of children were unearthed. The Police Pathologist who was present carefully lay down the skeletons on tables that where set up to have their picture taken before they were put in body bags.

The looks that Maggie began to receive changed from doubtful to wondering, how did she know? Most of the police department employees always have been skeptical about psychics and the painter refused that title, claiming that she did not feel the present of the dead children, rather, she dreamed about them in a vision.

"What now?" Paul asked KC and Matthews.

"They are going to determine their ages, hopefully their DNA's still can be harvested and the approximate time of their deaths," KC replied. "Once that is done, for the record, we are probably going to ask for your and Mrs. Anderson's whereabouts on those dates."

"Very well," Paul replied. "You know where we live."

The detectives thanked them for their collaborations and instructed one of the policemen to drive the Andersons' home.

CHAPTER NINE

MAGGIE WAS BUSY in her studio working on a landscape, which was a replica of her real life garden at the back of the house, when the ringing of her doorbell interrupted her work. "Paul," she yelled to her husband who was working in another bedroom that was designated as his study. She heard the sound of voices and Paul appeared in her doorway.

"The detectives are back," he said and rolled his eyes.

"I'll be right there," she replied with a grin of her own and cleaned her brush that she was using. Putting them down in their usual places, she went to the bathroom to wash her hands. A couple of minutes later Maggie joined Paul and the two detectives already sitting in the living room.

"Hello, again," she said and shook hands with them before sitting down next to her husband on the couch. "What can I do for you?"

Matthews cleared his voice before he began. "Mrs. Anderson, we thought that perhaps you wanted to know that the bodies of the four children were identified via DNA and through the missing children's network. Two were boys, age six and eight; the two girls were age six and seven. They were reported missing in Portland, Oregon two months ago. It took us two weeks to get DNA samples from their parents. I have to ask this, just for the process of elimination, where were you and your husband two months ago?"

"Actually, we were right here. After my procedure and what I experienced, I preferred to remain home. As for an alibi, I have been around town, and was questioned by the FBI, the CIA, also by Homeland Security, even by ATF, so there are great many people who can verify my presence."

KC smiled at her but it was not a smile of admiration and Maggie sensed that right away. And there was something else about KC, Maggie thought as she was looking at the young female detective. KC began to fade from her sight and a large tree appeared with a car in flames from hitting the tree. On the driver's' seat was a woman, possibly in her mid-fifties, dead from the head wound received when she was thrown against the windshield. The airbag was not deployed and the woman was not wearing a seatbelt. Maggie turned to the right of KC and she focused on a backseat where a small child, around eighteen months old was strapped into the child seat.

There were sounds of sirens and Maggie turned her head toward the living window because it appeared that sirens were very close to her house. When her eyes returned to KC, she could clearly see that the firemen were trying to remove the child from the backseat. The child was screaming and the firemen were working feverishly until they were forced back by the flames, and then the car exploded. The sound of explosion was so vivid that Maggie jumped up from where she was sitting.

"Maggie, are you alright? Maggie, look at me." She heard Paul's voice but she was unable to reply as she lost consciousness.

When she looked up, she was in a hospital's emergency room, surrounded by Paul, a nurse and KC; Detective Matthews was outside talking to the doctor. "What happened?" Maggie asked.

Paul told her about her odd behavior, how she was staring at KC, and toward the window and how she just collapsed into Paul's arms. As her husband filled her in about what happened, Maggie recalled her vision. It was the very first time that a vision came to her not in a dream, but while she actually was talking to people.

"Detective Calhoun," she said. KC stepped up to the bed.

"Yes, Mrs. Anderson, are you feeling alright?" She asked Maggie.

"Is your mother's car a red Toyota Corolla, with the license plate number QVC 911?" Maggie inquired.

"How did you know that?" KC asked with surprise.

"Do you have any children?" Maggie asked. KC looked at her surprised. "Do you?" Maggie insisted on an answer in a raised voice.

"Well, yes. I have a daughter, she lives with my mother in Lexington, Kentucky," she explained.

"Call her," Maggie said almost demanding. "Call her and tell her not to drive anywhere tonight."

"What are you talking about?" KC asked but reached for her cell phone anyway.

"Call her," Maggie screamed at the detective whose facial expression began to show concern. She pushed the automatic dial button.

"Hi Mom," KC said into the phone. "I am fine, how is my baby girl doing?" She listened to her mother's voice while watched Maggie who was also staring at her. "Mom, I cannot explain this just now, but please do not drive anywhere tonight, okay? You promise me?" She listened again. "No, Mom, you have to reschedule her appointment for another day. Yes, I know it's hard to get an appointment, but please do this for me. I will explain the reason later, okay. Promise?" She asked and then smiled. "I love you, too, and give an extra kiss to my baby girl." She pushed the off button and looked at Maggie. "What is this all about?"

Maggie looked at Paul and he nodded, that she should tell KC what she had seen. Maggie took a deep breath and she slowly told KC all the details she saw in her vision. KC shook her head. "I can't believe you, this is all bullshit. You have a lot of nerve to scare people like that."

"Now just a minute, detective," Paul intervened. "If it was not for Maggie, you would never have found those small children in the Arboretum."

KC turned around and without a word she left the room. A short time later, Detective Matthews knocked, and then entered the room. "You have my colleague all upset, Mrs. Anderson," he commented.

"I am very sorry but I had to tell her to prevent such a horrible accident," Maggie said. "Paul," she turned to her husband. "I want to go home."

"I'll go talk to the doctor," Paul told her and left the room.

"Detective Matthews, do you have any suspect or lead in the deaths of those children?" Maggie asked.

"We do know that they were not killed at the place where they were found. It is our opinion that they were murdered either in Oregon, or on the way here to Los Angeles, and then they were buried next to that cottage. The director of the Arboretum mentioned that employees noticed that there was some disturbance around the cottage but they assumed that perhaps a contractor was working in the area. They mentioned it to him and he confirmed that some soft earth was delivered earlier to the very same spot. We are checking on that lead as we speak."

"I would appreciate if you keep me informed," Maggie asked.

"We will do that, Mrs. Anderson," Matthews said and left the room when the doctor entered.

The doctor informed Maggie and Paul that they could not find anything wrong, he thought that perhaps Maggie was dehydrated or upset about something, but the MRI did not show any brain abnormalities. He ordered rest and signed the release form.

They barely got home from the hospital when the doorbell rang once again. Maggie opened the door and she saw KC standing in front of the door. She walked in and after Maggie closed the door, she turned to KC who unexpectedly hugged her tightly. When she finally let Maggie go, her face was covered with tears. "What happened?" Maggie asked and pulled KC by the hand to the sofa.

KC, who could not recall the last time she cried, was crying like a child. "I just got a phone call from my mother," she said and Maggie's heart began to race from fear. "Her neighbor came by and asked her if she could borrow my mother's car because her daughter, who serves in the Navy was at sea. She left her daughter in her mother's care and the child was running a high fever. Mrs. Wheeler told my mother that her car would not start and she asked my mother if she could use her car because she needed to take the child to the hospital. Of course, my mother loaned her the car. They almost made it to the hospital when for some reason Mrs. Wheeler lost control of the car; she drove off the road and hit a tree. Just like you saw it in your vision, the car burst into flames. Mrs. Wheeler died at the scene and the firemen were unable to remove the child from her seat before the car exploded. If it wasn't for you, my mother and my child would have died today." She explained and hugged Maggie one more time. "You are indeed the *Gifted One*. I no longer have any doubt about it."

"I am very sorry that Mrs. Wheeler and the child died," Maggie said. "I did not see the faces clearly, but I knew the car."

"What is going on?" Paul asked entering the living room. Maggie told her husband about the phone call KC just received regarding her mother's neighbor. He kissed Maggie's hand, smiled at KC and once again he left them alone.

CHAPTER TEN

"SIR," MARY ANN said as she opened the door. "You want to take this phone call."

The Deputy Director of the FAA looked at her questioningly. "You could just buzz me," he murmured. She shook her head and pointed at his telephone with the blinking "hotline" written above. He nodded and Mary Ann withdrew into her office just outside Roland Riggs'.

"Riggs," he said into the receiver.

"My name is Dr. Paul Anderson," introduced himself the caller. "I am calling on the behalf of my wife, Margaret, Maggie as everyone calls her."

Riggs was not in the mood for a chat, he was due to report to the White House on increase of security breaches at three major airports. "What is that I can do for you? He managed to say to the caller.

"Well, what I am about to tell you even sounds unbelievable to me, but my wife is convinced that there will be a major airline disaster which is going to take place in two weeks time, on August 11th." Paul informed the Deputy Director. He was also very certain that Mr. Riggs just rolled his eyes in his no doubt comfortable office.

"Dr. Anderson," replied Riggs after rolling his eyes and taking a deep breath. "Is your wife psychic or something like that?"

"No, Mr. Riggs," Paul told him. "She has a sound mine and she is only taking heart medication and beta blockers, nothing that would make her hallucinate."

"Dr. Anderson," said Riggs. "Do you have any idea just how many phone calls of this nature we are getting a day? The FAA takes all phone calls very seriously, but we simply do not have the man power to investigate every single case because somebody had a bad dream."

"I believe you, Mr. Riggs, and trust me that it is not in my nature to believe supernatural predictions, I am a physicist by profession. My wife is convinced that CU Airlines will crash after colliding with a commuter plane over West Virginia, on August 11th," Paul said and even he knew how it sounded.

"I suppose she even has the flight number," Riggs said and his voice oozed sarcasm.

"Yes, she does, sir," Paul informed him. "It is flight number CU 0617."

Riggs scribbled the number and the date down. "Is there any significance of that number perhaps," he suggested and was ready to end the telephone call.

"Well, technically her parents elected to drive, but for some reason my wife believes that they will be on that flight or they would have direct contact with the flight she saw crashing." Paul replied. Riggs thought, *bingo*. "Look, Mr. Riggs, my wife, Maggie is concerned that they may change their minds and that they are going to fly, that is why they were warned about that particular flight, not to mention the possible loss of many lives. If you think Mr. Riggs that there is bad blood between Maggie and her parents, you are very wrong. Maggie is their only child and her mother is her best friend. Parents cannot be closer to a child than my wife is to hers. How are you getting along with your in-laws Mr. Riggs? I am blessed with wonderful people and my father-in-law is closer to me than my own father was."

"Is there a reason for their upcoming visit?" Riggs asked and put his pen down.

"My wife had a close call recently," Paul explained. Riggs interrupted him.

"Close call? Would you please explain." He said. Paul thought, *that is what I was about to do.*

"Maggie had a heart procedure done recently and while it was successful, she went into a coma and could not wake her for several hours." Paul informed Riggs. "When she woke, she told me that she had a strange vision."

"Your wife had seen the light at the end of the tunnel?" Riggs asked grinning.

Paul swallowed his anger and tried to remain civilized. "No, Mr. Riggs," he replied. "Maggie did not see any tunnel, she saw the Messenger."

Riggs heard enough. "Dr. Anderson," he said to Paul. "As I mentioned, we are getting phone calls such as yours on a daily basis. As a matter-of-fact, we get almost a dozen a day, so you must understand my position, could you? We are having major budget cuts by Congress every opportunity they get, but at the same time, we are obligated to investigate all terrorist threats and strange phone calls that we find reasonably threatening."

"Listen to me, Mr. Riggs and listen to me very carefully." Paul said genuinely angry. "My wife and I not asking for recognition, rewards or anything else than to cancel that flight so people would not die. That plane is a Boeing 767 and holds more than 300 passengers and crew. You simply cannot allow those people to die, to leave widows, orphans and grieving parents behind."

"Dr. Anderson," Riggs said in the calmest voice he could muster. "Please leave your information with my office manager Mary Ann and we see what we can do."

"Mr. Riggs," Paul replied. "I am only going to say this once. I will personally hold you responsible if anything should happen to that plane and its passengers."

"Are you threatening me, Dr. Anderson?" Riggs asked with threats in his voice as well.

"Noooooo," Paul stretched out the word. "I am only telling you that if something should happen, I will make sure that the media will hear this conversation that we just had."

"What do you implying?" Riggs asked suspiciously.

"I have taped this telephone conversation, Mr. Riggs, for one reason and one reason only. I want to make sure that the world would know that you ignored our warning about an upcoming and avoidable disaster." Paul said and hung up the phone.

Mary Ann opened the door and entered Riggs' office. "Did you hear the whole thing?" She nodded. "Who the hell does he think he is, talking to me like that?" He glanced at Mary Ann who was looking at her shoes instead of him. "Speak up if you want to say something." He urged his long time confidant.

"Dr. Anderson is Nobel Prize winner physicist and those paintings on your wall," she pointed at three large, beautiful and peaceful landscapes on Riggs' office wall. "That was painted by Maggie Davis-Anderson, the caller's wife."

"You are kidding me, right?" Riggs asked while stared at his favorite paintings. He actually owned several of Davis-Anderson's painting at his home in the city as well as at his summer home.

"Why do you think I forwarded his phone call?" She asked and sat down in one of the chairs that waited empty in front of his desk. "Have I ever forwarded such a call to you?" Riggs shook his head and looked at Mary Ann.

"What now?" He asked her in return.

"I suggest we should contact the airlines, it never hurts to take precautions," she suggested and Riggs agreed.

"No media," he warned her.

"Don't even go there," Mary Ann replied and vividly recalled some of the headlines from the past. The FAA has always been a target of the news hungry media and even the smallest distraction in air traffic would cause an avalanche of calls and criticism.

"Before we call CU Airlines, I want you to check on Anderson and his wife's family background," Riggs said after a moment of hesitation.

"Is that really necessary in the case of a Nobel Prize winner?" Mary Ann asked as she got up from the chair. "All you have to do is to Google it."

"Yeah," Riggs commented with a smirk on his face. "Don't call the Police, the FBI or the Homeland Security, just Google it."

"That's technology of its best for you," she replied with a smile and left her boss' office.

CHAPTER ELEVEN

THE HEADACHE THAT woke Maggie was almost unbearable. She could barely open her eyes but when she finally managed, she glanced over Paul's side of the bed. Seeing that he already got up, she pushed herself out of bed and staggered into the kitchen where Paul was sitting drinking his coffee with two pieces of toast on a plate in front of him.

"You are up," he commented, but at the same time, he also noticed that something was wrong with Maggie. "Are you alright?"

Maggie shook her head but even that movement was painful. She sat down across the table from Paul and looked at him. "Can I get you anything?" Paul offered.

"May I have some coffee and some migraine pills please," Maggie mumbled and watched Paul getting the coffee and from the bathroom, he returned with a couple of tablets that he placed on a napkin in front of her with a glass of water. She took the two pills and buried her face in the palm of her hand.

"I can stay home you know," Paul remarked although truthfully he had a meeting with a building inspector and the Air Force representative for a final walk-through of his new building. Maggie slowly shook her head again, she was fully aware of the fact that Paul was under great deal of pressure and it was only a headache anyway probably brought on by the nightmare of the airplane crash again.

"Same nightmare?" Paul inquired. The date of Maggie's first prediction, August 11th was only a week away and Maggie had the same nightmare every single night. Paul called the FAA again but Riggs would not take his call again, so he once more, left a message.

"Yes," Maggie replied and asked Paul to give her the phone, which he did. Maggie dialed her parents' number in Connecticut. Her father picked up the phone at first ring. "Hello, dad," Maggie said.

Her father was very pleased to hear Maggie's voice. "Well, we were just talking about you," he informed her. "What can we bring you Maggie, what would you and Paul like from the East coast?"

"Yourselves," Maggie answered. "Dad, I just wanted to make absolutely certain that you and Mom will not fly on the 11th of August."

"I told you darling, and I told Paul, too, it is time to crank up the good old RV and take a nice trip. As a matter of fact, we are all packed up and ready to leave first thing tomorrow morning, that way we won't have to rush and will have plenty of time to get there for your wedding anniversary." He explained.

"Is Mom home?" Maggie asked.

"I am sorry honey, she just left for the supermarket to buy the last few items for our trip, but if you want, she can call you when she gets back." He offered.

"No, it's alright dad, we are going to see you real soon. Dad, please drive carefully, you promise?" She asked with concern.

"Of course, is there any other way to drive?" Her father laughed.

Paul cleaned up the kitchen table and kissed Maggie before leaving. "If there is anything you need, or if you need for me to come home, call right away," he instructed her and left for work.

After Paul left, Maggie debated on eating something but even the slowest movement caused sharp pain in her head. Paul did offer to make her breakfast before leaving, but she declined his offer knowing that he was in a rush. She got up from the table and returned to bed, hoping that perhaps a little more sleep would ease her headache.

The children unexpectedly came out of nowhere, two girls and two boys. They playfully run around in the beautiful garden, which later Maggie identified as the Arboretum. One of the girls ran up the steps leading inside the cottage and when she entered, the inside of the building was not like the one that Maggie visited with the detectives. It was a private home, a single family room, and very soon, she saw the other three children entering. They were following the sound of a voice coming from the basement and they went down the steps in single file.

Her vision changed and she was watching the house from the outside. There was an older model orange Chevy Malibu in the driveway and she tried to see the license plate, but she could only see the letters on it and not the numbers, it said SYL and the bottom of the license plate showed that it was issued in the State of California. All of a sudden sounds of screams forced her to reenter the house, but before she was able to open the door to the basement, a man appeared in the kitchen doorway and asked her who she was looking for. Maggie replied that she was looking for the children from Oregon. The man laughed and replied to her that they were in good hands, just like the others were. "Others?" She asked the man but he disappeared. Maggie opened the door that led down to the basement and very carefully stepped down on the concrete steps. She noticed a man's shadow on the wall but her attention was drawn to floor that was moving. To her horror she realized that it was a huge puddle of blood, as a matter of fact, there was so much blood that it created a small tide and was coming up on the steps. Maggie backed up and shut the door to the basement, and then she ran out of the house.

She sat up in the bed ever so grateful for the ringing of her bedside phone that woke her. "Maggie?" She heard KC's voice.

"Hello," she answered weakly. She began to shiver in her wet nightgown that was soaked with perspiration.

"Maggie, are you alright?" KC asked her again.

"I am sorry KC, I just woke up from a horrible nightmare," she said, with her eyes barely open.

"Do you want me to come over? I can get away," KC offered. Maggie thought about it and agreed. Because she was not certain if she was going to make it to the door when KC arrived, she gave the detective the security code to their front door.

She was still sitting at the edge of the bed when KC arrived and walked into the entryway, calling out her name. "I am in the master bedroom," Maggie replied.

KC walked in and she was shocked to see what bad shape her new friend was. "Maggie, let me draw you a nice bath," she offered. "You need to get out that wet nightgown before you catch a cold."

Maggie agreed and KC helped her into the spacious bathroom. They let the bathwater fill the tub three quarter high. Maggie, although she was somewhat shy, let KC pull the nightgown off from her and helped her to step into the bathtub. It felt good and the bubble bath made the water smoother than usual. KC got a hand towel and from the icemaker she put some ice cubes on the towel and rolled it up, just then she placed it on Maggie forehead that was burning up.

"Thank you, KC," Maggie said and she even managed to smile. When KC wanted to leave to give her privacy, Maggie stopped her. "Please, stay, I don't want to be alone."

"No problem," KC replied and sat down on the closed topped toilet.

"I had another vision about the children," Maggie said after a few moments of silence. KC straightened up her back when she heard Maggie's words.

"Can you tell me about it?" She asked.

Maggie told her everything she envisioned, the happy children, how they entered the cottage at the Arboretum that inside looked like someone's home, which she described to KC in details, even the color of the furniture, how the furniture was arranged, the basement, which was unusual for California unless it was a wine cellar.

She told KC about the screaming children, the two men, one seen and the other one's shadow, and the flood of blood. She took a brief break and she told KC about the car and the partial license plate.

"It is possible that the children were kidnapped, not all at once from Oregon and transported to Los Angeles where they were killed." KC suggested.

"I don't know how to describe this feeling, but it seems to me that there were most definitely two men involved, perhaps one kidnapped the children and the other murdered them," Maggie mentioned. KC nodded that was a possibility, she and Detective Matthews already talked about that, but not with Maggie.

When Maggie finished with her bath, KC helped her to get out of the tub but let Maggie dry herself and waited for her in the living room. Although she and Detective Matthews had been in the house a few times, it dawned on KC that she never really looked at the pictures that were arranged on the mantel above the fireplace. Since Maggie did not join her yet, it was a good time to take a look at family photographs of the woman whom she strangely felt a close kinship with since she saved her mother and child's lives.

There were no photos of children anywhere, but she already knew that the Andersons did not have any, so it was not a surprise. Most pictures were taken of Paul and Maggie and her parents, in their home in Connecticut. It was evident that the Andersons liked to travel as many of the pictures were taken in various places in the United States, in the Bahamas and several shots showed them in Puerto Rico. What got KC's attention about those photos was the fact Paul either looked at the right, or to the left, or even downward, but never into the camera.

"Hmmm", KC mumbled. She could not explain why, but for some reason she did not care for Dr. Paul Anderson. KC knew that he was a very smart man, obviously, after all, he got a Nobel Prize for physics, but his over attentiveness of Maggie was troublesome. When she mentioned this to her partner, Detective Matthews, he replied to her that probably it was her problem with men; they either were too attentive or not enough. The other thing KC observed was the lack of Paul's facial expression in the pictures, he never smiled, laughed or even grinned. She noticed that about Maggie's husband in real life, too.

When twenty minutes later Maggie still did not show, KC went to look for her in the bathroom and when she did not find her there, she checked the master bedroom. There were no signs of Maggie. She had to get dressed as her nightgown was in the hamper and the walk in closet door was left open. KC slowly made her way to the fourth bedroom that was designated as Maggie's studio.

Maggie did not look up when KC entered, nor that she reply when KC called out her name. She was completely involved with painting the story what she told KC about her dream. KC sat down on the daybed and silently watched her friend paint. When Maggie finished with painting the basement, which was a gruesome scene, she began to paint the portrait of a man whom she told KC, she encountered in the house in her vision. In the basement picture she only painted a man's shadow on the wall, while the portrait of the man was vivid, so vivid indeed as if it was a photograph.

Maggie worked feverishly without stopping and KC took out her cell phone and made a brief video of the portrait and the painting that Maggie already finished. The third painting showed a house, similar to the cottage, yet different as it looked more like a private home than a showpiece, and she also added the orange color Chevy Malibu with the partial license plate parked in the driveway. When she completed that painting as well, she just sat on her chair and stared in front of her not touching another canvas on the easel. KC tried not to make any noise, but when she touched Maggie shoulder, as if she was just waking up from a dream, she looked at KC and smiled.

"Are you alright?" KC asked her. Maggie nodded. "How about if I take you out for lunch, what do you think?"

"That sounds very nice," Maggie responded and got up from the chair. "What do you think of the paintings?" She asked KC. The detective looked again at all three and took a longer look at the painting that showed the house and then she smiled. There was something more on that painting, something additional other than what Maggie had told her, the house that Maggie painted had a number, 2550. No street name, just a number but that was enough to narrow down all the streets in Los Angeles County with that number. KC took a couple of pictures of each of the paintings on her cell phone and forwarded them to Detective Matthews with a comment that they needed to talk, but she also informed him that she and Maggie Anderson were going out for lunch. When they stepped outside, Maggie re-set the security system and they were on their way.

KC offered to drive and Maggie gladly accepted, as she had not driven for a while, not since her procedure, months earlier. KC asked her where she wanted to go and Maggie asked her in return if she ever ate the Bamboo Tree Chinese Restaurant. KC laughed and told her that it was also her favorite Chinese food place in LA. The place was getting crowded but the Maitre'd recognized Maggie and ushered them inside without any further delay. "I can easily get use to this kind treatment," KC remarked after they were seated.

The service as usual was very efficient and Maggie, as always, ordered her favorite, which was Mongolian Beef. KC decided to try it too as she always ordered chicken dishes. They were almost finished with lunch when KC's cell phone began to vibrate. "KC," she answered after she pressed on the *accept* button.

"Detective Calhoun, is my wife with you?" She heard Paul Anderson agitated voice.

"Yes, she is," she replied but did not offer to put Maggie on the phone.

"Where are you?" He demanded to know.

"Dr. Anderson, I invited Maggie for lunch and we just finished," she explained.

"I have been trying to reach her and there was no answer. You know her situation, she shouldn't be out alone, it's too dangerous," he objected.

"Dr. Anderson, she is fine and I am a trained police officer with a gun on my belt, she is more than safe with me," KC responded to Maggie's angry husband.

"I want her home," he said, trying to control his anger. "Where are you, I can go and get her," Paul suggested.

"I know that you are very busy and I can assure you that I will take her home safe and sound," KC told him. There was a moment of hesitation from Paul's part.

"I am sorry, I didn't mean to raise my voice at you," he apologized. "I am just worried about her so much."

"I fully understand," KC replied.

"Thanks for taking her home," Paul said and ended the phone call.

"It was Paul," KC informed Maggie who already figured that out. "As you heard, I promised him that I will take you home safe and sound." Maggie smiled at KC. "He cares about you a lot," she commented.

Maggie looked out on the window as she replied. "Yes, he certainly does."

The way she said that rubbed KC in a certain way. "Do you mind my asking, how the two of you met?" KC asked.

"Hmmm," Maggie turned back to her. "Actually that was very interesting. One friend of mine from college was from Puerto Rico and she invited me to stay with she and her family in San Juan during spring break. I really liked Puerto Rico and I told my friend, her name was Juanita Gomez, what if we stayed and attended college there. She told me that she wanted to finish her education where she started, but if I wanted to attend the University of Puerto Rico in San Juan, she would go with me to the campus to check it out. Since we had free time on our hands, we drove there and walked around the campus. We sort of got lost and I noticed a tall man, around late thirtyish who was watching us. He probably noticed that we didn't know which direction to go. He approached us and he couldn't take his eyes off me. He introduced himself as Dr. Paul Anderson, a faculty member at the university and he told us that he was a physics professor. He asked me if I was a student and when I said 'not yet', he asked me out for a date and the rest is history." Maggie explained.

"So you like older guys?" KC joked.

"Paul is almost fifteen years older than me," Maggie said. "He did not change at all since I have known him." She remarked.

"How did you two end up Los Angeles?" KC inquired.

"Well, as it turned out, I decided not to attend the university in San Juan after all and returned to the states with Juanita. Paul remained in Puerto Rico for another year. He left the university and with his friend, Christopher Collins joined a government research facility which was later transferred right here to Los Angeles. After I graduated from Columbia University, he flew back to Connecticut where I was staying with my parents and proposed. Good looking, charming and intelligent man, and living in California, how could I turn him down?" Maggie told her. KC noticed one thing; Maggie not once mentioned the word "love" when she talked about Paul.

KC looked at her watch, it was two in the afternoon. "Listen, Maggie, you can turn me down, but I was wondering if you would mind to stop by the station with me before I take you home. If you don't want to, I'll take you straight to home."

"Not a problem, I have never been in a police station before," Maggie agreed. KC paid their bill and drove her friend to her place of employment without telling her the reason. When they walked in and everyone welcomed them, just then Maggie understood the purpose of the stop. It was Detective Matthews last day of work before he retired from the Police Department. Many of the detectives were already in the meeting room and soon as they saw KC walk in with Maggie, Matthews waved them to the front.

There was a huge sign above a long table that had certificates, gifts, a large cake and plastic cups with soft drinks lined up on it. Speeches were made, laughter and tears were shared and Maggie actually enjoyed herself in the company of KC's colleagues. "You are going to miss him," Maggie remarked to KC.

"Yes, I will. I worked with him for the past five years," KC agreed. "However; my new partner is here, do you want to meet him?"

"Sure, why not," Maggie shrugged.

There were a group of detectives and police officers talking to Matthews when KC tapped on the shoulder of a tall dark haired man. He turned around and his smile became permanent on his face when he saw Maggie. "Maggie, this is Detective Tony Morales, Tony, this is Mrs. Maggie Davis-Anderson, I briefed you about her situation, remember?" KC asked and snapped her finger when Tony failed to respond. He turned her head toward her.

"What?" He asked.

"What is the matter with you, she is married," KC said, reminding her new partner of Maggie's marital status when she noticed that Tony and Maggie would not look away from each other.

Maggie had never felt like that before in her entire life as she felt when she looked into Tony's blue eyes. She could feel a tingling sensation rushing down from her head to her toes, and all of a sudden she felt an urge to be held by the man whom she just met. *Dear God,* she thought. *Snap out of this.*

"Maggie, are you ready to go home?" KC asked her when her friend said goodbye and wished good luck to the retiring Detective Matthews.

"Yes, sure," Maggie replied.

"Would you mind if I tag along?" Detective Tony Morales asked.

"Why in the world you want to do that?" KC asked grinning.

"Well," Tony replied. "I probably should get to know Dr. and Mrs. Anderson better if I am going to work with her, don't you think?"

KC rolled her eyes and asked Maggie if it was all right with her if Tony was going to join them. Her face turned red and she assured KC that she didn't mind.

Tony volunteered to drive and he was rather quiet as he drove through the downtown area toward the Andersons' household. When he pulled up to the driveway, Maggie made a comment that it didn't look like her husband made it home yet. She invited them inside for coffee, and while KC was ready to go home, Tony nudged her shoulder and she agreed to join them.

Maggie punched in the security code and when the light turned green she opened the door and let them in. She offered seats in the living room while she was making the coffee. KC noticed that Maggie came alive and she did not seem so lethargic as she was earlier. It was at that moment that she realized that her newly found friend, Maggie Davis-Anderson was a very lonely and many ways, ignored woman. Her husband, Paul was very attentive to her when she was in need of medical attention, perhaps because he wanted to make sure that nothing was said in her semi-conscious moment that was not supposed to be heard by anyone else. Those thoughts stuck in the back of KC's mind.

Maggie placed the coffee, cups, sugar, cream and some cookies on a tray and she was about to carry them into the living room when she heard Tony's voice behind her. "Please let me help you with that," he offered.

Maggie turned around and her heart skipped a beat, not because of her prior condition, but because Tony had such a smile on his face and in his eyes that would have melted a stick of butter in the middle of Antarctica. "Thank you," she whispered. When she let him take the tray from her hands and his fingers touched her hands, she thought that she was going to drop the tray, but it was already secured in his hands.

"I got it," he whispered back to her. "Here it is," he announced as he put the tray down on the coffee table as if it was his own home. KC tried to hide her smile as she put the magazine she was reading back down on the table where she found it.

"Are you new in the area?" Maggie asked Tony.

"No, I actually have lived here for the past ten years," he informed her. "I am originally from San Diego."

"So you were transferred in?" Maggie inquired.

"I was working in the cold case department and I put in for a transfer when I heard that Matthews was retiring, and here we are," he replied.

"Congratulations," Maggie told him.

"I understand that you are a wonderful artist," Tony said.

"I just do what comes naturally, I suppose," she replied quietly.

"I saw three of your latest paintings that KC forwarded from her cell phone. If you don't mind, I would like to see the originals," he requested.

"Of course," Maggie replied and got up to show Tony the way to her studio.

"Don't mind me," KC remarked with a grin on her face.

Inside the room that was designated as her studio, Tony picked up some of her paintings and he was surprised so see how beautiful her paintings with landscapes were with their vibrant and life imitating colors. Maggie seemed confused as he stood there. "It's strange," she mumbled. "KC, would you please come in here." She called out to the detective from the living room. She appeared seconds later.

"What's going on?" She asked seeing how upset Maggie was. She glanced at Tony but he just shrugged his shoulders.

"The three paintings, they are gone," Maggie said and stared at KC. "The house was locked and secured, you saw me coding the security alarm," she reminded KC and looked at her for an explanation.

KC thought about it for a moment and then turned to Maggie. "Call your husband and ask him if he had a chance to come home while you were gone."

"What are you saying? You think that he came home and took the paintings? That just doesn't make any sense." Maggie argued.

"I know, but would you please call him, that way we could find out if he took them or if someone else broke in here somehow," she urged her.

Maggie was very unhappy and concerned at the same time. If Paul did not take the paintings, they may have a major security problem in their home. She did not want to get upset over something like that, and besides, she didn't notice anything else missing, or was out of order. She picked up the phone and dialed Paul's private number. "Hi, Paul," she said as calmly as she could.

"Hi, honey," he replied cheerfully. "How was your lunch?" He asked.

"That was nice, KC treated me, so I owe her a lunch," she told him. "What time are you coming home?" She asked.

"I honestly don't know. I haven't been able to break away since this morning and someone had to bring me lunch. I didn't even have a time to go out and grab something. I am so pleased that you are doing alright, this place is a mass and the inspectors looking into everything, even into the toilet," he joked.

"I thought that perhaps you came home for lunch," Maggie commented.

Paul was hesitant with his answer for a couple seconds. "I just told you that I was very busy all day, did something happen?" He asked with concern.

"No," Maggie said and it was the first time that she ever lied to Paul. When she turned off her cell phone, she looked at KC. "He said that he did not come home for lunch and there are only three people who know the security combination, Paul, myself and you, KC, but I was with you while the paintings were taken."

"You need to talk to Paul about this for certain. Maybe you should be changing the security code," KC suggested and Maggie nodded that she would when Paul got home.

"I saw some of your paintings with the airplane on the ground in pieces and on fire, what was that about?" Tony asked. A cold chill ran through Maggie's entire body. "Are you all right, you turned as white as a wall," he remarked and looked at KC who also looked concerned.

Maggie looked directly in Tony's eyes and as if she was in a trance, she told him about her vision about a plane crash that supposed to happen on August 11, only a week away. She also told KC and Tony that they have contacted FAA and later on, she even called CU Airlines herself and warned them, but nobody called them back, despite their repeated attempts. "When Paul talked to Mr. Riggs, at the FAA, he promised that he would discuss it with the airlines, but so far nobody called, nobody came or expressed interest in saving lives. I was worried about my parents but my father decided to drive their RV across country, yet I am still very concerned about them."

"Do you know where the plane is going to crash, the location that is?" Tony asked. Maggie shook her head.

"I am very sorry but I don't know. It really troubles me that I cannot help those unfortunate passengers who will be on that plane," she said with genuine concern.

KC looked at her watch and motioned to Tony to get ready to leave. "Listen, we have to go but it was very nice to meet you finally. I hope to see you again, soon," Tony said and reached out to shake her hand. He held her hand and she did not make an attempt to pull it back. KC had to clear her voice to bring them back to reality. Tony smiled at Maggie and whispered. "We have to go."

"I know," Maggie whispered and reclaimed her hand. "I hope to see you too, soon." She repeated his words.

CHAPTER TWELVE

"YOU ARE AWFULLY quiet," KC remarked as she was driving toward Tony's apartment to drop him off before she headed home as well.

Tony glanced at her direction as he replied. "I was thinking about Maggie." He confessed.

KC already knew that Tony took an immediate liking to Maggie Davis-Anderson, but she was now her friend and Tony just became her colleague. "Look, Tony," she said to him. "You have to keep in mind that she is off limits to you."

"Why is that?" He asked, wanting to know.

"Because she is happily married for one, secondly, because I am worried about her," she admitted.

"There is where you are wrong," Tony replied. "She is only married, but not happily. Have you looked at those pictures in their living room? That man doesn't smile and you know what my mother use to say?" He asked.

"You actually listened to your mother?" KC chuckled.

"Hell yes, she is the smartest woman I have ever met, with the exception of you of course," he laughed, too.

"Of course," KC repeated. "So what is that your mother said?"

"She said that if a person never smiles, that person is hiding something," he told her. "I like Maggie," he continued. "Something about her is so delicate, so fragile that I want to take her in my arms and protect her."

KC was surprised by Tony's confession and she actually believed that her new partner fell in love with Maggie at first sight. "Look, her husband is a super smart guy and she is indeed fragile. Those visions she has are taking a toll on her. She gets depressed after each of these visions. She always recovers, but we have to be very careful when we talk to her."

"What do you know about her husband?" Tony asked.

KC shrugged her shoulder. "Not much really other than that he received the Nobel Prize for physics that he shared with his colleague and friend Christopher Collins. Collins perished in the explosion at their company, along with few other people."

"Yes, I remember that, it happened a couple of months ago, right?" He looked at her for confirmation. She nodded. "So what did they find out about the explosion?"

"Actually, it was a federal investigation because his company was working on federal contract projects, so we were left out of the loop about the outcome. I would not be surprised if the investigation is still on-going." KC informed him.

"Where were they when it happened?" He asked.

"According to Maggie, they were in the hospital that afternoon. Paul was at work and she fell ill and called him home. He insisted to take her to the emergency room and after spending hours there; she wanted to go to his company. They stopped at an eatery and Maggie told everyone to move away from the windows that faced the street toward the industrial park where his company's building was located, actually just a block from the restaurant. Although two patrons who did not listen to her warning died, she actually saved many lives."

"Well, it is certainly a good alibi," he remarked. "How about if he planted the explosives and went home to take care of her as an alibi?"

"What are you saying? He had a good thing going, multimillion-dollar contracts with the Air Force and other companies. Why would he do that? Why would he throw all that away?" KC asked.

Tony remained quiet for a couple of minutes, and then he asked KC to pull over which she did once it was safe. "What if you and I take a closer look at Paul Anderson's background and his business activities?" He asked.

"Is that what your private parts or your brain telling you?" KC asked and she was dead serious. What her new colleague was asking from her far exceeded their authority and they would have to do it in their spare time, not to mention they had to do it very carefully.

"Look, it is just a gut feeling," he said. "Sure, I like her, but something is very wrong in that household."

"I don't know about wrong, maybe unusual because of what she can do," she said hesitantly.

"I don't doubt her visions. I understand that she found those four children's bodies, too. I am just wondering about her husband's background, that is all," Tony explained.

"I don't care for Paul either, although I must admit he had never done anything that would have raised any suspicion. I suppose there is one thing that kind of stands out, but I would not call that a suspicion, just sort of standing out. It is his absolute devotion to Maggie. I can understand that he worries about her health and well being, but he was always there, I mean always there, as if he didn't want to miss anything she might have said, you know what I mean? Sure, there are good husbands who are taking care of their spouse's every need, but according to Maggie, who by the way called this devotion, this attending to her every need started right after her first vision."

"So are you in?" Tony asked.

KC took a deep breath. "We have to do our jobs first, and this project would come second, after working hours and very discretely."

Tony nodded. "Understood, and thank you."

CHAPTER THIRTEEN

MAGGIE WOKE AND screamed at the top of her lungs. The shadowy figure bent over her to try to stop her from screaming. "Maggie, it's me," she heard Paul's voice whispering. When he felt that she relaxed somewhat, he lifted his hand off from her mouth.

"Paul," Maggie said and swallowed hard. "What are you doing? You almost scared me to death," she complained.

"The power is out in the neighborhood," he explained as he sat down next to her on the couch. "What are you doing here in the living room, it's after eleven o'clock?" He asked.

"I must have fallen asleep waiting for you. Wow, already that late, you must be exhausted working all day. Did you eat something?" She inquired.

"Yeah, we had food brought in for lunch and for dinner, too. Basically we just sat around and tried to settle things with the government requirements, again," he emphasized the word. "It was so much easier when Chris was around, he handled the negotiations much better than I can," he said and sighed.

"Is everything settled?" Maggie wanted to know.

"We signed all the necessary paperwork, but this time we even have more security added than before and that was a pain." Paul said. All of a sudden the light came on in the living room and the security system beeped letting them know that it was also back on. "How was your day?" He asked.

"Well, as you know, I had lunch with KC, and then she took me to her police station to say goodbye to Detective Matthews. It was his last day of work, he retired," she explained. "Oh, yes, I met his replacement, Detective Tony Morales, he seems like a nice person, too."

"Hmm," Paul murmured and yawned. "I am sorry, I am totally exhausted. I think I am going to bed and you should too," he suggested and Maggie agreed.

After Paul showered and got into bed, Maggie debated on telling him about the three missing paintings but seeing how tired Paul appeared to be, she decided not to burden him with the subject. The security part of the problem did trouble her, but that had to wait too, there is nothing he could do about it in the middle of the night.

As soon as Paul's head hit the pillow, he was sound asleep, snoring slightly. Maggie lay on her side of the bed, her eyes wide open and many things rushed through her mind. She took inventory of the days events, her meeting with Detective Antonio Morales, who encouraged her to call him Tony, the questions that KC asked, the missing paintings, Paul's absence all day. It was most definitely the busiest day she had lately. Her thoughts returned to Tony and how it felt to have her hand held by him, how his fingers gently rubbed her hand, how his incredibly blue eyes, a startling contrast from his jet black hair, was looking at her, how his glance penetrated all way down to her inner core, to that live wire that was dormant for the past ten years.

She glanced over to Paul who was still sound asleep and she slowly got out of bed and went into her studio. Maggie closed the door behind her, not wanting to wake him with any noise she may make and flipped through the paintings that were leaning against the wall under her window. There were dozens of paintings; most of them were landscapes that waited to be framed. It was a project that she usually put together with the galleries directors. She still needed to get in contact with her usual gallery owner, not that there were no phone calls made from their part about the next gallery opening of her work. She was looking through the second row of paintings when some of them seemed out of order; the canvases were longer and higher than the landscapes canvases she normally used. Maggie turned those painting over and she was shocked to realize that they were the three missing paintings.

She sat down in her armchair and stared at them, the painting with the car, the house with the number and the portrait of the man whom she saw in her vision standing in the hallway. Maggie was certain that the paintings were not there, she was not the only person who was looking for them earlier in the day; KC and Tony were looking as well. There had to be only one explanation, one that she did not like and one that she did not want to admit.

When she returned home from the lunch and the visit at the police station in the company of the two detectives, the security alarm system was up and running. She had to punch in the code to get the front door open. The code controlled the other two doors, the back door, through the kitchen as well as the French door that led to the backyard. Despite his denial, Paul must have been home and took the paintings with him for some reason and he returned them when he got home, *so very late,* she thought. It was the very first time that Paul left her all by herself for an entire day since her heart procedure was done, a couple of months earlier. He did not even call her; she had to call him, another first as he usually called her a few times while he worked.

Maggie refocused her attention to the painting of the house and the number on the house's eaves, she distinctly recalled that she painted the numbers 2550 and now, on the paintings it showed 22550. She picked up the painting showing the orange Chevy Malibu with the license plate she painted, which was QVC, but the painting was showing GVC, she moved on to the third painting, the portrait and she concluded that it was not tempered with.

She glanced at her cell phone that was resting on the small end table but she decided not to bother KC until the morning. She placed the paintings back where she found them and sat down in the armchair. For the first time since they were married, Maggie felt doubts about Paul's honesty and she questioned herself about the reason for that. Did a certain detective by the name of Tony have anything to do with doubting of her husband of ten years? She was not certain.

She and Paul had a good, solid marriage. She knew that but not always with clarity. Paul was always busy with various projects and Maggie made sure that she was not in his way when he worked in his home office. It was the same way about Paul, he never interrupted her work, other than reminding her to take her medication or if it was time to have lunch or dinner. She called it a marriage of convenience because it was certainly not a marriage that involved passion, or even love. As a matter of fact, Maggie was unable to recall a single occasion when Paul told her that he loved her. They had not been intimate for the past few years and Paul repeatedly apologized to her, claiming a medical condition which she believed in because he told her, not that he ever showed her a medical note stating the reason for him being impotent. It was all right with her because she was not in love with him either, at least not anymore.

When they met it appealed to her to have an older and perhaps wiser man in her life who would provide her with security. She was not the kind of woman who was seeking financial stability, rather, Maggie wanted to have a man by her side who was not a philanderer and who treated her with respect. Paul did all that and for a while, for ten years it was enough for her, but now, meeting someone who took an interest in her, her feminine side, she admitted to herself, was a pleasant, refreshing and yes, even exciting feeling.

CHAPTER FOURTEEN

"DID YOU SLEEP well?" Paul asked when she entered the kitchen. He already prepared coffee and as appeared, he was ready to go to work. She was sleepy, yet, her adrenaline was working at full speed just thinking about the day ahead of her.

"Yes, I did despite the fact that I woke up a couple of times," she replied and watched Paul who was busy with putting some fruit into a brown paper bag. It was something he routinely did for years, claiming that if he didn't have time for lunch, at least he could grab an apple; banana or whatever was his fruit choice for the day.

"What is you plan for the day?" He asked her again and he closed his briefcase.

"I thought that I'll paint this morning," she answered. "I saw some lovely flower arrangements yesterday and I think I got the inspiration to paint flowers again."

Paul smiled at her response and bent down to kiss her goodbye. "Please take it easy, get plenty of rest. I will check on you later." He promised.

"Around what time you are coming home?" Maggie inquired when Paul opened the door leading toward the garage.

He replied to her half way out the door. "With Chris is gone, I have to do two jobs, so I am sorry but I may be home late again." He turned around one more time. "Of course, as always, if you need me I can break away no matter what. You were and always will be my priority." He remarked.

Maggie nodded that she understood and watched Paul drive out of the garage and disappear into the distance. She poured some coffee but changed her mind and poured the coffee down the sink and made a fresh pot before she dialed KC's phone number. "Detective Calhoun," KC answered the phone.

"This is Maggie," she introduced herself. "I need to talk to you this morning, it's very important."

There was a moment of hesitation before KC came back on the phone. "We have a new homicide to investigate but I will try to make it to your house as soon as I can."

"Thank you KC, I'll see you later," Maggie said and pushed the "end call" button on her cell phone. After having a light breakfast, she usually had some cereal with fruit, she entered her studio and began to paint the bouquet of flowers she had seen in the restaurant on the day before. Around ten o'clock in the morning she heard the doorbell and she was certain that it was KC. To her surprise, it was Tony who stood in the doorway.

"May I come in?" He asked as Maggie nervously just stood there and she could feel that her face was turning red. She showed him in.

"I am sorry, I expected KC to come," she mumbled as they sat down on the couch.

"She was planning on it but something came up. However, she said you told her that it was important that you speak to her. Since we are partners, here I am," he said with a smile on his face.

"Yes, indeed it is important, please come with me," Maggie said and led Tony into her studio. "Remember the three of us were looking for those paintings that I painted of my vision, the portrait, the house and the car? KC, you and I could not find them. I could not sleep so I went into my studio. They were back in the studio last night," she explained and showed them to Tony. "To make matters more interesting, take a look at the house number, it was changed from 2550 to 22550, and the letters on the car's partial license plate were also changed from QVC to GVC. It was a good thing that KC took pictures of them. The house was secured and Paul denied that he came home during the day. So who took the paintings, changed them and brought them back?" She asked visibly upset.

"I know that KC mentioned to you on the phone that we were working on a new homicide case," he said and when he saw that Maggie nodded, he continued. "We ran the portrait you painted through our database and we came across with a name of a drifter who happened to live 2550 Tombstone Road. KC and I went there first thing in the morning and when we got there, we found an orange Chevy Malibu on his driveway, the license plate of the car was QVC 465."

"He was dead?" Maggie asked.

"Yes, he was." Tony confirmed.

"How did he die, can you tell me?" Maggie inquired.

Tony did not respond right away. "Normally we don't release that information but I suppose you are part of that investigation, so I can tell you that he was found in the living room of the house in a pool of blood."

"Was anybody or anything else there?" Maggie asked.

"No, but there was a lot of dry blood. The CSI folks will let us know if it matches any of the unsolved crimes. We," he stopped for a moment as he looked at Maggie's concerned face. "We found a lot of pictures of nude children and that is all I can say about that."

Maggie stood there with tears streaming down on her face. "I want this to stop," she said quietly. "I want this vision business to go away."

Tony stepped up to her and put his hands on her shoulders. "Maggie, you may have to consider this as a gift," he said quietly. Maggie looked up at him with tear soaked face.

"A gift?" She asked. "I said this before, it not a gift, it is a curse. I am afraid to go to sleep because I may dream something horrible, and so far I have done that more than once. I want to be normal again; I want to have a sweet dream, flowers and grass instead of flood of blood by my feet."

Tony lifted her face up with his finger and bent down to kiss her. It was a soft and tender kiss, totally unexpected and Maggie was surprised how much she wanted him to kiss her again. She didn't pull away which he would have considered a sign of objection; instead she put her arms around Tony and offered her lips for another kiss. Tony pressed his lips down on hers with such passion that Maggie went limp in his arms. He picked her up and rushed to the bedroom because he wanted her as much as she wanted him. At first there was no time to take off their clothes, he pulled her panties off quickly and he entered her with the desire that she never experienced before. She moaned as he moved inside her and enjoyed every touch of his fingers and kisses of his lips.

"Maggie," Tony whispered to her when she clung to him upon climaxing for the first time in her life, truly climaxing not just a fake one to please her husband. Tony came inside her when his pleasure reached its peak and he collapsed on the top of her still whispering her name.

Sometime later, as he rested next to her, he touched her flushed face. "Are you alright?" He asked her softly. She nodded as she turned toward him. "I wanted to have this happen from the moment I saw you," he confessed as he caressed her face, her breasts, kissing her, wanting her again.

"I thought about you, too," Maggie told him.

"God, Maggie," he whispered as he pulled her closer. His hands gently touched her breasts that became exposed after Tony piece by piece removed her clothing. Maggie helped him undress as well. He felt an incredible desire and passion when he made love to her again and he was immensely pleased when

Maggie welcomed his lovemaking for the second time. "You feel so good," he murmured and pasted his lips on hers. His tongue danced around inside her mouth and it found her tongue so they could dance together in a rhythm of their own.

Maggie opened her eyes and touched his shoulder to stop. "What is it?" He asked.

"It's Paul," she replied and pushed herself away from him. "He is heading home," she informed him.

It seemed to Maggie that Tony did not comprehend the seriousness of their situation. "He will be home in twenty minutes."

"How do you know?" Tony asked as he was unwillingly getting dressed.

Maggie turned around to look at him before heading to the bathroom. "When I closed my eyes, I saw him driving." Tony did not argue with her and while she used the bathroom, he straightened out the bed and went into the living room. As soon as Maggie joined him, the cell phone rang and Maggie picked it up. "Hello," she answered.

"Hi, honey," she heard Paul's voice. She nodded to Tony that it was Paul. "Are you alone or someone is there?" He asked. Maggie's face turned snow white and Tony noticed that right away.

There was the moment when Maggie had to make a decision, to lie or to tell the truth and she was certainly not a liar. "Detective Morales is here," she finally told Paul. "Where are you?"

"I am just a block away, but I noticed an unknown car in the driveway," Paul told her and Maggie's hand began to shake.

"He stopped by about twenty minutes ago to ask some follow up questions about the findings at the Arboretum." She mumbled.

Paul hesitated with what he was about to say. "Are you alright?" He asked.

"Yes, I am fine," Maggie replied.

"Honey, if you don't mind, I would rather not come home right now. I will grab some food somewhere. I don't want to spend any more time sitting around while he is questioning you about something you don't know much about."

"I know exactly what you mean and I have no problem with that," Maggie said going along with Paul's suggestion.

"Okay, then, I will see you later tonight. Take care and get some rest," Paul told her and pushed the end of call button.

Maggie looked at Tony who was watching her and when she put the phone down, a smile appeared on the corner of his lips. Maggie smiled, too, and got up where she was sitting and walked up to Tony. "Where were we?" She asked with a sheepish smile.

Tony reached under Maggie's skirt and pulled down her panties once again. Maggie was ready for him; ready to finish that was unexpectedly interrupted. She positioned herself on Tony's lap and lowered herself on his erection. "Maggie," he whispered into her ears. "My Maggie."

CHAPTER FIFTEEN

SHE LAID ON the couch with her head on Tony's lap when his cell phone went off. "Morales," he answered. "Yeah, I can be there in twenty minutes."

Maggie sat up. "You have to go?" She asked.

Tony leaned forward and kissed her. "Sorry," he told her. "It was KC, she needs to meet me at a murder scene. She also asked me if you would come with me, too."

"Me?" Maggie asked with surprised.

"KC asked me not to tell you details until we get to the scene, I hope that it's alright with you?" Tony inquired. Maggie shrugged her shoulder. She did not quite like that idea but at least she was going to be in the company of Tony and her new friend, KC.

As Tony drove, he gave her side looks with a smile that almost made her embarrassed, recalling their intimate times together, the feeling of his touch, his passionate kisses and the feeling of his hardness inside her. She was not a child and although she was still only thirty-two years old, she felt like a schoolgirl meeting her first love for the first time. Maggie felt warmness toward Tony, not just physically, but emotionally as well.

"Maggie," Tony said when they were getting near to their destination. "I want you to know that I care about you and I would never let anything happen to you."

Maggie gently touched his arm. "Yes, I know. Thank you."

The car stopped and as Maggie looked at their destination, she realized that she knew that place despite the fact that she had never been there before, at least not in real life, only in her dreams. It was the house that she saw in her vision, the very same house that she painted. The orange car was still sitting in the driveway, exactly as she has dreamt it.

At the door, Tony bent down and put plastic shoe coverings on the top of Maggie's shoes, just like the one the surgeons used in the hospitals and handed her latex gloves just in case she touched something by accident. "There is a body inside, KC was wondering if you recognize it." Maggie noted that she understood.

Inside the house, especially around the living room had blood splatters all over while in the middle of the living room was a dead young man, covered in blood. It was obvious that he was brutally stabbed over and over. Nobody had to be a specialist to conclude that the person who did such a savage job on another human had either had some very serious anger issues or was a psychopath.

KC asked the CSI specialist to turn the body over so Maggie could take a look at the victim's face. For some reason Maggie thought that she would immediately recognize the man who appeared in her dream, but to her surprise the brutally attacked victim was not familiar to her at all, she had never seen him before. She told KC and Tony who were waiting for her to confirm if it was the person in her vision or not. KC already told Tony that the man's face did not match Maggie's painting or the picture that the Police Department's database came up with.

Strangely, Maggie was not terribly disturbed by the sight, perhaps because she had seen it in her dream but when she looked at the door that was half way down the hallway, she pointed at that direction. Tony followed her finger. "That is the basement, but I guess you already knew that."

Despite the fact that Maggie's heart was racing, she wanted to see it, she wanted to know if she would feel something when she went down there. KC, who joined them a few minutes after their arrival at the homicide scene walked in the front as they made their way down the cement steps. Both KC and Tony turned on their heavy-duty flashlights and when they got down to the floor level, Maggie was once again surprised that although the place looked somewhat familiar, it was also somewhat different. Where they were was very clean and the tools appeared to be arranged on shelves attached to the walls in a certain order.

There was absolutely no sign of a struggle and the floor seemed spotless. Eventually, when they went upstairs, the CSI technician sprayed the entire floor and the walls of the basement with luminal but she came up empty handed, there wasn't as much as a drop of blood anywhere, not even on the steps that led to the basement.

"Maybe I was wrong," Maggie said as they walked through the house where everything seemed to be in order with the exception of the living room with the dead body.

"I am here, me too," Maggie heard children's voices loud and clear. She turned around but only Tony, KC and two CSI technician were in her vicinity, the uniformed cops were standing outside the door so they would not overcrowd or contaminate the crime scene.

"Did you hear that?" Maggie asked from Tony. He looked at her questioningly.

"Hear what?" He inquired.

"Two children said that they were here," she replied.

"Maggie, there are no children in this house, not even a picture of them," KC informed her.

"Have you checked the backyard?" Maggie asked again and without waiting for an answer she headed outside through the backdoor. She stopped on the patio and looked around. It was a very nice size yard; flower gardens occupied most of the space with the exception of a large wooden shed that was painted red with pink trim. She stared at the flower bed and a thought occurred to her, it seemed like part of the flower bed seemed higher than others, maybe the gardener wanted to try something different for the variety of flowers planted, or maybe there was some other reason behind it.

"Detectives, you have got to see this," yelled one of the uniformed policemen assisting in the search. He was yelling at them from the shed. KC and Tony walked right up to it and they disappeared inside for a few minutes. Tony reappeared and motioned to Maggie to join them. She walked up the three steps that led inside and with surprise she realized that there was a trap door that led downstairs to yet another basement.

"Are you sure you want to see this?" Tony asked Maggie. She nodded; she had to so she could confirm her vision.

Each step that she took gave her a sense what was waiting downstairs. The smell of old and drying blood attacked her nostrils with full speed and as a natural gesture; she covered her nose and mouth. They did not go all the way down to the floor level; they wanted the CSI technicians to precede them. They stopped midway down the steps. The light was working and the place was worse than she had ever seen in horror movies, movies that she seldom watched or read about. The floor was completely covered with blood, darkened with age; it was obvious that the crime that was committed there had taken place a while back.

On the walls and from the ceiling various sized and types of equipment were hanging, some of them had noticeable dried blood on them. "Maggie, this is the place where we died," the child voice said to her.

"Tony," she whispered to him as he stood in front of her, on a step lower. "A child is telling me that this is the place where they were killed."

"The same children whose bodies we found in the Arboretum?" KC asked. Maggie nodded.

"Let's get out here it and let the CSI guys do their jobs," Tony remarked and motioned to Maggie who stood a step higher than him. A cold breeze rushed by Maggie so strongly that she stopped and turned around. She saw him, the same shadowy figure she saw in her dream.

"Oh, my God," Maggie whispered. "He is here."

"Who is here?" Tony asked her.

"The killer," she said still whispering. She could feel the person approaching them and then she felt the cold breeze again. All of a sudden Maggie could not breathe and she lost consciousness, falling into Tony's protective arms.

CHAPTER SIXTEEN

THE VOICE WITHOUT a doubt was familiar and still scary, as she recalled. "Do not forget who you are," said the voice. "You have been given a second chance to live, you must fulfill your destiny."

"I don't understand, who am I?" Maggie whispered.

"You have become *The Gifted One*," the voice echoed but the person who spoke those words was not visible. "Remember the day," said the voice as it faded out.

"She is coming through," Maggie could hear a woman's softer voice and she recognized the voice that belonged to KC. She looked up and saw her friend and Tony's worried faces bending over her. She soon realized that she was in the inside of an ambulance and the EMT just finished checking her blood pressure.

"She seemed to be okay," the EMT informed them. "Her blood pressure and pulse are normal. How are you feeling Mrs. Anderson?" He asked turning to her.

Maggie tried to sit up and with the help of Tony she did. "I am fine. What happened?" She asked.

"Mrs. Anderson, according to the detectives, you fainted. Do you wish to go to the hospital to have you checked out?" He asked.

"No, no hospital," she objected right away and motioned to KC and Tony that she wanted to get out of the emergency vehicle. Tony escorted Maggie to his car and helped her get into the passenger seat. KC remained with the EMT to do paperwork.

Tony was concerned despite the fact that Maggie's vital signs were good, she still seemed very pale. "Maybe you should go to the hospital for a check-up," he suggested.

"Then Paul would come and ask questions," she replied. Maggie looked at Tony and in a very quiet voice she asked. "What is today's date?"

"August 10th," he replied.

Maggie grabbed Tony's hand. "That is what the voice was warning me about," she whispered to him.

"What voice?" Tony asked wondering if Maggie was hallucinating.

She burst into tears. "I do not want this, you understand me Tony? I do not want this," she cried into his chest where she buried her face.

Tony kissed her forehead and gently stroked her hair. "What is it that you don't want Maggie? You don't want us?" He asked with hurt in his voice.

She pulled away and shook her head. "I want us, Tony, I don't want to be *The Gifted One*." Maggie replied and explained to Tony what the voice said to her while she was unconscious. She also told Tony that she recognized the voice from their first encounter, and then she asked him if he knew about what happened to her before. Tony admitted that KC filled him in with the details of her vision of the pure white man and the white dog, the things about what happened so far and what is supposed to happen on the following day. Tony already knew and heard of some of the things that she was telling him. KC mentioned of them to him before he ever met Maggie.

"KC told me that you and Paul notified FAA. Did they do anything about it or did anyone contact you?" Tony inquired. Maggie shook her head.

"My parents are supposed to arrive in a couple of days," she informed Tony. "Our wedding anniversary is on August 11th, that is the primary reason for their trip here. Thank God my father insisted on driving, but for some reason, it doesn't make me feel better, perhaps because I know that so many people may lose their lives." Maggie glanced at her watch, it was getting late and she said so. "Would you mind to drive me home?" She asked. Tony asked her to wait a couple of minutes while he told KC about his whereabouts. While Tony talked to KC ever so briefly, Maggie closed her eyes. It was then that the vision appeared so unexpectedly that it made her gasp for air.

Maggie watched in horror as the airplane nosedived toward the car where they were sitting. She could feel the earth trembling around the vehicle and she could clearly see the terror stricken faces of people who had a split second left to realize that their lives were about to end. Maggie stared ahead as the plane crashed into parked cars alongside the road when it broke into three pieces and then burst into flames. She covered her face when she realized that the tail section from the plane was sliding toward Tony's car. She could smell the high-octane airplane fuel all around them as it fed the spreading flames. She took her hands off from her eyes because she had to look; she had to see the plane's the numbers painted on the tail section. The large white letters and numbers were screaming at her as the broken up plane section stopped in front of the car, it read, CU-INH7431.

"Maggie, are you alright?" She heard Tony's welcoming voice. She turned her tear filled eyes to look at him. "Did you just see something, like a vision?"

"I saw the plane crash, it happened right here, but this will not be the place. It was just a reminder," she mumbled and with a Kleenex she wiped the perspiration from her forehead and face. "Please take me home," she asked him again and he immediately started the car's engine.

They drove in silence. Maggie kept thinking about her vision and Tony was deep in thoughts about his feelings concerning the beautiful woman sitting next to him in the car. As he pulled up in front of Maggie's garage, he stopped her before she got out of the car. "Just a moment of your time," he asked her. She remained seated although she nervously looked toward the walkway that led to her front door. "I know that it is probably not the best time to talk about what is happening between you and I, but I wanted you to know that I am in love with you." Tony confessed to her.

Maggie smiled as she replied. "I have feelings for you, too. However, I owe Paul for everything he has done for me. I do not love him, not for a very long time, but he is a good man. He took care of me when nobody else was there to do so. He cares about me and loves me."

Tony lowered his head; it was not what he wanted to hear. "You and I have something very special," he said and reached for her hand. "I don't want to think that it was just a passing thing between us. I have hopes for a future that includes you too, Maggie."

"I have no regrets about what happened. As a matter of fact, you made me very happy. Please understand, I just can't walk out on Paul." Maggie said and got out of the car.

"Be careful," Tony yelled after her. She turned around and waved at him as he drove off.

Maggie entered the security code and when the light turned green she stepped inside her house. She reset the security alarm and went through the kitchen toward the bedroom to change clothes. Paul came out of the master bathroom and startled Maggie so much so that she grabbed her chest. He immediately apologized and asked if she was all right. "I did not know that you were home," she mumbled. "I didn't see your car."

"I parked it in the garage," Paul explained. "I was surprised that you were not home and you did not answer your cell phone either." He said in an almost complaining tone of voice.

Maggie could not explain why she did not hear the ringing of her cell phone, but sometimes she unintentionally set it on vibes, off the ring tone. She did not do that often, and she could not remember doing at that particular time either. "Where have you been, I was worried about you?" Paul inquired as Maggie was changing clothes.

"KC and Detective Morales asked me to join them at a crime scene," she told the truth, leaving some important activity details out.

"Isn't that unusual taking an outsider to a crime scene?" Paul asked somewhat suspiciously. Maggie thought about her response when she came out of the walking closet. Instead of answering, she asked Paul to follow her into her studio. Paul did as she asked. Once inside, Maggie pulled out the three paintings of the crime scene, one from the house, one from the car and one of the portrait of a man she saw in her vision.

Seeing the portrait, Paul took a step back and Maggie could not help but to notice that the color of his face turned ashen white. "Do you know this man?" Maggie asked. Paul shook his head as he replied.

"No, I don't," he denied it. Maggie was one hundred percent certain that he was lying. Paul's reaction spoke better than words and when he rushed out of the studio it was proof that indeed he knew the person that the police identified as Mitch Johansson.

She followed Paul into the kitchen and gently put her hand on his shoulder. As if electricity shocked him, he span around and his eyes were sparkling from anger. "I am sorry," Maggie apologized. She did not understand Paul's behavior, so she went back into the studio and closed the door behind her. She needed to think. She needed to collect and evaluate her thoughts, but most of all; she wanted to make sense of some of the feelings she was experiencing in recent days, as well as the feelings that she was harboring for a very long time.

Sitting on the daybed she stared at the door. Paul has changed, there was no doubt about it, she just did not know why. Ever since her heart procedure and it's aftermath, the vision she had while unconscious, her prediction of the explosion at Paul and Christopher's company, her identification of the place where four murdered children's corpses were buried and the vision of the still upcoming airplane crash has most certainly changed her too. She fully acknowledged that Paul was attentive to her especially since her heart procedure and he cared about her. There were times when he didn't want to leave her sight. Maggie tried to remember the time when she first noticed the changes in Paul's behavior, and she concluded that it all began after he and Christopher began to establish their company.

She began to wonder if Paul was actually blaming her for the explosion and for the death of his close friend and employees. Her loyalty to Paul had also changed in a major way beginning a few months earlier. For reasons she could not fully explain to herself, she no longer trusted Paul. Of course, the truth was that Maggie thought that she was actually falling in love with Tony and she wanted to be with him. *Did Paul sense that?* She wondered.

There was a knock on the door. "It's open," she said loud enough for Paul to hear. He slowly opened the door and hesitantly entered her studio.

"Maggie, I need to apologize for my behavior," he said and looked her straight in the eyes, the way she preferred while she conversed with other people. "I know that I acted rather strangely and I also must admit, I wasn't telling you the truth when I said that I did not know that person in your painting," he admitted.

"Who is he and how is he related to you?" Maggie asked.

"His name is Marcos Trujillo," he informed Maggie. It was a name she never heard of and she wasn't sure if she should mention to Paul that the police identified the person as Mitch Johansson. "He was a student of mine in Puerto Rico, at the university and there was an accident, an experiment that went terribly wrong and he died in the explosion."

The words he was saying reached her in a certain way and Maggie had the odd feeling that it was not even close to the truth about Paul's relationship with the man in the painting. She was becoming deeply troubled by Paul's evident lying but she made the decision not to approach him about it without first talking to KC and Tony.

"Paul," she said and picked up the other two paintings with the car and the house. "Have you ever seen these paintings before I showed them to you earlier?"

Paul shook his head. "No, I haven't." He replied.

"Then we have a security problem," Maggie informed him by telling him the disappearance of the paintings on the day before and about the changes that were made to them before they were returned.

"That is very strange because other than you and me, and the security company, nobody else knows the combination," Paul said. "I think I better contact them about the break in." Maggie nodded that it would be the best. However, she did not mention to Paul that KC also knew the combination. KC was with her when the break in happened and she trusted KC with her life.

Paul got his cell phone out and was about to dial when it rang. "Anderson," he said into the phone. "My wife, why?" He glanced toward Maggie's direction. "She seemed to be fine. Okay. Thanks," with that said, Paul ended the call and turned back to Maggie. "Do you want to tell me what happened this afternoon?" He asked.

"Nothing really," Maggie said as casually as she could. "I was overcome by something in the basement at the scene of the homicide and I fainted."

"That was an EMT calling to check on you because you refused to go to the hospital," he said almost angrily. "What is wrong with you Maggie, how come you failed to mention something that important to me?"

Maggie took a deep breath. "You have enough on your plate Paul and my parents are coming and all those things that are happening. I just did not want to burden you with them."

"Maggie, damn it," Paul cursed. "I know that I am not the husband I used to be, but I care and I am concerned about you. If for no other reason, I expect that you at least be honest with me."

Should I tell him the whole truth? Maggie wondered but remained silent, it was most definitely not the right time to tell Paul about her feelings for another man. "Of course, you are right Paul," she said instead. "You have always been good to me and I am so sorry for not letting you know what happened this afternoon."

Paul looked at her and the door, and back at her again as if he could not make up his mind. "Did you have dinner yet?" He asked. Maggie shook her head. "Would you like me to pick up something?"

"If you feel up to it," she replied.

"I can get some Olive Garden," Paul suggested.

"That would be nice," Maggie agreed and watched Paul leave her studio. It hurt her to hold back the truth and she was determined that sometime soon, perhaps after her parents departure, she would confess to Paul how she felt about Tony and about their affair. In the meantime, she acknowledged with sadness, she and Tony would have to keep their feelings and desires for each other on a back burner.

She laid down on the daybed and closed her eyes for a moment, which unknown to her, turned into a couple of hours. Maggie would have slept even longer if the doorbell did not wake her. When she looked at the clock, she realized that Paul had been gone way to long. The restaurant was an easy fifteen minute drive away, which meant thirty minutes round trip, ordering and preparing the food would have taken another twenty-five minutes, so either way, Paul should have been home by the time she woke up, besides, he would have wake her up anyway.

She gathered herself together and made it to the door where the person pushed the doorbell once again. Maggie noticed through the two narrow side windows next to the door that there was a police car outside her house with a flashing light, but no siren. She looked at the security monitor and saw two uniformed policemen standing outside her front door. She punched in the security code and opened the door.

"Mrs. Anderson?" Asked the taller police officer who stood closer to her.

"Yes," she replied curtly. "What is this about?"

"Mrs. Anderson, is your husband's name Paul?" Asked the second, a younger officer.

"Yes, but please don't keep me guessing. Did something happen?" Maggie asked.

"May we come inside?" Asked the taller officer. Maggie nodded and opened the door wider. They somewhat nervously stood there when the younger officer politely asked her if she would like to sit down. Maggie shook her head. "Mrs. Anderson, we are sorry to inform you that your husband was involved in a fatal car accident not far from here. He died on impact when his car hit a cement wall in a shopping mall's parking lot." The tall officer informed her after taking his hat off.

Maggie stared at him and the only word that went around and around in her head was "fatal". "Where did they take him?" She asked in a raspy voice.

"If you like, we'll could drive you to the city morgue to identify him," offered the younger officer.

She nodded. "Yes, that would be kind of you, I just have to get my purse."

"Mrs. Anderson, we wait here until you are ready," said the taller officer.

Maggie moved in a daze, not completely comprehending what the policemen were telling her. She understood that something horrible happened to Paul but she wondered why she did not have a premonition about what just happened to her husband. What kind of *"Gifted One"* was she if she could not even predict what was going to happen to a family member?

From the kitchen counter she grabbed her purse that she left there when Tony drove her home earlier in the afternoon. Thinking of him began to trouble her; it was not the time that any decent wife who just lost her husband thought about a lover whom the deceased husband did not even know about. Guilt conscious began to build in her heart and mind as she headed out the door. She was so troubled by the unexpected event that she was halfway down her walkway when she remembered that she did not set the alarm. She returned and re-set the security system and then walked down to the waiting police car where the younger police officer opened the door to the backseat for her.

All the way to the morgue she thought about calling KC and/or Tony but she just couldn't make the call. It was not that she did not want to talk to either of them, Maggie simply did not want to say the words that Paul was "dead" and that he had a "fatal" accident. Maggie knew that Paul was an excellent driver and she began to wonder what caused the apparently one car accident. The restaurant itself was located in the vicinity of a shopping mall, but she could not visualize how and why Paul would drive with full speed into a cement wall. There were things she must find out, she knew that much already.

Arriving to the morgue, the two policemen escorted her down to the area where the unidentified or just recently received bodies were located. They politely directed her to a small room that had a long window for reviewing the body in question. She asked but was denied to identify Paul's remains by standing next to the gurney. One of the policemen stepped back while the other; the younger one stayed next to her just in case she may become sick or lose consciousness. They were just about to let the person in the other side of the curtained up window know that they were ready when the door opened and KC and Tony appeared.

"How are you holding up?" KC asked and hugged her shoulder. Maggie turned to her friend and KC was shocked to see Maggie's guilt ridden face. "It wasn't your fault." She whispered to her.

"I like that you are here, but why are you here?" Maggie mumbled to Tony and KC. She couldn't help but notice that the two detectives exchanged looks. Just then the curtain parted and there he was, Dr. Paul Anderson, her husband of almost 10 years of marriage lying dead on a cold stainless steel table. It was strange that other than how long they were married, no personal thoughts came to Maggie. She thought about Paul's accomplishments, about him receiving the Nobel Price for Physics along with his longtime friend Christopher Collins and how badly the US government wanted his ideas and suggestions about the technology that he mastered, and now all that remained was a body on a table, badly bruised.

Maggie quietly said. "Yes, he is my husband, Dr. Paul Anderson." The curtain unceremoniously closed but Maggie just stood there, deep in thoughts. Tony wanted to take her into his arms and comfort her but they both knew that it would have been very inappropriate under those circumstances. KC took her by the arm and they left the morgue. KC released the two policemen and they escorted her to their car, parked not far from the exit door.

They were quiet during the drive as Tony was driving and Maggie was sitting in the backseat, holding onto KC's arm. "Why were you at the morgue?" She asked.

KC cleared her voice and squeezed Maggie's hand. "Maggie, it wasn't just an accident," she informed her. "Paul was shot in the head, the Medical Examiner who came to the scene could tell that right away. Actually he was able to determine as a preliminary finding that there were at least two bullets that entered his forehead. That is why he lost control of the car and hit the cement wall."

"But who and why?" Maggie asked. KC shook her head.

"We have no idea at this point," she admitted. "Is there anything you can tell us?" She asked Maggie.

Maggie sat back in the car and tried to think. "Truthfully, Paul never shared his work with me, they were usually government contracts and they were very hush, hush projects. He told me that after the explosion, the government beefed up security at the new company, he had to negotiate more money for that, too."

"Did he say anything about having problems with any of the employees, contractors, and such?" KC asked.

"No, he never mentioned anything like that. He was a genuinely liked person. Something did happen earlier, before he left to pickup some food from the Olive Garden Restaurant." Maggie said and went on telling them what happened when she showed the paintings to Paul, what his strange reaction was and that he identified the man in the painting as Marcos Trujillo and not Mitch Johansson."

"Did you mention to him about the disappearance and reappearance of the paintings?" KC inquired.

Maggie nodded. "Yes, I did and he was about to call the security company to change the codes. He was also very upset when he found out that I fainted and did not call him or tell him about it."

"Do you need any help with the legal matters and the funeral arrangements once the Coroner releases Paul?" KC asked.

"I'll be alright," Maggie replied. "Thank you for your offer though. We have a family friend who has been our attorney for a very long time, he should be able to assist me." She informed them and became very quiet.

"Maggie," KC said after a lengthy silence. "Is something troubling you other than what we already talked about?" She asked.

"I found it very strange that I can *"see"* where bodies were buried and I predicted his company's demise and now I am facing an airline disaster, but there were no clues, no visions or warnings of any kind about what was about to happen to Paul. Why not about him? Why was I unable to predict or even paint a picture of what was about to happen? I could have prevented the shooting and consequently the accident too." She replied.

KC squeezed Maggie's hand. "Maggie, I do not know how this "thing" works with you, but what is written in God's big book cannot be stopped. We can investigate after what happened, but only in movies can be stopped what was about to happen. We will find out who killed Paul, you can bet on that." She promised.

"Thank you, you are a good friend." She said and looked into the rearview mirror in which Tony glanced at her while he drove. It seemed strange to him that with all that happened, Maggie was calm and collected and without any doubt about her honesty, KC mentioned to him the same thing. Later on Tony reminded KC that people react differently to the news of death of a loved one. Perhaps Maggie was stunned and in shock, that was the best explanation the two detectives came up with, as they were unable to explain Maggie's calmness and her lack of tears and lack of visible sorrow. It never crossed their minds that perhaps Maggie was lying about her whereabouts at the time of Paul's death. It would have been very easy to check as the security alarm system was monitored and registered all exits and enters of the Anderson's household. Indeed, they found it strange that Maggie did not have any "vision" about the coming tragedy, but KC emphasized once again to Tony that nobody really knew how some people, like Maggie was able to "see" things ahead, or seen after they happened like where the children were buried in the Arboretum.

"Thank you for the drive," Maggie said as she was getting out of the car. She turned around to add. "And for everything."

They waited until she entered the house before driving away. Maggie barely re-set the security system when her landline began to ring. "Hello," she answered the phone.

"Honey, it's your dad," she heard her father's voice.

"Hi dad, it's so good to hear your voice," she told him. "Where are you calling from?"

"Maggie, I am calling you not far from Albuquerque, New Mexico, we are at a camping site for the night, but we should be able to get to your place by tomorrow afternoon. So are you and Paul planning anything for your anniversary?" Maggie did not reply to her father's question. "Are you okay, honey?" He asked with concern. He could feel and sense from her voice that something was not right.

"I am fine, dad, I'll see you tomorrow night, drive carefully please," she said quietly. She almost hung up the phone when she caught her father's voice.

"Maggie, wait. Is everything all right, you sound depressed," he commented.

"I am fine dad, just take care of mom and yourself." She repeated and hung up the phone. For a brief moment she thought about telling them the bad news about Paul, but she just could not make herself do it. She decided that it would be the best to tell something like that face to face, but she prayed that the news media would not get ahold of the news that the Nobel Prize winner physicist, Dr. Paul Anderson had died, before her parents arrived.

She glanced at the answering machine and already there were seven messages waiting to be answered. *The vultures are out for flesh*, she though as she went to her bedroom's closet to change clothes. She stepped to Paul's clothes and gently touched them with her hand. Maggie couldn't deny the fact that although it was not love, but she still had some feelings for Paul, spending ten years day in and day out, in sickness and in health just could not be set aside and to forget in a moments time.

Maggie thought about Tony, and she wished that he was there with her to share the burden of pain that followed Paul's untimely death. Strange as it may sound to others perhaps, she actually loved Paul for what he had done for her, but the feeling she was developing toward Tony was an entirely different kind of love. Paul stopped being intimate with her at least for the last five years that she could recall, and while they remained together, it was from more out of friendship, companionship and sincerity with deep respect for each other.

She heard the doorbell and she looked at the small screen by the security code box. She recognized Tony standing by her front door. She sighed as she opened the door. "I couldn't stay away," he said when she appeared in the doorway. "I am worried about you."

"Come in," she replied and re-secured the system after closing the door behind Tony. "Do you want some coffee or tea?" She asked Tony when he sat down on the couch, the very same couch where they made love what seemed like a very long time ago.

"Tea would be nice," he replied. "Do you want any help?" He offered. Maggie shook her head and went to the kitchen. A few minutes later she returned with a tray with two cups on saucers, with a steaming pot of tea, sliced lemons and sugar. Tony took the tray from her and placed it in the middle of the coffee table that was located between the couch where he was sitting opposite from the loveseat where she slowly sat down after pouring some tea for herself.

She sipped from her hot tea and finally looked at Tony who was staring at her direction. It was impossible for him not to notice the tears in her eyes. "It has been a very long day," she said finally as she began to reflect on the day's events. Earlier on that morning, Tony and she made love for the first time, her visit at the scene of a horrible crime, the argument with Paul and last, Paul's questionable death. When she woke up that morning, she had no idea that by the time the sun retired on the horizon, she would be a widow.

"KC and I believe that perhaps your life is in danger," Tony said quietly. "That is one of the reasons why I came back."

"Why would anybody want to hurt me?" Maggie asked. "I don't know anything about Paul's business, I have no idea why I am capable to see, to visualize things. I am just a painter, that is all, but right now I feel very lost."

Tony hesitated for a moment and then he got up and changed seats, he sat down next to her and wrapped his arm around her. "I feel so bad," Maggie continued. "I should have been honest with Paul, I should have told him about us." She mumbled.

"You have no reason, no reason at all to feel that way," Tony told her. "I know that eventually you would have told him how we feel about each other, right?"

Maggie nodded and wiped her tears. "He was a good man," she remarked.

"I have no reason to doubt that," Tony replied. "I can assure you that we will find out who shot him and why."

"My parents are arriving tomorrow," Maggie reminded him. "There is so much to do and I don't even know where to start."

Tony looked at her for a brief moment and took out his cell phone, then pushed a button. "Hey, Captain, this is Tony Morales. Sorry to bother you but I need to take a couple of days off." He listened and then he replied. "Yes, I know, but I would not ask you if it was not important, just two days, the most." He promised. He listened some more and he nodded. "Yes, I will do that, thanks Captain."

"That is very generous of you," Maggie told him.

"Maggie, I am so in love with you, you surely know that and I cannot just leave you alone at a time like this. If he wouldn't have given me those days off, I would have quit." Tony told her and Maggie could tell from his facial expression that he meant what he said. "Look," he said. "I respect Paul's memory and I will wait as longer as it takes for you to feel that we can move forward in our relationship. We can take this one step at a time and right now, we have to face what is coming at us."

Maggie leaned forward and gently kissed him. "Thank you Tony, I will never forget your kindness."

"I just love you Maggie, from the moment I saw you for the very first time," he confirmed to her and smiled. "So, what is the first thing you need to do?"

Maggie looked toward the telephone answering machine with the unplayed messages. "I think I should call our attorney before the news of Paul's death hits the airwaves."

George Brandt, the Anderson's family attorney simply couldn't believe what Maggie was telling him, but he knew that it was the truth. He knew Paul and his wife since he moved to the city at the same time as they did. He became their lawyer as soon as he passed the California bar examination. In his opinion, they were just about the nicest and caring people he ever represented. Paul was extremely bright in his field of work, and his office walls proved what he thought about Maggie's painting.

"Have you received any phone calls from government agencies?" George asked.

"There are seven phone calls on the answering machine but I didn't have a chance or patience to listen to them yet," she confessed.

"Okay, Maggie, listen to the messages, write down who called and their phone numbers, and then call me right back. Do not return any of those phone calls, leave that to my office. Are you alone?" He asked.

Maggie looked at Tony who was sitting next to her on the loveseat. "Detective Morales is here with me," she informed him.

"That's good, keep him around for a while," he suggested which made Maggie smile briefly. "I am concerned for your safety. I am thinking that perhaps you should check into a hotel."

"No, George, I want to stay in this house, I feel safe here and we have a security system. The silent alarm at the company and the alarm in this house would go off if anybody tried to break in."

"Alright, Maggie, please put the detective on the phone," George asked her and she complied. She listened as Tony introduced himself and then he, too, listened to what the attorney had to say.

"Yes, Mr. Brandt, I would do that," Tony promised something to the lawyer and then he ended the call. "He wants me to keep him informed how the investigation is going," he explained George's request.

Maggie took a pen and note pad and began to listen to the messages that were left on their answering machine. The first call was from her dad, he was concerned about Maggie as he was unable to reach her all day. He informed her what he also told her later, when she did answer the phone that they would be arriving not later than the evening of the following day.

After her father's first call when he actually left a message, the next two phone calls were from various government agencies, including the Pentagon and Maggie wrote down all their names and numbers so George's office could take over the answering. One of the messages came from KC, she acknowledged that she knew that Tony was there with her, yet, she wanted to Maggie know if there was anything she could do for her, she did not want Maggie to hesitate to call her for anything. She also asked Maggie to tell Tony to behave himself and promised her that she will be in touch if anything new comes up. The fifth phone call came from a supplier and the sixth message came from a security firm that confirmed their appointment with Paul on the following day. The last call was her father's second call when he was about to leave another message but she arrived home.

Maggie looked at Tony and reached for the phone to call George. Tony pointed toward the kitchen and Maggie nodded that it was okay for him to go there. She left all the information with George's paralegal and followed Tony into the kitchen where she found him busy preparing two sandwiches. "You need to eat something," Tony said and cut a ham and cheese sandwich in half and pushed the plate in front of her. Indeed she was hungry, poor Paul left for food, their dinner but obviously never made it home.

They ate at the breakfast bar and after they finished, Maggie stopped Tony before he returned to the living room. "You know that I don't need a babysitter. If you want to go to back to work on the investigation with KC, I would not mind. I understand that the first 48 hours is the most critical."

Tony smiled and reached for her hand. "You are watching too much television," he said and pulled her to him. "There are more than just KC and I working as detectives, there are a lot of good and capable people in the department. They will keep me informed and if I have any ideas or suggestion, I will let them know, don't worry about that."

"I am totally exhausted," Maggie said and Tony could easily see it on her face and movements that she was telling the truth. "I am going to bed."

"Do you want me to sleep in the guest room?" Tony asked. Maggie thought about it for a moment and shook her head.

"You can sleep next to me. I would feel much more secure knowing you are beside me," she said with a painful smile on her face.

After a quick shower, they both went to bed, holding each other tightly. Maggie, for the first time since early that afternoon was finally able to relax, but sleep did not come that easily. "Who would want to kill Paul?" She whispered into the silence of the bedroom.

Tony shook his head. "I don't know, but I have some ideas that perhaps his death was related to the original explosion of his company that killed his partner and employees." He replied.

"I thought about that as well," Maggie confessed. "I hope that you don't mind when I talking about him," she remarked.

"Of course not," Tony assured her. "Maggie, you mentioned something about Paul being upset upon seeing that painting you painted with that man's portrait. He didn't give you any clue, how the accident happened and where that person supposedly died?"

"No, he just said that an experiment went terribly wrong and that a student of his died," Maggie repeated what she told him earlier. "When he first denied knowing the man, I knew that he was lying and he did apologize for it later. It was then that he acknowledged knowing him and he gave me his student's name. He was just acting so strange, I never saw him behave like that before. During our ten years together, he never ever raised his voice at me and never cursed at me until today."

"Why did he curse at you?" Tony asked.

"Because I didn't tell him that I fainted and that I refused to go to a hospital to have me checked out," Maggie explained.

"He was just concerned about you, that is all," Tony said.

Maggie began to cry softly and sat up in the bed. "I used to love him you know. It was never a passionate love, or anything like that. Paul did have so many good qualities that were more important to me in those days than being in a passion filled marriage. I changed too throughout the years and perhaps it was my fault as well that his interest in me changed. I just don't know."

Many other men would have felt strange, perhaps even offended listening to a lover talking about her husband, but Tony was a different kind of man, a man who within a short period of time fell so deeply in love with Maggie. He was the kind of man who loved her and respected her even more for being able to reflect only the good things about her late husband, and who felt sorrow for losing someone who cared about her. There was no bitterness in Maggie's voice only regret that she was not honest with her husband before he died about their love affair. At the same time, Tony was also relieved, as despite the fact that he trusted Maggie one hundred percent, KC and he were wondering about Maggie's calmness after reviewing and identifying Paul's body.

"It now seems strange that the day of his death, he actually apologized for not being the man that he used to be. He probably meant that we hadn't made love for years," Maggie said and sighed while she wiped her tears away.

Tony leaned over her and kissed her shoulder. "Maggie, I know that it hurts, but there is nothing you can do to change what happened. I also know that it may sound cold, and much too soon, but some things had to be let go. You can hold onto the pleasant memories of Paul and the good times you had together, but you should not blame yourself for things that were not said or done."

Maggie nodded. "Yes, I know Tony. You are a good man and I am very fortunate that I met you."

"You need to get some sleep, we will talk some more tomorrow," Tony said and covered her when she laid back down. He watched her as she struggled to fall asleep and he smiled thinking about all the teasing he had done when a friend of his in college told him that he saw a girl in the library and he thought that he was in love with her without even talking to her once. It was true, the moment KC introduced them and he held her hand in the process, there was some kind of connection made that he was hoping to make some day with someone decent, someone kind and passionate. Maggie told him that she felt lucky to meet him; she had no idea how lucky he felt for the same reason. He looked at the clock on the nightstand; it was almost one in the morning already. He felt exhausted and as soon as he relaxed with Maggie's head resting on his arms, he fell asleep.

He woke up to the ringing of bedside phone and when he looked at Maggie's side of the bed, she was gone. Tony thought that perhaps she was in the bathroom that is why she was unable to answer the phone. After the steady ringing, he picked up the phone. "Hello," he said in the receiver.

"Who is this?" The man on the other line asked.

"This is the Anderson residence, who is calling please?" He asked.

"This is Robert Davis, Maggie's father," the man introduced himself.

"Good Morning Mr. Davis, this is Tony Morales, a friend of Maggie. She is in the shower at the moment, but if you would like to leave a message she could call you right back," Tony offered.

"Son, I am calling from a payphone, we don't have those fancy cell phones," he explained. "Would you please tell my daughter that we wouldn't be arriving this evening after all, but tomorrow for certain. We stuck at the KOA campground with our RV with a major fuel pump problem. The part is coming sometime this evening and the fellow here at the gas station promised that he would fix it right away so we could be on our way."

"I will make sure that Maggie gets your message," Tony assured him.

There was a moment of silence, and then Robert Davis just had to ask the question. "Is my son-in-law there?"

"I am sorry Mr. Davis, he is not here," he informed him without telling Davis the whole story. Tony felt that Maggie should be telling her father what she knows so far about what happened to Paul.

"Hmmm," David mumbled. "Tell Maggie, that I will be calling again."

"Will do," Tony said and hung up the phone.

He got dressed quickly and went to the master bathroom, which had its door closed and knocked on it. When he did not receive any response, after knocking and calling Maggie's name out several times, he turned the knob and the door opened effortlessly. There was no one in the bathroom and Tony, after glancing in the mirror; he noted that he needed to shave. He noticed Paul's electric shaver but there was no way that he could use it because he knew that within the next couple of hours, KC will be arriving in the company of some uniformed cops to serve a search warrant. He actually expected that on the previous night but he was sure that out of sympathy and trust for Maggie, KC delayed serving it.

The house was quiet and Tony called out Maggie's name several times while he walked through the house, looking in the other two guest rooms and Paul's home office where he made a mental note of the laptop computer on the desk. The second bathroom was also vacant and before he reached the living room, he stopped by the room that was designated as Maggie's studio. He knocked on that door too and when he did not hear any response, he drew his Glock and slowly opened the door.

Maggie was sitting in front of a canvas and feverishly painting a picture. "Maggie," Tony called out to her but she did not even flinch, he wasn't even sure if she heard his voice. He slowly made his way to get behind Maggie as she sat on her usual rolling chair so he could look at the painting. He put away his gun and his eyes widened realizing what he was seeing on the painting.

The painting had dark and vivid colors and the scene appeared to be at a KOA campground. In the forefront of the painting was a large RV, what was left of it that is. The roof was gone; windows shattered and so were several equally damaged and variety of size of RVs and Vans with camping extensions. On the ground there were bodies and body parts, the ground itself looked soaked with blood. Next to the RV in the front of the painting what looked like an airplane's cockpit, she even painted the pilots with bloody faces in the window. In the background and around the camping vehicles were other airplane parts were visible and opened suitcases with scattered belongings of the perished passengers were everywhere. Tony narrowed his eyes so he could focus on the license plate of the RV on the front and he wrote the number down in his notebook.

He gently touched Maggie's shoulder but she was still painting details on the canvas so he left her studio and he went into the living room to call KC on his cell phone. He told her about Maggie's father's phone call and the painting that Maggie was working on. "She is in what I would call a catatonic state, she would not react when I called out her name or when I touched her shoulder," Tony informed her. "I need your help KC."

"We are on our way with the search warrant," KC announced.

"Grab us some breakfast and coffee, please," Tony asked her.

"Typical man, always thinking about his stomach," KC teased him and ended the call.

CHAPTER SEVENTEEN

TONY WASHED HIS face and combed his hair; he didn't want to look like a slob when KC and the uniformed cops arrived. He made the bed in the master bedroom where he and Maggie spent the night, and just then he went into the studio to prepare Maggie for the news about the upcoming search of her house.

The painting was finished and it was drying on the easel, he found Maggie sound asleep on the daybed. She still had her bathrobe on and nothing underneath. That was the way she always slept, and which she told him before. He sat down at the edge of the daybed and gently moved the hair from her face, and then Tony bent down and kissed her warm forehead. She opened her eyes and seemed confused. "Why I am in the studio?" She asked.

Tony explained what happened and told her about her father's phone call. He could easily tell that Maggie was in a state of panic, especially after she noticed her latest painting. He had to ask her to turn back to him because he had something important to tell her. "Maggie, you know that when a crime is committed, as a routine police procedure, the investigators usually obtains a search warrant to the victim's or the suspect's home. KC and some cops are on their way here to serve you that warrant."

"I don't mind, but there is nothing here. Paul seldom ever bought work home and if he did work on some project, he usually worked on the computer," she recalled.

"They are going to confiscate the computer for the time being, eventually you will get it back, if there is nothing on it that is. I am also fairly sure that the FBI would want that computer as well," Tony informed her. Maggie shrugged.

"Sure, they can take it. I have never used his computer, I have my own," she pointed at a laptop on the small desk in the corner, away from the paintings. "Actually, I have not been on my computer for a couple of weeks now," she told him and looked up at Tony. Her face was wet with tears. "I am so worried about my parents," she whimpered. Tony could not do anything else other than to take her into his arms and hug her tightly. Knowing the history of her predictions and visions, he was concerned as well, especially for the airline crash that she predicted months earlier and which Paul reported and was ignored by the FAA.

He glanced at his watch and carefully pushed her away and led Maggie into her walk-in closet to get dressed. "Do you need any help?" He asked before leaving her to go to the living room. She shook her head.

Only a few minutes passed when Tony heard cars stopping in front of the house and went to open the door. As he stood there, he realized that he did not know the security code. Tony called out for Maggie who joined him a couple of minutes later and opened the door for KC and four policemen to enter. KC reminded the cops that it was a friendly home, she asked them try to be careful with things around the house. As Tony predicted, Paul's computer was taken away and KC asked Maggie if she could take Paul's comb with some hair samples for a DNA test.

"You may take whatever you think is necessary," Maggie told KC, who thanked her. Maggie and Tony were in the dining room eating some croissants that KC brought to them for breakfast along with some freshly brewed coffee from a local coffee shop.

After a couple of hours of careful searching, other than some of her paintings, especially the ones with the portrait, the house and the orange car was bagged and labeled. In a box they took some of Paul's work that they found in his desk where Maggie never snooped or looked around. They did not find any illegal substance or guns, and KC told her, not that she did not know in advance, they had a clean search, meaning that they did not find anything out of the ordinary. KC also told Maggie that she will keep her informed about anything that comes up, including if there was anything interesting or pertaining Paul's case on his computer.

Maggie and Tony thanked them for the careful search and KC for the breakfast and then the cops and KC departed. Only minutes passed when the phone rang and Tony handed the receiver to Maggie to answer. "Hello," she answered.

"Hi honey, its dad," she heard her father's voice. Tony could hear a big sigh and Maggie's face lit up a little bit.

"Oh, dad, I am so glad that you called. I had a terrible dream again," Maggie told her father. She said "dreams" as her parents did not know about her visions. "Please, dad, don't go back to the campground."

"Maggie, I am at the campground," her father informed her. "A nice young man who is camping next to us let me use his cell phone. I guess it's a good thing to have, I will look into it once we get home."

"I thought that you were at the gas station, having the fuel pump put in," Maggie said and she sounded concerned again.

"Well, the part has come in but they will be doing the repairs right here. I can't drive the RV without the fuel pump," her father explained and then he added. "I refused to pay hundreds of dollars for towing it."

"Dad, I dreamt that an airplane crashed into the camp ground. Please, I am begging you, tell people that there will be a crash and everybody is going to perish in the plane and on the ground. Please, please dad, take mom out of there," Maggie begged him.

"Is that the same plane crash you mentioned months ago?" Davis asked.

"Yes, it is, the day is today," Maggie reminded him.

"Hold on," he asked her and she could hear her mother's voice. "What?" He asked. "That is non-sense."

"Dad, what is going on?" Maggie asked and she had to repeat her question because her father was taking to her mother.

"Maggie," she heard her mother's voice. "How are you darling?" She asked and Maggie immediately knew that something happened.

"Mom, what is going on?" She asked on a verge of panic.

"You tell me, Maggie." Her mother replied. "I just heard on the radio that Dr. Paul Anderson was shot to death and they are investigating his murder. Is that your Paul?" She asked. Maggie sighed.

"Mom, I wanted to wait with telling you and dad in person when you got here," Maggie tried to explain. "There is nothing much I could say. I don't know anything else other than somebody shot Paul and his car hit a cement wall, but apparently he was already dead."

"Oh, my dear God," Maggie's mother replied. "I was wondering what was going on because you father said that when he called earlier this morning, a strange man answered the phone."

"Mom, he is Detective Tony Morales, he is a close friend of mine," Maggie informed her mother. He is staying here to keep an eye on me." The moment Maggie said that she knew that she made a mistake and she was right.

"Are you in some kind of danger?" She asked with concern.

"I don't know mom, I don't think so, but Tony wants to make sure that nothing will happen, okay?"

"Alright, I guess. We are going to be there as soon as we can. Take care of yourself my child," her mother said and then she added. "We love you very much."

"I love you too, mom and dad," Maggie replied with tears in her eyes. When the line went dead an incredible sense of loneliness crept upon her mind and in her heart. She looked at Tony and because he loved her, he knew that it was the time when he needed to be with her the most. He picked her up in his arms and walked with her to the bedroom, laying her down on the bed gently and without a spoken word, he undressed her.

Maggie watched him taking off his clothes and she wanted nothing more than to be with him, right then and if it was possible, perhaps forever. He joined her in the bed while he kissed her softly and caressed her unruly hair. "I love you, Maggie," he said to her in a clear voice that sounded nothing but the truth to her.

"The feeling is mutual, Tony," Maggie replied, but for a reason, she could not confess her love for him the same way he told her.

He leaned over her and laid kisses on her breasts and his hands caressed them when lips began to move down on her body. Feeling his presence relaxed Maggie and in those moments she could think of nothing else than that Tony loved her as a man should love a woman. He knew what she wanted and he gladly obliged to her demanding tongue, his entered her mouth to dance as long as they could.

She was more than ready for him and when he entered her slowly, steadily, Maggie cried out from feeling his body completely. "Oh, Tony," she whispered and hugged his back, pulling him down for more kisses while he moved inside her. Sometime later he turned her around and she was on the top of him, moving with him in a steady rhythm that matched their equal desire and passion.

Tony sat up and held onto her while they moved, still together until he laid her down again on her back and continued making love to her. Her climax came seconds before his and afterwards, they lay side by side of each other. "I always hoped that someday I will find someone like you," Tony said quietly. She gave him a tired smile.

"I like being with you, Tony," she said softly and drifted into a restless sleep.

They slept until four in the afternoon when Tony's cell phone rang. "Hello," he said quietly, not wanting to wake up Maggie. He hurried into the bathroom to answer the phone.

"This is KC," she introduced herself. "Are you guys watching the television?"

"No, we haven't. Why, what's up?" He asked sensing a sound of urgency in his colleague's voice.

"Is Maggie there?" KC asked before telling Tony anything further.

"Yes, she is but she is asleep," he told his partner. She did not ask the reason.

"Tony, it's bad, really bad," she said finally. "That airplane crash Maggie predicted, it happened outside Albuquerque, New Mexico. They don't exactly know what happened, some witnesses said that they saw the plane explode in midair and after breaking apart, all the parts fell into a KOA campground. You are not going to believe this, but everything she painted came true."

"Oh, God," Tony whispered. "Any news on her parents?" He asked.

"Nobody knows for sure, there are so many casualties from the plane and on the campground, it will be a while before they can identify all the bodies. Break it to her gently, okay?" KC suggested and even she knew that it was not necessary to say.

"Of course," Tony replied and ended the call.

"It happened?" Tony heard Maggie's voice as she sat on the edge of the bed. He nodded and he repeated to her what KC told him. Maggie leaned to him and kissed him before she pushed herself off the bed and went to use the bathroom. Tony became concerned when Maggie was in there longer than usual, he just couldn't help it, he had to go to check on her. He knocked and he didn't hear a response, he turned the knob and the door opened.

Maggie was sitting on the top of the toilet her face was puffy from crying. She looked up at Tony. "I don't know if I can handle all this," she said, trying to catch her breath. Tony hugged her and helped her to get dressed, and then he escorted her to the living room where she sat down on the couch, opposite from the television. "Please turn the news on," she asked him.

"Are you sure that it is a good idea?" Tony asked before he reached for the remote control. Just one look at Maggie's face he immediately understood that not only Maggie wanted to know, but also Maggie needed to know what happened.

CNN as usual had not one but a few reporters at the scene of total devastation. There were ambulances, fire engines, policemen and airline personnel all around the area. Maggie went down on her knees and leaned on the coffee table in front of the couch and her eyes were glued to the screen. One of the reporters was interviewing campground survivors and all of a sudden Maggie yelled out and jumped up from the floor. "There, look on the stretcher," she shouted at Tony's direction.

Tony saw several people on stretchers at one of the hospitals in Albuquerque that was receiving injured survivals for treatment. Of course, he never met Maggie's parents, but he followed her fingers as they pointed at the screen.

"That is my father and the third stretcher is my mother. Tony, they are alive," she sobbed into his shoulders. He kissed the top of her head.

"God was watching over them," Tony remarked and took out the cell phone to call KC. She promised him that she was going to be there shortly, but before she left the station she wanted to get the information hotline number so Maggie would be able to call that number to inquire about her parents.

Tony left Maggie in the living room and went to fix something to eat, as they hadn't had anything to eat since that morning, it was already close to five in the afternoon. He found some eggs and cheese and made some omelets and after putting them on a plate with a couple of slices of toast, he brought them to the living room. It took him all his charm to make Maggie eat some of it. Naturally she was extremely upset, yet relieved at the same time knowing that her parents were alive, but also concerned because she did not know about the extent of their injuries.

They did not have to wait until KC give them the information hot line number as they appeared on the screen, although Tony guessed that KC would have an "inside" number to call for better details. There were two reporters at the actual scene where the plane fell out of the sky, although the debris covered not only the KOA campground but the surrounding area as well.

Most of those folks who were interviewed lived nearby, or were driving by when the plane appeared to have exploded. Hearing the unusual sounds coming from above, and being New Mexico after all, home of the city of Roswell, at first they thought that perhaps some spaceship was about to appear in the sky. Within seconds they realized that it would be best for all concerned if they would get out of the area because of the falling debris.

The first question for everyone to ask, what caused the explosion of CU Airlines, flight number CU 0617? Tony remarked that it would take a long time to investigate what exactly happened, although the black box, if they were able to locate it would give them a general idea as to what had taken place. Did some sort of electronic malfunction caused the explosion or was it a terrorist act? It was a question that begged to be answered.

KC arrived an hour later and brought them fast food from Arby's. She discovered that they had already eaten, so she began to consume one of the sandwiches. Maggie thanked KC for her thoughtfulness. When Tony brought her the telephone, she dialed the number he wrote down for her. The information hot line was not directed to the hospital; rather, it was a CU Airlines phone number. The person at the other end of line was very helpful and she told Maggie that although her parents' name were not on the flight manifest, the local police provided them with information on the people who were injured or deceased at the campground. "I am pleased to tell you Mrs. Anderson that your parents are going to be alright. By some miracle they only suffered superficial injuries. The only reason they were taken to the hospital is because the first response team wanted to make certain that they did not also suffer some internal injuries." Maggie thanked her for the information and for the hospital phone number where her parents were treated.

Maggie's hands were trembling when she made her next call to the Albuquerque hospital. After the second ring, a soft-spoken man answered the phone. Maggie introduced herself and told the man that her parents were involved in that plane crash and accordingly the information she received, they were treated at that hospital. The man asked her if she could hold the line for a couple of minutes and when she agreed, the line went silent.

"Hello, Maggie?" She heard her father's voice.

"Oh, dad, it is wonderful to hear your voice," Maggie told him while her tears began to roll down her pale face. "How are you and how is mom?"

"We had some minor bumps and bruises, but all things considered, we are doing fine," her father told her. "Maggie," he said with hesitation.

"Yes, dad," she replied waiting for her father's words.

"Just how did you know? How did you know not only about the plane was going to crash, but also about which airlines and flight number? I have been asking that question ever since your prediction came through." Davis asked her.

"Dad, it is very complicated, I will explain it to you when you get here, which brings me to the subject as how long are they going to keep you?"

"A couple of days I suppose, but I was told by one of the FAA investigators that they would appreciate if we stick around for another couple of days in case they have any questions. Actually I think it would be better if we stick around to rest up before we head in your way," he told Maggie.

"Would you like me to go where you are?" Maggie inquired.

"Oh, no, honey, we are going to be alright and we will see you real soon," her father assured her and they said their goodbyes. Maggie just sat there with the silent phone in her hand but her mind was hundreds of miles away.

"Maggie," she heard Tony's voice. "Is everything all right?"

She looked up and tried to smile. "Yes, I think so."

KC had a folder with her and she asked Maggie if she would mind to turn down the volume of the television for a few minutes. She needed to discuss something with her. Maggie complied with her friend's request and sat down next to her on the couch. "Maggie," she began. "I know that this is a very difficult time for you. I don't think that I'm wrong when I felt that we could safely call each other friends. Am I right about that?" She asked. When Maggie nodded in agreement, she continued. "Before I say anything further, I want to make certain that you are okay to hear some very unpleasant information." She said to Maggie and she also glanced toward Tony's direction whose eyes were asking her *what?*

"I seriously doubt if anything can be worse than what I just went through the past couple of days, or even months," Maggie replied. "I really would like to get some answers to what happened."

"Alright," KC agreed. "When I returned to the station from your house this morning, I had two FBI agents waiting with pertaining information to virtually everything you have predicted, or had visions about. Lucky for me, for us, one of the agents, Chuck Forester, is an old friend of mine and he was kind enough to give me some additional information that we would normally have to beg and threaten for." She stopped and took a sip from her coffee.

"First, let's talk about the child murders and the body we found in that house you saw in your vision and what you have painted. The first time we ran your painting through our database, we indeed came up with the name of Mitch Johansson, but as it turned out, he was well known to Homeland Security as Ricardo Lugo. The body, although you did not recognize his face is the same person, we confirmed that with a DNA test. Is that name familiar to you?" She asked, but instead of looking at Maggie, who shook her head, KC looked at Tony's direction. She most certainly detected an element of surprise upon hearing the name, but Tony remained silent. "Ricardo Lugo's DNA matched two DNA's in the FBI's database. I must also mention that our "friendly" agency, the CIA was also involved in some aspect of what we learned so far."

"The CIA?" Maggie repeated. It was KC's turn to nod.

"Yes, I know. What was happening around Paul is truly fascinating and equally troubling. Back to Ricardo Lugo, the FBI was searching for him because similar murders took place in San Juan, Puerto Rico during the time of his presence there. Eight children disappeared at various times and locations. We confirmed that Ricardo Lugo was in those vicinities."

"Whose DNA matched his?" Tony asked.

KC ignored his question and refocused on Maggie. "Do you know a person by the name of Paulo Lugo?" She asked. Maggie shook her head.

"Oh, yes, my friend, you know him better by the name Paul Anderson, your late husband," KC informed them and Maggie just couldn't comprehend what KC was telling her.

"KC, forgive me for saying this, but what you are saying about Paul just doesn't make any sense," Maggie said. "We were married for ten years and I have never heard anything about him being Hispanic, there was no accent, nothing like that."

"Well, his DNA made it to the FBI's DNA database courtesy of the CIA and it is a partial match for both, Eduardo and Francesco Lugo." KC told her.

"Who are those people?" Maggie asked and looked at Tony who was staring at the door, he was acting somewhat strangely.

"Eduardo Lugo is the brother of Paul, you late husband, they were identical twins. Francesco Lugo is Paul's son, while Ricardo was Eduardo's son," KC explained.

"Where are Eduardo and Francesco?" Maggie inquired.

"Well, this is where the entire story becomes interesting. I do not know how my FBI friend Chuck found this out, but evidently Paul's partner, colleague and friend, Christopher Collins was also a CIA informant. I suppose they released his name now because he died in that explosion. Eduardo and Francesco Lugo are members of a Puerto Rican terrorist organization who call themselves *Red December*, in the memory of something that happened at least a couple of hundred years ago." KC said as she looked at some of the pages in her file.

"The FBI was able to salvage some of the computer hard drives from Paul's old business after the explosion, and on Collins' computer they found emails from Eduardo Lugo offering money for something that Paul and Collins were working on. There were some emails from Eduardo to Paul on his computer, but evidently he deleted them all without opening them," KC continued.

"I am sorry to interrupt you," Maggie said to KC. "May I ask you about Francisco who is supposedly Paul's son. Paul never mentioned that he was married before or that he had a child. What do you know about that?"

"Paul was a twenty year old college student and was still being called Paulo Lugo when he married a young woman who was pregnant with his child, Francisco. She was eighteen years old when she died from complication of childbirth. Paul's brother, Eduardo who was also married at the time took in the child and raised him too. Paulo changed his name just before graduated from college, that is why all his diplomas and everything else only reflected his new name, Paul Anderson," KC explained and she showed copies of Paul's diploma and also a certificate of name change that was done in the Spanish language.

"You live with a man for ten years and it turns out that you didn't know him at all," Maggie said bitterly and looked at Tony. His face lost his color and Maggie sensed that something was wrong; something was out of the ordinary with him.

"According to the FBI reports, one of Paul's employees, you may remember him, Miguel Ponce de Leon, evidently he was a sleeper cell from the *Red December* terrorist organization and he planted the bomb in the building. Something must have gone wrong and the bomb exploded earlier than it was planned, perhaps that is why he also became one of the victims."

"Ponce?" Maggie asked. "He was in this house several times for dinner, he was a very nice quiet man." She shook her head.

"According to Homeland Security, Eduardo, Ricardo and Francisco Lugo entered the USA a year ago, and while it was their intention to track them, they fell out of sight until now. Ricardo was on the FBI's ten most wanted list for the child murders in Puerto Rico, he also served five years in jail for child molestation. It is now a question who killed him?" KC stopped and looked at Tony who was sitting in an armchair deep in thought. He looked up at KC and tried to smile.

"If you'll excuse me, I need to make a phone call. Maggie, may I use your landline?" He said unexpectedly and walked down the hallway toward the master bedroom for privacy. Maggie glanced at KC and turned her head. KC nodded and watched Maggie as she quietly made her way to the guestroom that had a connecting wall with her bedroom. She carefully lifted up the received and listened.

"*Monsignore, es Antonio. Sé que se supone que no tengo que llamar a menos que sea una emergencia, pero tenemos un problema.* (Monsignor, it's me, Antonio. I know that I am not supposed to call you unless it's an emergency, but we have a problem.)" Tony said into the receiver of the phone and glanced at the door that he closed.

"*¿Cuál es el problema?* (What is the problem?)" Asked the man at the other of the line.

"*El FBI y la CIA están involucrados. Ellos saben acerca de Anderson cambiando nombres, ellos saben acerca de la historia familiar de Lugo. Ellos conocen casi todo. ¿Qué te sugieren que debemos hacer?* (The FBI and the CIA are involved. They know about Anderson's name change, and they know about the Lugo family's history. They know almost everything. What do you suggest that we should do?)" Tony inquired from the person he called Monsignore or Monsignor in English.

"*¿Cuál es su relación con esa mujer, Maggie Anderson?* (What is your relationship with that woman, Maggie Anderson?)" He wanted to know.

"*Todo es fino, yo no pienso que Maggie sospecha nada.* (Everything is fine, I don't think that Maggie suspects anything.)" Tony replied.

"*Eso es bueno. Sugiero que usted no cambia su estatus, no abandone su cobertura.* (That's good. I suggest that you don't change your status, do not give up your cover.)" The man answered, and then he added. "*¿Comprende que nada puede suceder a ella?* (You understand that nothing can happen to her?)" He asked.

"*Sí, comprendo. Tomé algún tiempo de estar con ella, para estar alrededor de ella asegurarse de que ningún daño viene a ella.* (Yes, I understand. I took some time off to be with her, to be around her to make sure that no harm comes to her.)" Tony informed him.

"*Sea muy cuidadoso, el Lugos es personas muy peligrosas.* (Be very careful, the Lugos are very dangerous people.)" The man advised Tony.

"*Haré Monsignore. Adiós.* (I will do that Monsignor. Good-bye.)" Tony said and ended the phone call. He buried his head in his hands and rubbed his face with his palms and then, he took a deep breath. "Oh, Maggie," he whispered and a few minutes later he joined Maggie and KC in the living room.

"Did I miss anything?" He asked and both of the women thought that he seemed much more alive than before the phone call he made.

"I spoke to the Captain and we think that something went wrong between the brothers after Paul Anderson won the Nobel Prize for physics and got involved with high cost government programs. Just as a brain rush, we figured that perhaps Eduardo was involved planting a bomb on the CU airlines flight as a treat against the United States government. Perhaps it is part of a new wave of terrorist attacks that began because the US government refused to release Puerto Rico from its commonwealth status. Evidently the *Red December* terrorist organization's primary goal is for Puerto Rico to become a separate and independent country. Any thoughts on the subject Tony?" KC addressed the unexpected question to her partner. He seemed surprised.

"Why are you asking me that?" He inquired.

"Well, well no offense Tony, but aren't you Puerto Rican by national origin?" KC asked.

"I was born right here in LA," Tony responded in an offensive tone of voice. "Are you implying something?"

"For Christ sake," KC snapped at him. "What is wrong with you? You act as if you want be someplace else, making a telephone call in a middle of a discussion and now you are acting like I offended you with a question. Your parents came from Puerto Rico and I was just wondering if you ever heard them talking about something like that, that is all."

"I am sorry," Tony apologized. "You are right, my thoughts were on the Lugos' and there are some troubling questions in what you have told us so far."

"What about what I just asked you?" KC tried to go back to that subject.

"I was getting there," Tony said. "The answer is nothing, they had mentioned a couple of times about what would happen if Puerto Rico received its independence. On the political side, they have never discussed how Puerto Rico could accomplish that. I personally thought that Puerto Rico had the best of both worlds with some limitations. All Puerto Ricans are American citizens and they enjoy the same economic assistance as mainland Americans. The only big difference is that they cannot vote during the presidential election," he told them. "On the other hand, I do not see anything wrong about a country who wants to be independent from a controlling country, being a commonwealth country that is." He added.

"Hmmm," KC murmured. "Okay, let's move back to the subject of the Lugos. From the evidence we found at the murder scene, it appears that Ricardo strayed away from the political movement and followed his own murderous ways. It may have been too dangerous for the Lugos', perhaps they were concerned that Ricardo's action may lead the police to them, therefore their reign of terror would be stopped. Perhaps, just perhaps they decided to get rid of their problem child, Ricardo. Perhaps one of the Lugo's, the killer was the shadow you have seen in your vision." KC suggested to Maggie. She nodded that it was possible.

"It means that Eduardo and Francisco are still out there," Maggie said quietly.

"My gut feelings are telling me that Maggie, you may be their target," KC said and turned to her friend. Maggie did not seem surprised.

"You may be right," she replied and looked at Tony who was also watching her. "Although for the world of me, I cannot imagine the reason why would they want to harm me? Ransom would not make any sense because they have killed Paul who would pay the ransom? I just don't understand what would they possibly want from me at all." She declared.

"Perhaps they want you because you can see things that are going to happen," Tony suggested. KC and Maggie looked at each other.

"Tony," Maggie said. "It doesn't work that way. I don't just go asleep and dream up things. These visions appeared to me for certain reasons. Before my heart procedure, I seldom ever dreamt. It all began when I could not gain consciousness. Although some people may call it a gift, but as I told you, it is truly not a gift, at least I don't think so. I would consider it a gift if I could heal ailing people, if I could prevent things from happening." As soon as she said that she covered her mouth with her hands. "Oh, my dear God," she mumbled. "I did try to prevent that plane crash didn't I?" KC nodded.

"You have absolutely no reason to blame yourself," Tony said to her. "You told Paul and he called the FAA not once but multiple times and you called them as well. They are responsible for not preventing the tragedy and not you."

They were quiet for a few moments, gathering their thoughts when KC's cell phone went off. "KC," she replied. "Yes, Captain, I am here with her." She glanced over to Maggie while she listened to her superior officer. "Will do sir, right away."

After putting her cell phone away, KC stood up. "Maggie, please pack up some essentials and clothing, we have to move you into a safe house."

"But why?" Maggie asked, wondering.

"The Captain did not go into details over the phone, but he said that there is a reason to believe that there will be an attempt on your life. Other than the three of us, no one would know your location, not even the Captain." KC informed her.

"I am not going anywhere until I know why all that is necessary," Maggie said stubbornly and looked at KC for an answer.

She glanced at Tony and turned to Maggie. "The Medical Examiner determined that the bullets that killed Paul came from a police issued Glock revolver."

"I have a Glock," Tony said and put his hand on his gun.

"And so do I and many of our colleagues," KC replied. "It would be the best for all concerned if only a minimal number of people would be aware of your location until it all clears up."

"What about my parents?" Maggie asked.

"You can call them on your cell phone and explain the situation. It would be a very bad idea right now to visit you under these circumstances." KC suggested.

Maggie, without any further hesitation went into her master bedroom closet and packed carry-on luggage and collected her essentials from the bathroom. She was ready in less than ten minutes and then she looked around in her house if there was anything else she would need. A thought occurred to her and she rushed back into her studio and grabbed her laptop and just then she picked up her purse and waited until Tony called them that it was safe to go outside. Maggie got into KC's car and Tony followed them with his.

The safe house was located in Malibu, not far from the beach and tourist area. It was a small but tidy place, two bedrooms, small kitchen and bathroom, something what a recent college graduate and young couple would buy for a starter home. Once Maggie was situated in her temporary home, KC left her to go back to the station but not without giving her straight instructions about not opening the door to anyone, even if they claim that they were from a law enforcement agency. She and Tony were the only ones who had keys to the house. KC told Maggie not to go near, or by any of the windows and not to use the landline phone. Tony also left to go back to his own place to get some clean clothes and to shave and shower, not to mention to buy some groceries.

Having not much to do, Maggie booted up her computer and read several articles on the subject of Puerto Rico, just to refresh her memory from those seemingly long ago times when she went there to visit her college roommate's family. She clearly recalled the beautiful clean beaches, and at the same time it also brought her back memories of how she met Paul for the first time. Although she no longer loved Paul, she had respected him for many reasons, most of all because he stood by her when she was ill and while she was recovering.

Paul and Maggie were married only three years when Paul won the Nobel Prize for physics along with his friend and colleague Christopher Collins. After winning the most prestigious prize known to human kind in the field of science, their lives changed forever. From the beginning Maggie wanted a child, or even children but despite the fact they did not use any contraceptives, she never got pregnant. According to physical examinations it was determined that there was nothing wrong with her, but she choose to never bring up the subject to Paul, as his new "fame" took him away from home even more than before. Maggie began to feel alone and her discovery that she had a talent for painting came as a blessing.

Maggie was healthy most of her life, except for an occasional cold or flu, she had never been sick, until she woke up one morning with her heart racing hundred miles an hour. It was then when their lives was turned upside down. Just two years earlier, Chris Collins and Paul became involved with the Federal Government to design a military missile system. Maggie told the truth to Tony and KC, that Paul never shared his work with her.

Thinking about Paul made her sad and angry at the same time. How could they live under the same roof and lay in a bed of lies like they did. How could a man not tell his wife that he was married before and that he already had a child, a son named Francisco. Since Maggie learned that, she bitterly thought that there was no wonder why Paul did not force or was not interested talking about the issue of having children.

She checked her emails; she had three different accounts, one for her private emails, another one for fans and business, and the third one for ordering merchandise over the Internet. Because she hadn't looked at her emails for at least two weeks, there were hundreds of emails. She took a deep breath and looked at the sender's email address before she opened any of her emails. There were over twenty emails from someone who used the initial as EL. Maggie's heart began to beat faster thinking about one person whom she knew or heard of with those initial, Paul's brother, Eduardo Lugo. After a long debate with herself, she clicked on the first email from EL; it read, *"I will find you."* She opened the second and the third, but all said the same thing. She looked at the date and time when they were sent, thinking that perhaps the servers messed up and sent the same email several times by accident, but there was no accident, Lugo sent those emails every two hours or so. She thought about deleting them but she changed her mind, she forwarded one of them to KC's email and told her that there was another nineteen of those identical or similar messages.

Maggie had enough from her computer, she walked into the kitchen and looked for a tea bag or something she could quickly make but all the cupboards were empty, she had to wait until Tony returned from his home and from shopping for food.

She went back into the living room, turned on the TV and looked for the CNN news channel. Maggie leaned forward despite the fact that she could see just fine from the place where she was sitting. On the screen a picture was shown with a comment that it was taken five years earlier at an opening of one her exhibits. Paul was standing next to her smiling with a glass of champagne in his hand, looking at her. Maggie was smiling too, why not, she thought. Those were seemingly happy days.

The reporter went on saying that someone from the FAA leaked an audio tape of a phone call made by the well-known painter Margaret (Maggie) Davis-Anderson's husband, the recently mysteriously murdered Nobel Prize Physicist Dr. Paul Anderson, whose murder was still under investigation. On that tape Dr. Anderson mentioned that his wife had a vision of some sort, and he went on describing what his wife's vision was in such details which should have been a motivator to FAA to at least look into a possible plane disaster, which is now being labeled as a terrorist act by Homeland Security. She asked the viewers to listen and/or read part of that taped conversation between Dr. Anderson and Mr. Riggs, FAA Director.

Maggie watched the call played on the screen with the words typed so the viewers could follow easier. She vividly recalled that day, months earlier when Paul made that call, she was sitting right next to him on the sofa in their living room. Hearing Paul's voice as he was pleading with Riggs was heart breaking for Maggie to hear, not as much as hearing his voice itself, but the way he fought to be heard which meant that he actually believed in her.

She couldn't take it anymore after one of the female reporters questioned her vision and called her psychic that she was not. Maggie turned off the television in disgust and decided to lay down until Tony returned. As soon as her head hit the pillow, Maggie immediately fell asleep.

CHAPTER EIGHTEEN

MAGGIE COMPLETELY LOST track of time and had no idea how long she slept, but the noise at the entry door woke her up. "Open up, we are Federal Agents from Homeland Security," yelled a man after banging again on the door. Maggie immediately reached for her cellphone on the nightstand and pressed the number for KC.

"Hello," Maggie said in the phone not giving the other person a chance to answer. "KC, is that you?" She asked.

"Yes, what's up Maggie, did Tony get back yet? He went to shop for some groceries when he called about twenty minutes ago." KC informed her.

"KC, I don't know how many men are outside there but they are banging on the door. They claim to be from Homeland Security," Maggie said in a hurried voice as the banging on the front door continued.

"Shit," KC cursed. "I am on my way, don't open the door."

"What if they break it down?" Maggie asked. There was a momentarily silence on the other end of the line, and then KC replied.

"We will find you," KC said and ended the call.

The banging continued and suddenly there was quiet outside, which gave Maggie a false since of relief. It did not last long, just as she thought, the men broke the door down and with gun in hand searched from room to room, finding Maggie calmly sitting at the edge of her bed. "Are you Margaret Davis-Anderson?" One of the three men asked, pointing their guns at Maggie. She nodded. "Mrs. Anderson, you need to come with us."

"Gentlemen, first things first. I would like to see your identification cards and badges please." Maggie said calmly. The men rolled their eyes but after putting their guns away, they whipped out their badges and the ID cards, both in the same holder. Maggie looked at all three of them and when she was satisfied that they were indeed Federal Agents that they claimed to be, she turned to the man nearest to her. "As you can tell, I just woke up. I am going with you without any resistance, but please give me the courtesy to let me use the bathroom."

The men looked at each other and one of them went into the bathroom to check out the window and look for weapons. When he motioned that it was clear, Maggie went inside, used the toilet, washed her hands and face and combed her hair in no particular hurry. It only took ten minutes with only one of the men telling her through the door that they have to get going.

Leaving the bathroom that opened from the master bedroom, she picked up the cell phone from the nightstand and put it in her purse that was also on the nightstand and looked at the men. "Do you want to handcuff me?" She asked with a smile.

"Do you think that it is necessary?" Asked the taller man. Maggie shook her head.

"No," she replied and followed the first man into the living room that led to the small entryway. Just as they were about to leave the house, Tony appeared with two bags of groceries in his arms. He dropped them immediately and drew his gun just to find himself face to face with three men with guns in their hands.

"Who are you?" Asked the man who was holding Maggie's arm, trying to shield her from Tony.

"If I can reach in my pocket I can show you," Tony replied. The man nodded, and while still holding his gun in one hand, he took out his detective shield and his ID. The men lowered their guns and so did Tony. "I don't know how you found Ms. Anderson, but she is in protective custody." He informed them.

"We need to question her in reference to the terrorist attack on the downed passenger airliner," one of the man told Tony.

"Where are you taking her?" Tony inquired.

"To a safer place than this," said the man shielding Maggie, after letting her arm go.

"You cannot detain her without representation," Tony tried to argue but he knew exactly how the men were going to respond to him.

"Yes, we can, under the Patriot Act we can detain and hold a person under suspicion of terrorism as long as it's necessary without any formal charges, but you knew that didn't you?" The man in the middle of the three said. Tony nodded. "We are leaving," the man declared and went outside by himself to secure the street, just like Tony did when KC and Maggie left her house. Within minutes three of them were sitting in the back of a large black SUV, the tall man was driving and Maggie was sitting between two agents on the back seat.

The vehicle barely reached the middle of the street when they passed a large truck with a sign on its side that read "Morton's Garden Supply" when the explosion rocked the entire street. Maggie felt a tremendous pressure in her chest and everything went black. Within seconds Tony was on the phone calling for an ambulance, police and the bomb squad. He ran like a maniac toward the heavily damaged vehicle and tried to open the backdoor that was stuck as the frame was bent.

Tony thought of many things, but his first concern was that the car could burst into a ball of fire in any second and blow up. The door finally opened and the man on Maggie's left fell to the ground. He was dead and so was the man who was sitting on Maggie's right in the backseat. Maggie was still alive, her breathing labored and Tony suspected that she probably had collapsed lungs. In a short distance he could hear sirens and he prayed that they would get there very shortly. He didn't want to disturb the crime scene but he had to do something about Maggie in case the car blew up. He took out his cell phone and took several pictures before he pulled the dead man on the right side out and gently as he could he pulled Maggie out and carried her in his arms to what he considered a relatively safe distance.

He could see the first fire truck turning on the corner when the SUV indeed burst into flames and then exploded. Tony used his own body as a shield over Maggie's, trying to keep her from suffering further harm. The fire truck finally arrived followed by two ambulances, several police cars and the bomb squad which quickly searched the area while the police evacuated those who were home on both sides of the street.

Maggie was clearly suffocating from lack of oxygen and the EMT had no choice but to do a temporary tracheotomy on her, and then they were on their way to the hospital. Before the ambulance departed the scene, the EMT also told Tony that he suspected that Maggie also suffered a concussion. Tony wanted to go with her in the ambulance but he was needed at the scene so he asked the EMT which hospital they were taking Maggie. Once he got the information he rushed to KC who just arrived at the scene of a massive car bomb explosion.

CHAPTER NINETEEN

THE SCENERY WAS familiar, Maggie was certain that she had been there before and then she remembered that it was a place that if once someone visited and lived to tell, they would never forget. She passed between the white trees and her hands brushed white flowers. At this particular time, she knew that she was not alone; she saw the shadows but not the faces of others in the white forest. It was more like a feeling than a visual thing to experience.

Her walk ended when she reached a white grass and vegetation clearing. She slowly walked out of the white forest, but did not quite make it to the center of the white field as white bars appeared in front of her preventing Maggie from further movements. She immediately thought about the white man and the white dog that she had seen in her first original vision, when she was told that she was *"The Gifted One".*

"Hello," she said quietly. "Is anybody here?" She turned back toward the forest because she heard quiet, yet audible murmurs behind her. When she returned her attention to the white bars in front of her, she almost screamed. The white man and same white dog were in front of her, behind the bars. She took a step back, yet not far enough to have her hand wrap about the bars in front of her. "Why am I here?" She asked. "Did I die?"

The man's cold stare tore into her heart and she knew the answer. She was in limbo; she was not dead, not yet. "Why am I here?" She asked again.

"You have committed a sin," the man said and it seemed to her that his voice thundered, when it did not. "And you have not followed the word of the Lord."

"What sin did I commit?" She asked and the man's stare made her understand that her sin was to cheat on Paul with Tony. "It is not a deadly sin to love someone," she said quietly.

"You were given a gift not many humans possess, yet you did not take full advantage of it," the man accused her. "The Lord made you one of his *Gifted Ones*, but you did not fulfill your obligation to your Master."

"Forgive me, but I am just a human being who only wants to do one thing, to live a normal life. I don't want to sound ungrateful, but this "gift" gave me so much sorrow and anguish that I could barely stand it." Maggie said.

"You do as the Lord tells you," echoed the white man.

Maggie bowed her head, thinking that perhaps it would be just as well if she died because she was not sure if she could live a normal life to dream and paint about murders and bloodsheds. Her surroundings became quiet again. She looked at the white man and the white dog who picked up his ears; he sensed that someone was approaching. "Maggie?" She heard the familiar voice.

She turned around in shock to see Tony approaching. He was not white like everything around her, and he smiled right away when came close to her. "What are you doing here?" She asked.

Tony pointed at his chest and his right arm. There was no blood, only one small hole on both. Maggie turned around to look at the white man. "No, you cannot take him away from life. He is a good man and he loves me as a man should love a woman."

The man did not reply he just stared at them. The white dog laid his head down on the man's feet, ignoring them both. "What is this place?" Tony asked and looked around while put his hands on Maggie's shoulder.

"I am not sure. I think that this is a place before people allowed to go to Heaven." She smiled. "I don't really know." She confessed.

"I was so worry about you," Tony said, ignoring the white man and his white dog. "You came into my life and I finally knew what real love was. If we are dead, and if there is such place as Heaven, I hope that we go there together and never leave each other's sight." Maggie smiled and gently touched Tony's face, then they looked at the man who was quietly still sitting on a white chair in front of them, as if he was waiting for something.

After a few moments of silence, he raised his right arms. "He has spoken. The man must stay and you, woman, must return to life to fulfill your mission." He declared.

Maggie screamed and it echoed through the forest. The white dog jumped up and perked up his ears. "NO," Maggie screamed again. "Please take us both then because my life would be worthless without him. Oh, please, dear God, don't take him away from me." Maggie begged. "I'll do whatever you want me to do, but with him in my life."

Tony hugged her and said to the white man. "Her life is more important than mine. Do not listen to her. If you want to take my life, than do it, but not her life. She needs to live, she needs to love, she needs to be happy." It was Tony who did the begging at that time.

The white man remained silent and the white dog settled down once again but kept an eye on Maggie. She looked down at the dog and on an instinct she reached through the bars to pet him. The moment she touched the dog, she and Tony were thrown backwards and were unable to move or open their eyes, but they heard a voice that not as much thundered, rather echoed around them.

"Do not forget your mission. Go back to life and sin no more," said the voice.

CHAPTER TWENTY

"MAGGIE," SHE HEARD KC's voice. "Open your eyes," she encouraged her. Maggie blinked a couple of times but she had a throbbing headache and everything was blurry, so she closed them again. She tried to talk but she could not. She lifted her arm that had an IV in it and tried to touch her throat, but KC's hand stopped her. "You cannot speak because you have a tube in your throat. You could not breathe and they had to do a tracheotomy on you. Do you understand me? Squeeze my hand if you do." KC asked her. Maggie squeezed KC's hand gently; nevertheless, KC was glad as it was a squeeze. Maggie motioned with her hand that she wanted to write something. "Hold on," KC said and reached into her small purse to take out a notebook and a pen. She placed the pen in Maggie's hand and held the notebook. "Go ahead," she encouraged her to write.

Maggie's hand moved slowly as she carved the word with the pen. *Tony?* She wrote and placed a question mark after his name. KC smiled.

"He is here in the same room with you, he is sleeping now," KC informed her. "Do you want to know what happened?" She asked. Maggie wrote the letter "*Y*" as her answer meaning, "*yes*". "Alright," KC agreed and glanced at Tony but he was still asleep from the medication he received through his IV. "After the ambulance brought you to the hospital, we had to compare notes with the FBI and Homeland Security on the failed attempt to take you to a secure location so they could question you. More than ever they are anxiously trying to find out how those individuals knew where you were, to place the explosive in that truck almost across from the house where you were saying. Needless to say they were upset over the deaths of three of their agents, of course, it made us sad too as no matter how you looked at them, they were just doing their jobs."

KC stopped talking when the nurse entered to check on Maggie's and Tony's IV and to take their vitals. She was done in no time and left the room without a single word. "Okay, so after a couple of hours comparing notes and ideas, Tony and I decided to go back to your house just to take a second look around. I don't want you to get upset, but your front door was unlocked. At that time we didn't know who, but someone had to either know your code or disconnected the security system. Both of us had our guns in hand when we carefully entered your house. We heard activities coming from the studio and then we smelled smoke."

Maggie grabbed KC's hand in panic hearing her words. "Please calm down, we got there just in time. Most of the smoke came from the paints and we were almost run down by two men. One of them jumped at me, and when you get your eyes open all the way, you may see the proof that I didn't let him go without a fight. I am okay but my shoulder and back is killing me. Anyway, the man who jumped me was Francisco Lugo and Tony got into a fight with Eduardo. Tony had two dilemmas, he had to tackle Eduardo who was a strong guy and Tony also wanted to save your paintings because he knew that they could get serious smoke damage, not to mention that the whole room and perhaps even your house could blow up with all the chemicals in your room, like your cleaning fluids and such."

KC heard a sound coming from Tony but her partner just moved in his sleep, so she continued. "Tony finally managed to tackle Eduardo Lugo down by hitting him with one of the big vases in your hallway, sorry about that. Eduardo went down and I was cuffing Francisco when Tony saw the first flames, luckily they were just blank canvases. Like a maniac he ran inside your studio and started tossing your paintings out through your window to your yard. I was helping him but neither of us realized that although Tony cuffed Eduardo's wrist, somehow he managed to get out of the cuffs and use his gun. He fired two shots at us, one hit Tony in his chest and another one hit him on his arm, Eduardo did not have a chance to fire another shot as I took him down. Thank God I was a better shot than he was. I immediately called for an ambulance and the fire department of course and here we are." Maggie's hand eased on KC's arm and reached for the pen, she wrote the letter "*T*" at that time for "*Tony*" again.

"Tony was in the ICU for a couple of days and had two surgeries. Once again, do not panic, but they had to resuscitate him on the operating table because his heart stopped for a few seconds. They extracted both bullets, from his chest; it barely missed major arteries in his heart and from his arm too. Just that you know, you were out for three days my friend," she informed Maggie.

While KC was talking, Maggie tried and finally succeeded to fully open her eyes. When KC noticed that, her lips curved into a happy smile. Maggie pointed at the tube in her throat and in the notebook she wrote a question mark. "I will ask the doctor," KC promised. "Hey, listen, I have to leave for a little while, but I'll be back later." Maggie nodded.

KC turned around from the door before she left. "Maggie, I almost forgot, there is a policeman outside the door and he has a list of names of who can visit you. It is a short list, if you know what I mean."

After KC left the room, Maggie desperately tried to turn to look at Tony but she was unable to do so until she sat up in bed. She immediately fell back as she became terribly dizzy. She decided to wait until the nurse came in to help her up. She felt extremely tired and before she fell into another sleep, she thought about what KC told her about Tony, how he technically died on the operating table until he was resuscitated. Maggie concluded that perhaps it was the time when Tony appeared in her vision with the white man and the white dog.

Maggie's sleep was troubled from the moment it began. Her vision began at the police station where Tony and KC were based. She watched as KC was interrogating Francisco Lugo whose left hand was handcuffed to the heavy table that was between two sets of chairs. KC was talking when there was a knock on the door and a rookie cop entered. Maggie didn't know the cop but in her vision, she just knew that he was a rookie. The cop stood next to the table and was handing KC some paperwork when Lugo, with his free right hand reached for the cop's weapon and ripped it out of is holster. Francisco pointed the gun at them and he yelled at KC to remove the handcuffs. KC told him to remain calm; she will do as he asked. Maggie was able to see clearly as the rest of the KC's colleagues also realized what was going on. Luckily for KC the young cop left the door of the interrogation room open when he entered.

Seconds later after KC calmly as she could unlocked the handcuffs, Francisco grabbed KC around her neck by wrapping his left arm around her throat and with the gun in his right hand, he forced her to walk toward the door while he nervously looked around in a threatening fashion. Maggie noticed in her vision some SWAT team members hiding behind the visitor's desk and behind a thick column by the police station entrance door, waiting for Francisco with his hostage to leave the elevator at the lobby level.

A couple of minutes passed and people began to move away from Francisco who was acting like a mad man. The SWAT member behind the column fired one single shot hitting Francisco in the back of his head. He died immediately, collapsing to the floor in a pool of blood. Maggie watched as the blood began to spread on the floor, growing into a bigger and bigger puddle.

She felt a hand on her forehead and when she looked up, a nurse was standing by her bed along with a doctor. "How are you feeling?" The doctor asked. Maggie had to concentrate on every syllable what he was saying, waking up from some vision she just had, into reality was a hard task. She nodded that she was okay. "We are going to remove the tube, okay?" He asked. Maggie nodded that it was okay.

CHAPTER TWENTY-ONE

THE MINOR SURGERY went well but Maggie still had difficulties speaking and swallowing. The doctor explained to her that it was normal after having a trachea tube removed. He also told her that she could consider herself lucky because they used a smaller tube to make her breathing possible.

Maggie understood what the doctor was explaining but she had other, bigger concerns. KC did not return to the hospital yet, which was her reason to worry about the correctness of her vision. What if something happened to KC, a worse ending than what she had seen? She got out of the bed and pushed the IV stand next to Tony's bed. She sat down in a chair that she pulled closer to him. The medication that was given to Tony made him very drowsy, but he looked up at her and tried to smile. "We make a good pair," he whispered and he was out again.

Maggie felt genuinely bad for Tony, he had medicine and blood was going through IV's in his arm, a tube was draining excess fluid from his chest and another bag was hanging on the side of the bed collecting his urine. *This all happened to you because of me,* Maggie thought and kissed Tony's hand.

Around five thirty in the evening dinner arrived in the form of a bowl of soup, Jell-O, an orange juice and her choice of beverage, which was tea. She forced herself to eat because the nurse threatened her that if she was not eating than they would have to feed her through her IV. She did not feel hunger because they were feeding her the threatened way earlier, when she had trachea tube in her throat. Now that it was out, her stomach made it clear that it wanted to be fed.

The cream of potato soup wasn't too bad, she agreed, although she also knew that when a person was hungry any food would have tasted good. She finished her cherry Jell-O; actually it was her favorite even at home when she made Jell-O on a few occasions. The orange juice was cold and it felt good going down her dry throat.

While Maggie was slowly consuming her food, she kept her eyes on the TV screen, and on the clock, high on the middle of the wall. Time past by quickly and by nine of clock she was on edge. KC did not call and did not stop by, something had to happen, Maggie suspected. She went back to bed and as sleepy as she was, she had great difficulty falling asleep.

It was past ten o'clock, way past visitor's time, but being a police detective had it perks and KC talked herself into Maggie and Tony's room. Tony was awake earlier, but by the time KC arrived, he was asleep again. Maggie who was just dozing opened her eyes when she sensed a presence in her room. "Sssss," KC told her. "It's me."

"Oh, thank you, God," Maggie murmured her first words of the day with a raspy voice. "I was so worried."

"I am so, sorry," KC apologized. "We had another murder, unrelated to your case and we are short of people. I didn't even have time to eat until on the way here. I should have called you but I thought that perhaps you were asleep. Anyway, why were you concerned?" She asked.

It would have been too long for Maggie to explain by talking, so she said some of the things and wrote down some other things. "I was afraid that you were hurt," she said finally.

"We didn't interrogate Francisco yet, so your vision did not happen yet. Now I know what I have to be careful about," KC smiled and squeezed Maggie's hand. "How are you feeling?"

"I feel okay," Maggie said. "My head doesn't hurt that much anymore either."

"How is Tony?" KC asked and glanced at her partner.

"In and out of sleeping, but I know that he is going to be all right," Maggie said and she gave KC a weak smile.

"How can you be so sure? Something that a doctor said?" She asked. "Did you have another vision before the one I was in?"

Maggie nodded and slowly and with only a very few words, she told KC how she saw Tony also in that place she had seen before they ever met. "When his heart stopped, that was a brief moment when he joined me in front of the white man." Maggie whispered.

KC sat by Maggie's bedside and listened to her friend with amazement, but also with concern for her safety. There were a lot of bad people out there who could translate Maggie's capability to see visions of upcoming disasters or terrorist attacks they were planning to do themselves, and they may want to prevent Maggie to tell and warn the police about those planned attacks in the future. CNN already mentioned Maggie's name and her husband's phone call to the FAA in reference to the pending plane crash, and when she checked Maggie's phone messages being in her house earlier in the day, there were over thirty phone calls. The callers were various news agencies, television news reporters, and even many religious organizations that were asking her to speak to their congregations, and yes, there were also threatening phone calls from people who accused her from being a devil's advocate. She did not erase the phone calls because the phone was not her property, but she made notes to warn Maggie about them when she was allowed to return home.

It was very late in the evening and KC bid goodnight to Maggie with a promise that she will return on the following morning after first taking care of some office business. Maggie reminded her about the vision of the interrogation that almost turned deadly and KC promised her that she would be cautious.

As soon as KC left, Maggie said her nightly prayer and went to sleep. Her dream began slowly but her subconscious mind recognized the scene she had seen once before involving KC. The beginning of the vision was the same but the ending was much different than in her first vision and shocked even her.

CHAPTER TWENTY-TWO

KC ASKED ONE of the uniformed policemen on duty to bring up the prisoner, Francisco Lugo from the holding cell and take him to interrogation room two. The policeman nodded and headed for the man in custody. KC knocked on Captain Vargas' door and when he waved her in, she entered and asked him if she could close the door.

"What's up KC?" He asked pushing his computer keyboard away.

KC briefed the Captain about Maggie's vision of a possible incident that might occur in the interrogation room. There was a look on the Captain's face that KC knew was hesitation. "Look Captain, I grant you that Maggie and I have become friends and that we are concerned for each other's safety, but you must admit, so far everything she has predicted came true."

Captain Vargas nodded in agreement. "What do you want me to do? You want someone else to do the interview?" He asked. KC shook her head.

"No way, he is my case," she objected.

"Why don't you take Jack in with you, he is after all your temporary partner," Captain Vargas suggested. KC thought about it.

"I want to do the questioning alone. The perks sometimes think that a woman is easier to handle and they may brag about some things," she said. "I would like to ask you a favor, do not let anyone enter the interrogation room with a weapon, while I am in there."

"Okay, I can do that," Captain said and got up to talk to his subordinates.

He asked for everyone's attention and told the detectives and police personnel present not to enter interrogation room two with a weapon while Detective Calhoun was conducting the questioning of Lugo.

Many of the detectives automatically removed their guns from their holster upon entering the office, but some of them who were just stopping by and ready to leave quickly, did not. Everyone got the Captain's order and KC gathered her file on Lugo. After putting on her jacket, she joined Lugo in the interrogation room where he was sitting with his left wrist handcuffed to the stainless still bar on the table.

"How is your cellmate treating you?" KC asked Lugo as she took off her suit's jacket and wrapped it around back of the chair that was across from him, then she took a seat herself.

"I prefer to be on the beach," Lugo replied with a smirk on his face.

"Don't we all," KC murmured and opened his file. She shook her head. "There are so many questions, I don't even know where to start." She stated.

"How about you un-cuffing me?" Lugo asked.

"Maybe later when they take you for the lethal injection," KC commented without looking up from the file. "So, let's start with the four children's murder."

"Why don't we start with making a deal?" Francisco said and tapped his right hand's finger on the table. KC looked up and stared at the young man in the eye for a considerably challenging moment.

"Depends what you are offering," KC said slowly, deliberately.

"To start with, take off the death penalty from the table," Francisco tossed in his first suggestion. KC raised her eyebrows.

"You were offered a lawyer, right? I just wanted to know for the record," she asked Lugo.

"Yeah, yeah, I know all that. I don't want a lawyer, not just yet," he declared. KC shrugged her shoulder, well knowing that the interrogation was being videotaped.

"Okay then, talk to me Francisco," she said calmly. "What do you know about the child murders?"

Francisco began fidgeting on his chair. "My uncle and I never liked what Ricardo was doing. He liked young kids, boys or girls, he was sick that way you know," he said and KC got the impression that indeed Francisco didn't agree to his cousin's activities for real. "We had to move from place to place even back at home because he just couldn't control himself, you know," he tried to explain.

"So what happened here, in Los Angeles?" KC asked.

Francisco Lugo took a deep breath and stopped tapping on the table. "Ricardo came back from Oregon before my uncle Eduardo and I arrived from New York. Before Ricardo left for Portland, just as my uncle instructed him, he rented a house in Los Angeles. We arrived two weeks after his arrival back and…," he took another deep breath. "Well, he told us that he had a work shop in the back of the house and he asked us not to go there. My uncle didn't like when someone told him something like that and one day, when Ricardo was on a mission, we went down to the basement of the work shed. It was totally gross. Those poor kids, he kept there, you know, he did stuff to them. They were dead, all four of them were dead." He took a break, KC silently waited for him to continue. In her experience, many times stories like that wanted to be told by a suspect who knew about it but did not commit the crime himself or herself.

"Ricardo came back and by that time my uncle was furious. He ordered Ricardo to get rid of the bodies. Evidently he was stupid enough to bury them in the backyard, but it angered Eduardo even more and he told him that he had to dig them out and bury them someplace else. It was then that Ricardo took the bodies to the Arboretum during one night, after they were closed."

"What happened after that?" KC asked quietly.

"Eduardo told Ricardo to clean up the mess and that he was going to have a serious talk with him," Francisco replied.

"Did he?" KC inquired.

Francisco lowered his head and remained quiet for a couple seconds. "My uncle loved my cousin but he had enough of his molesting and killing so many young children," he sighed. "They got into a huge fight in the living room, I was in the kitchen preparing dinner. I couldn't help but hearing what was happening. I did not know what to do; I really wanted them to stop arguing when I heard the sound of a commotion. They actually got into a physical confrontation and I saw a knife in Ricardo's hand. I couldn't believe that he actually pulled a knife on his own father, but he did. Eduardo challenged his son to stab him if he could and I knew that Ricardo was capable to do many vicious things. Eduardo usually carried a gun but not a knife and his gun was not on him at the time. I picked up a long butcher knife and when he backed up into the kitchen, I shoved it into his hand. He nodded and went back to the living room. I heard a scream, it was Ricardo's. I ran inside the room and I saw Eduardo stabbing my cousin over and over. It was kind of sad in a way, because he was actually crying while he was stabbing him." Francisco stopped and finally looked up at KC who was silently listening to Francisco's explanation of the child murders.

She wrote some notes down, and then she looked up at Francisco. "You mentioned earlier that before the discovery of the children's bodies, Ricardo was on a mission. What kind of mission?" She asked.

It quickly became evident to her that Francisco was reluctant to speak about anything else than his murderous pedophile cousin, Ricardo Lugo. When he looked at KC, she soon realized that it wouldn't be as easy to get an answer out of Francisco than it was before. "Roll up your sleeve," she ordered him.

"Why?" Francisco asked stubbornly. "I am not a junkie," he commented.

"Prove it," KC challenged the young man. He slowly unbuttoned his shirt's sleeve and rolled it up, taking his time. "Turn it sideway," KC told him, he did as she asked. It was then that she saw what she wanted to see, a lightning bolt between two words "*Diciembre Rojo*" (Red December). Just as she suspected, the Lugo family was connected to the Puerto Rican terrorist organization. It was the same organization that was in the news very recently due to reports that the members of *Red December* stepped up their activities in Puerto Rico against American held interests on that soil. Part of the organization moved their activities to the continental United States as well.

KC immediately understood Homeland Security's involvement in the investigation and behind the reason why they wanted to question Maggie. Paul Anderson, Maggie's husband changed his name from Paulo Lugo, and probably was involved in some ways with his brother's organization. Perhaps he was, what was known as a "sleeper cell" who laid low while waiting for orders. There was only one major exception, Dr. Paul Anderson hardly laid low, after leaving his job at the University of Puerto Rico, he and his friend, Christopher Collins has became Nobel Prize Winners. How is that for a perfect cover?

"Okay, you can pull the sleeve down," KC agreed.

"I told you that I was not a junkie," Francisco said with sarcasm. KC concluded that he was most definitely not the brightest member of his now almost defunct family. However, he knew people back East, in New York who by the time that particular interrogation took place, were suspect of placing a bomb on the downed passenger CU Airlines plane that took the life of hundreds of innocent people travelling on the plane and also on the ground as well.

"What do you know about the *Red December* organization?" KC asked and her question surprised Francisco.

"What organization?" He asked, mimicking KC's voice. She smiled and put her pen down on the top of the file.

"You surely cannot be that stupid that you thought that we were not aware of your organization's activities? What was your father's role in *Red December*?" She asked a more specific question. Francisco didn't reply, KC decided on another approach. "Okay, so tell me Francisco, who gave you access to Paul Anderson's home? Did he give you the security combination?"

Francisco grinned at her. "He...was...my...father..." he replied mockingly.

"Did you see your father often?" She asked what sounded like a fairly innocent question.

"Lady, are you deaf?" Francisco asked angrily. "I just told you that he was my father."

"So what you are telling me that he was a good father and the two of you kept in touch on a regular basis?" She inquired.

"Sure," he replied.

"How well did you get along with Maggie, your stepmother?"

"Real well, she is a cool lady," Francisco said and looked at KC. "Why are all of these questions?"

"I just tried to figure out about your family," KC said casually as she could. "When did you see Maggie the last time?"

"The same morning you arrested me," he lied without missing a beat. KC nodded a couple of times.

"It's sort of ironic because Maggie Anderson did not even know that you exist," she commented calmly and looked up at him. He turned his head and looked at the door.

"Are you expecting someone?" She asked, and then she felt a light breeze brush her face.

"KC," heard a voice that sounded very much like Maggie's. She looked at Francisco but he was staring down at his left handcuffed hand on the table, his lips were not moving. She heard the voice again. "KC, put on your jacket."

"What?" She murmured under her nose but she did as the voice told her and touched the right pocket of her suit's jacket once she was wearing it.

"Are we done?" Francisco asked when he saw KC was putting on her jacket.

"Not even close," KC replied when she heard a knock on the door. "We are busy," she yelled back, but the person knocked again. "What do you want?" She asked.

The door opened and a young, uniformed policeman entered. KC had never seen him before. He was holding a folder in his hand. "Detective Calhoun, I was told to give this to you." He said and handed the folder to KC. She immediately knew that something was very wrong with that uniform, it was ill fitting on the young cop. Her eyes dropped on the nametag and it read "Olson". She knew Olson and he was a veteran cop whom she not directly only occasionally worked with at homicide scenes. The uniform belonged to another cop and not the one who entered the room, it was clear as the sky. She sat back down at the table and put her hand in the right pocket of her jacket.

Only a few seconds passed when she looked up into the barrel of a Glock service revolver that most definitely did not belong to the uniformed person in the interrogation room. "Stay seated and don't do anything stupid," said the stranger still pointing the gun at KC while with his other hand tried to unlock the handcuff. The more Francisco fidgeted the more difficulties the fake cop encountered. He finally yelled at Francisco to remain still.

It only took a minute and a half to get Francisco's hand free just to be cuffed behind his back. "Stay here and don't leave this room until you count up to two thousand, you understand?" The stranger in the stolen police uniform asked from KC. She nodded that she understood.

The uniformed man opened the door and began to lead Francisco out of the interrogation room as if he was escorting him to another location. KC stood in the door and yelled. "Drop your weapon." The uniform man turned around and fired a shot at KC's direction, but she ducked behind the still open doorway, then quickly appeared again and fired two shots in succession, hitting the uniformed stranger in his shoulder and leg. He turned around and wanted to fire his weapon again, but the detectives who for a brief second were stunned managed regain momentum and tackled the injured man to the ground along with Francisco Lugo who tried to get the weapon that landed only inches away from him.

Captain Vargas rushed out of his office and looked back and forth between KC and the men. "What happened?" He asked.

KC briefed him and he just stared at her when she told him that she clearly heard Maggie's voice warning her about the imminent danger. She concluded that something must have changed in Maggie's vision as she found it necessary to warn her about it and somehow, in some unexplained way she managed.

When everything settled down, they found Olson's body in the basement of the building; the man who stole his uniform killed the veteran policeman. The fake cop was taken to a hospital for surgery of the wounds that he suffered when KC fired her shots. The Captain called Homeland Security and some time later two of their agents took custody of Francesco Lugo. The large office finally returned to its normal activities and KC was able to concentrate on her work. She began to read the forensic reports on Paul Anderson and she was genuinely surprised what she was reading. All of a sudden everything began to make sense to her, but some of the details remained sketchy. She knew that there was the inevitable; she had to question her own partner who was shot by Eduardo Lugo himself.

Before leaving her work for the hospital to visit Maggie and Tony, KC unlocked one of the drawers of her desk and pulled it out. She removed Tony's gun and put it inside an evidence bag, and then headed down to the lab. Her friend Stacey, a friendly woman in her mid-forties gave her a big smile seeing her entering the lab. "Oh, my, goodness, girl, I haven't seen you in ages. What brings you here?" She asked after giving KC a big hug.

"My two good feet," she replied with a smile. "Actually, I came to see you to ask you a big favor." KC said and placed the evidence bag with a gun in front of Stacey. "Would you mind to test this gun and compare to the bullets removed from Paul Anderson's wounds?"

"Sure thing," Stacey said and looked at her suspiciously. "What's going on?"

"I would have been surprised if you didn't notice that something was out of the ordinary," KC remarked. "For all concerned, and this is the asking you a favor part, this is a for-my-eyes-only situation. I do not want to get you into trouble, if you cannot do it my way, I'll just walk out of here."

Stacey stared at her friend for a moment and reached for the evidence bag. "I don't want to know. I will call you with the results."

KC got up. "Sorry about the short visit, there is a lot crap going on, but now I need to visit some friends in the hospital."

"Yes, I heard about the shooting in your office," Stacey said and pointed at KC's gun on her hip. "I suppose you had a lot of witnesses because the Captain still allowed you to carry your piece."

"There were at least twenty people in and around the office who saw what happened, it was a clean shooting," KC confirmed. "Of course, I have to do the usual reports tonight, after I return." She hugged her friend again before she left.

CHAPTER TWENTY-THREE

"THANK GOD, YOU are alright," Maggie said in a stronger voice when KC entered the room. KC smiled at her friend and glanced at Tony who was awake and murmured "hello" to her. *Later,* KC thought and concentrated on Maggie. She pulled a chair next to her bed and took her hand.

"I got your message," she said quietly. Maggie nodded that she understood. "You, Maggie Anderson, you are the real thing."

Tears flooded Maggie's eyes and her lips quivered. "I wish I was not."

"You have saved my life today, perhaps even others," KC told her. "Maggie, I need to show you a picture and I need you to tell me if you have ever seen this man before?" She asked and pulled out an envelope from her pocket with Francisco Lugo's picture. Maggie held the picture close and took a long, hard look at it.

"No, I have never seen him in my life, but his face reminds me somebody," she said quietly.

"That would not be a surprise," KC remarked. "He is your stepson, Francisco. He claimed that you two got along."

"KC," Maggie replied. "As I said, I have never met him in my life."

"And I believe you," KC told her. "Hey, Tony," and turned to her partner.

"I thought that you are never going to talk to me again," Tony replied. "You have been ignoring me lately, so what is going on?"

"Francisco claims that his uncle, Eduardo killed his own son because he was a pedophile and child murderer. Apparently, and he did not say this, Ricardo endangered the *Red December* Organization's mission with his behavior and they had to silence him," she explained.

"What was Paul's role in this whole thing?" Maggie asked.

"That is still not clear, Homeland Security took over that part of the investigation with a promise that they would keep us informed." KC told them.

Maggie asked KC to help her out of the bed so she could use the bathroom. Once she realized that she could walk without feeling dizzy, she made it to the bathroom on her own. When she closed the door, KC stepped to Tony's bed and bent down to him.

"Did you shoot Paul Anderson?" She asked whispering.

"Are you asking me as a detective or are you asking me as a friend?" He asked her in return.

"It depends," KC replied. "It all depends that if you had done it, why did you do it."

Tony nodded. "I want you to write down my logon name and password and check it out yourself. You will find an eFile under the title of *'Maggie'*. You find almost everything there that would give you an answer." KC wrote down the information just as Maggie exited the bathroom.

"Maggie, I am sorry about the brief visit but I have a long report to write before I can go home," KC said. "I'll stop by tomorrow." She promised.

"I am going to find out tomorrow morning when I can go home," Maggie informed her.

"That's great." KC said genuinely pleased to hear that.

"Did something happen today?" Tony asked suspiciously. KC looked at Maggie who nodded that go ahead and tell Tony. KC told him briefly what happened and Tony was getting upset by the minute. "How could this happen at a police station? What kind of security do we have if something like that cannot be prevented?"

KC tried to calm him down. "Nobody got hurt but the perp, so chill out Tony."

"But if it wasn't for Maggie, you could have been killed," he yelled at her. Maggie made her way to Tony's bed and sat down on the chair next to him. Her presence calmed him down a great deal and KC quietly waved at them as she left their hospital room.

CHAPTER TWENTY-FOUR

KC BARELY GOT out of her car at the police station's underground parking garage when her cell phone went off. "KC," she replied.

"Hello girlfriend," she heard Stacey's voice. "Where are you?"

"I am heading toward the office. What are you doing still in the lab this late?" She asked.

"I have your answer, want to stop by?" She asked, not wanting to give the information over the phone.

"I'll be right there," KC replied and changed her route to go to the lab first before her office. Since it was later in the evening there were hardly any people around, the night crew just arrived and their number were limited, their presence was required for emergency's only. "Hi BFF," KC said seeing her friend sitting behind her desk.

It was hard to read the look on Stacey's face but years of experience and knowing her friend so long, her demeanor gave a clue to KC that the news was not good. "It's a perfect match." Stacey said and placed the comparison picture and the evidence bag with the gun in front of KC. She nodded. Every instinct that she had supported and believed that Tony was involved with Paul's murder. The main question remained, why? Was the reason personal for him being in love with Anderson's wife, or that was just an additional reason for ending the man's life?

Another thought occurred to her and it showed on her face, giving Stacey concern. *Was Maggie safe with Tony?* That was a big and unanswered question.

121

"What is it?" She asked immediately seeing KC's facial expression. She shook her head.

"You better not know it just yet," KC replied, got up and picked up the picture and the gun from Stacey's crowded desk. "I promise that I will explain everything." She said and rushed into her office. She sat down and saw a note from the Captain, which read that she did not have to do a full report, only a statement was required as the entire incident was caught on tape, and a preliminary view from the Internal Affairs said that a statement from her would be sufficient for the time being.

She completed the typed statement in no time and after printing it she read it. Being satisfied with what she wrote, she signed, dated and delivered her statement to the Captain who had already left for the day, so she placed it on the Captain's chair.

There were only a couple of detectives working at their desks, finishing up reports or working late on cases, nobody paid attention when she took Tony's lap top from his desk that was facing hers and booted up the dormant equipment. She looked around and confirming that no one was in her immediate vicinity, she typed in Tony's identification code and his password that her partner willingly provided to her. There were dozens of icons on his desktop, she scrolled through them until she found the name *"Maggie"* and clicked on it.

The eFile was rather extensive and she soon realized that it would have been impossible to read all the saved emails that Tony, who, in an unexplained way, somehow managed to download from Paul Anderson's computer. She clicked on one email that subject line got her attention it read, *"Termination".* KC began to read and her anger grew with each line that she read in the email that was addressed to Eduardo a day before Ricardo's murder, and a couple of days prior to Paul's death.

"TO: Eduardo Lugo
FROM: Paul Anderson

"Eduardo, you must be patient. It is not only a virtue, it is a necessity. Our cause is bigger than us, bigger than what we have to endure. Think about the outcome of our mission; think about an oppression free country, our very own liberated Puerto Rico. What our forefathers could not accomplish with actions and negotiations, we will succeed honoring their memories and sacrifices. Our sacrifices are minor considering what they have to endure by occupying forces.

You, Eduardo are cursed with a son who is unable to control his sick urges and the taking of lives of innocent children. You must stop him at any cost, at ANY cost as I have my own curse to deal with. You were correct; Maggie must cease to live, especially after discovering her latest talent. Yes, she predicted the plane crash that we have planned for so long. Whatever she predicted, I counted on the ignorance and the arrogance of those who would not believe a "psychic's" prediction. While you complained about your son's activities, I had to endure almost ten years of marriage to a woman I disliked a great deal. What someone would consider a blessing was a curse to me. Just looking at her for the past five or six years made my stomach turn and playing the good and caring husband exhausted my ambition to find a true and genuine soul mate who would march alongside with me in our desperate fight for our beloved island's independence.

While Maggie has served the purpose of covering my real life, she has become dangerous in multiple levels. Now, that she can predict upcoming disasters and events, she has become ever so dangerous to our cause. I have never under estimated her intelligence and that combined with her vision, she would have caught up with us sooner or later. It is now only a matter of days before you and I will be free of the heavy loads of burden that was necessary to carry on for so many years to assure our mission's success. Nobody would ever suspect that a Nobel Prize winner physicist, who was a loving and doting husband to his troubled wife, ended her life.

In conclusion, my dear brother, you must do the painful thing of ending your son's troubled life as I do to end my wife's.

Please remember to erase this email after reading it.

Your loving Brother and Compadre,

Paul.

KC took out the thumb drive and downloaded the entire eFile that was titled *"Maggie"* and once finished, she put it in a padded envelope and addressed it to Maggie Anderson with a note inside.

Once the eFile was downloaded onto the thumb drive, she made another copy and after that, with one smooth move she slipped Tony's laptop computer into her large bag that she had on her desktop. She booted up her own computer and sent a brief message to her friend, Stacey at the lab downstairs. It read, "Stacey, the information I am about to give you once again, for the time being is for *YOUR EYES ONLY*. The gun that you tested this morning belongs to my permanent partner, Antonio Morales. I will explain everything later. Love you girl, KC." She clicked on the "send" button and logged off. Once she closed the top of her computer, she placed it on Tony's desk that nobody occupied while he was out on convalescent leave.

She almost sealed both of the envelopes with the thumb drive inside when she scribbled two notes, one was addressed to Maggie in which she informed her that the emails were downloaded from Tony's computer, and the other thumb drive was addressed to her friend, Dr. Stacey Hernandez. On her way out, she dropped the envelope for Maggie in the out-going mailbox, and the one for Stacey in the internal mailbox, both located next to the Duty Sergeant's desk. KC looked around as if she forgot something. She thought for a second and returned to her desk and removed the comparison picture from the matching bullets and Tony's gun, she put them in her bag. KC decided to call it a night, to go home and get some much-needed sleep.

There were some people in the multi-level underground garage and a couple of police cruisers just parked as KC got into her car. She started the engine and put the car in reverse to pull out of the parking place when her car exploded in a large fire ball from the powerful bomb that was strategically placed underneath her car. The entire garage shook from the explosion and within seconds emergency vehicles were on their way, but it was much too late for Detective Kathy Calhoun, also known as KC.

CHAPTER TWENTY-FIVE

MAGGIE'S SCREAM WAS heard all way down to the end of hospital corridor and it prompted all nurses and passing by doctors to rush toward her room. The police officer standing guard rushed inside her room and turned on the lights in the semi dark room. Tony was sitting up on his bed and pointed at Maggie who was also sitting at the age of her bed sobbing uncontrollably. The Charge Nurse wrapped her arms around her and asked her what happened.

"She is dead, oh, dear God. Why? Why? Why?" Maggie cried out loud and her entire body was shaking.

"Honey, what happened?" The nurse asked again. Maggie pushed her away and staggered to Tony who somehow managed to get out of his bed and was just standing there, not knowing what to do to calm her down.

"Tony, KC is dead." She whimpered to him as if she was telling a secret.

"How do you know?" Tony asked, but deep down inside he knew that Maggie would not say anything like that if it weren't true.

"I know, I just know," Maggie yelled at him.

The doctor ordered one of the nurses to administer a mild sedative to Maggie to calm her down. Maggie's throat was sore and for several minutes she had difficulty breathing. Once the injection took effect and she calmed down, they led her back to her bed where she fell asleep.

Tony called the police station and got a hold of his Captain who just arrived there a few minutes earlier after being informed about the car bombing of KC's vehicle. The Captain cursed into the phone, he was not mad at Tony but at the entire situation and told Tony to get well soon to get his "ass" back to work and clear up the mess of Anderson's case.

Maggie woke up in the middle of the night with a broken heart. She felt that in KC she lost a new but trustworthy friend and she felt extremely bad that she had no way of predicting or knowing what was going to happen to KC. In her thoughts she asked God that if she was given the "GIFT", why couldn't she have it all the time? Why was she not able to see what was about to happen to someone so dear to her? There was no answer and there was no dream or a vision. She came to realize that she could not predict all ills and catastrophes of the world and there must be other "gifted" people out there other than herself. She kept her word and had not sinned again, yet she felt punished for something that she had not done. Maggie was not questioning God; she questioned the way her visions appear to her in a selective manner.

Two mornings later, the doctor gave her a clean bill of health and told her that she could leave the hospital. It dawned on Maggie just how much KC helped her in the past and that there was no one she could call to pick her up and take her home. Tony was still hospitalized and he was informed that since the tube in his chest was removed and there was no sign of infection, he may be able to leave the hospital in a couple of days' time, but with a prescription for physical therapy for his arm once his chest wounds completely healed. Until then, he had to do minor exercises with his arm, a physical therapist was assisting him with that while he was in the hospital. Maggie and Tony agreed that they will stay in Maggie's house after Tony was released, so at least they could look after each other's possible needs, but they would keep separate bedrooms for the time being.

Maggie asked Tony a couple of days earlier if he remembered anything about a vision, seeing a white man and a white dog. Tony told her that he only saw her, but he did hear a voice telling them to go back to life and sin no more. Maggie smiled and confirmed to him that it was her vision, too, but with an additional appearance of the same white man and white dog that she had before, actually only a couple of months earlier, before all of her visions began and when she was told that she was *"The Gifted One"*.

Before leaving the hospital, Maggie was surprised to see Captain Vargas to appear in the doorway to take her home. Tony confessed to her that it was he who called the station and the Captain himself offered to give her a ride.

On the way toward Maggie's house, Captain Vargas expressed his sympathy for her loss of Paul as well as for losing a friend in KC. She quietly thanked him and remained silent during their drive. Her throat was still sore from screaming, but she did not want to mention that to her doctor as she did not want to stay in the hospital any longer.

Arriving to her house, the Captain removed some of the left over yellow crime scene tapes; most of them were already taken down. The security alarm was off and entering the house, Maggie expected to see bloodstains on the floor and smoke damage that Tony mentioned in her studio, but the house was spotlessly clean and her studio was already repainted. She questioningly looked at the Captain who turned his head. "KC?" Maggie asked. He nodded and told her that it was KC who made the arrangement with a special cleanup crew to clean up the mess, when a day earlier he authorized the release of the crime scene. Maggie thanked him and after that the Captain checked in every room. Before leaving, Captain Vargas asked her if he could be any further assistance to her. Maggie told him that she was grateful for everything that he and his department had done for her, but she will be all right.

"There is just one more thing," Captain Vargas said. "It is difficult to talk about such a subject, but what are your plans for Paul's funeral?" He asked.

"I want him to be cremated," Maggie said and explained that they have discussed that once in the past and they both agreed to that.

"I'll let the morgue know and they will contact you," he assured her and after saying goodbye, he left her alone in the big house. She sat down on the couch and remained there until she heard her cell phone ringing.

"Hi Maggie, it's Tony," he said. "Is everything alright?"

"Yes, it is. I suppose I should get busy. Just glancing at the answering machine shows over 45 messages, I didn't even think it held that much." She said nervously.

"Make sure that you contact the security company," he reminded her. "Please, do that first, let them know that you are there and that you need to change the lock combination."

"Okay," she promised and ended the call. She could not understand why, but all of a sudden she felt nervous talking to Tony. However, she did take his advice and called up the security system provider. They walked her through how to change the combination and after she completed their instructions, they did a test run and it worked.

She looked around in her studio and began to rearrange her paintings that were moved around by the hand of inexperienced people. At first Tony tried to save her painting from the fire, and then someone, very likely KC moved them back from the living room and from the outside. She lined them up in no particular order. She did not blame KC or Tony, or the firefighters, far from it, she was actually grateful for them for saving her the paintings because she put her heart and soul into them.

Maggie returned to the living room and look around. She had never felt so lost, so alone in her entire life. What was she going to do? How could she continue her life on her own? There was Tony and according to him he loved her, but then why did she developed sudden feelings of uncertainties. She could not pinpoint out anything particular, but her brain told her to be cautious.

In the kitchen she made some tea and slowly consumed it while sitting in her favorite armchair. She thought about the time when she met and married Paul. She desperately tried to remember the feelings that she had at that time but she no longer was certain how she felt almost ten years earlier. She was sure that she had feelings for Paul, otherwise she would not have married a man fifteen years her senior. Most of her life she liked older men and she could not tolerate young people with big ideas that they would never follow through, because there was one thing dreaming about something and another really doing something about it. Even in her younger years, before she met and married Paul, she wasn't sure how she was going to approach the idea of marriage to a young man. She wanted stability in her life and she didn't want to worry that a friend of a young husband would influence him to stray away from the sanctity of marriage.

Tony, oh, Tony, she thought. It was almost painful for her to think about him when it should have been happier thoughts. They both survived assassination attempts and physically suffered through them and then, they both lost someone close to them, Tony lost his partner and she lost her husband and her friend in the person of KC. Maggie could not explain the nagging feeling about Tony, something was not right and she could not put a finger on it.

"I'll have to snap out of this," she murmured and went back into the kitchen. As she opened the refrigerator door she laughed out loud, it was almost completely empty, only some nearly expired or about to expire items laid in there seemingly abandoned. "I need to get some groceries," she said out loud and after a moment of hesitation, she grabbed her purse and car keys to go to a nearby home town grocer that both Paul and she used to favor.

When she opened the garage door she looked around carefully, but there were no media reporters at the front, just as Captain Vargas explained to those folks who waited for her while she went into protective custody. Yes, it was the Anderson's home, but Mrs. Anderson will not be returning anytime soon. Her hospitalization made the news as well and the reporters were avoided by leaving the hospital through a back entrance.

The small grocery store was not busy and she bought some fresh meat, including some steaks, some chicken breasts and fresh vegetables as well as frozen ones. She also got some other necessities, such as milk, butter and dark rye bread, her favorite. The checkout clerk was a young woman, Maggie guessed that she was on her summer school break and she was glad that the girl either did not recognize her from the news on television or just did not let her on that she knew her. She paid and drove home without any problems.

Maggie busied herself with domestic work and soon she finished in the kitchen. She began to listen to her 47 messages, deleting most of them as she moved along. Among the calls, just as KC listened to them as well were some threatening calls, some of them called her vision as an act of blasphemy, some called her the devil's advocate, some praised her being a God sent angel to warn the world of it's evil deeds, and then there was one call that welcomed her and thanked her for being a fellow *"Gifted One"*. The woman left her phone number and told her if she needed to talk to someone about how she felt, she was always available. The only important call she found among the 47 was the call from her parents who were still in Albuquerque, New Mexico. She decided to call them a little bit later in the evening.

The biggest task for her was to sort out the mail that Captain Vargas brought in for her before he left. He commented that her mailbox was almost full and he was not joking. She went through them and used the method of process of elimination. She tossed out all the junk mail that included advertising, and then she sorted out the bills and any other mail that was addressed to her and Paul. It dawned on her that Paul never received any personal mail at their home address, which prompted a thought in her mind, what if Paul had a post office box in his name. She made a mental note to check on that.

There was a small square size padded envelope with *"KC"* and *"Official Mail"* written on the upper left corner where normally the sender's address was located. The envelope was addressed to her and when she opened it, she pulled out the thumb drive with a note from KC that read that she found the contents of the disk on Tony's computer and that she was going to explain some things to her. "What KC? What did you want to tell me?" She asked out loud without expecting any answers.

Maggie realized that she took her computer with her to the safe house and when she thought of that, she got up and walked back into her studio. Her laptop was sitting on its usual place. She concluded that KC must have brought it back from the supposedly safe house after what happened to her at that location. It was already in the afternoon, so she decided to wait with checking out what was on the thumb drive, instead of that, she wanted to pay a quick visit to Tony at hospital before it got too late. She preferred not driving once the sun went down for the day. She called Tony and asked him if he wanted anything. He laughed. "Why not a nice Subway sandwich," he told her, and then he added. "Only if it's not too much trouble."

"No trouble at all," Maggie replied and after turning off the lights in her house, leaving only the light on over the telephone console, she was on her way to see Tony. Maggie smiled and accused Tony for being happier to see the food that she picked up for him, than seeing her.

"That will never happen," Tony replied and kissed her.

"How are you feeling?" Maggie asked as she watched him almost inhale the fresh pastrami sandwich that he liked.

"The doctor said I can be released in a couple of days," Tony said and took her hands. "You are an inspiration to me. I love you very much Maggie."

She smiled again and bent down to kiss him without responding to Tony's declaration of love. Maggie's eyes wandered off from Tony and stared at the picture on the wall without seeing anything on it.

"Is something wrong?" Tony asked. "Maggie," he called her name out when she didn't react to his question.

Maggie looked down at him upon finally hearing her name. "Tony, you have to promise me that you will always tell me the truth."

"Maggie, where is that coming from?" Tony asked her suspiciously.

"Answer my question, please," Maggie asked him.

"I will never lie to you," Tony promised. While his reply seemed sincere, somehow Maggie felt that his words were not entirely honest. She couldn't explain how she knew that, she just did.

"Tony, I have mentioned to you how important trust is to me. I am going to be honest with you now so I don't want you to say that I have never told you. If I catch you lying, I will never speak to you again," Maggie promised. It was Tony's turn to wonder what Maggie was up to. *What did she know? How much does she know?* He wondered.

"I understand," Tony replied and kissed her hand. He looked at her long and hard, and then he smiled. "Have you ever been in Italy?"

Maggie looked at him with surprise and wondered why he was asking her that question. She shook her head. "No, but I always wanted to go there. What made you ask me that?"

"I would love to take you there some day," he said and watched her reaction. She smiled as she replied.

"I would like that very much," Maggie said quietly.

"What is your plan for tomorrow?" Tony asked.

Maggie sighed. "I have to make arrangements for Paul's body to be cremated, make something nice to eat and perhaps bring you some," she said teasingly.

"That sounds very nice," Tony replied. "I think you should get going before it gets very late," he suggested looking toward the window. She nodded, got up and kissed him goodbye.

"I'll see you tomorrow," she promised and left the hospital room.

As soon as she arrived home and secured the house, she made herself comfortable in her favorite chair and called her parents. She was most pleased to hear that they were doing fine and her father informed her that their insurance company authorized them car rental and by taking advantage of that, they were going to leave the following day to finally visit her. Maggie could not emphasize to them how careful they should be and her father and mother made multiple promises that they were going to do just that.

After a leisurely shower, she put on her favorite bathrobe and taking her laptop to the bed with her, she inserted the thumb drive into its side and opened its contents. She read message after message of the correspondence that was exchanged between Eduardo and Paul and she could not believe that she did not know the man she was married to for almost ten years at all. One of his last emails truly got to Maggie, the one in which Paul told his brother that he actually planned to kill her himself and not someone else do it for him. That loving man who seemed to genuinely care about her through her ordeal after her heart procedure, who seemed to be concerned about her well being was nothing but a cold hearted killer? How could that be? Paul Anderson was a liked person who was kind to everyone he encountered. He was highly intelligent, smart and what she believed, that he was a borderline genius. Now, it seemed to her, he was nothing but a borderline psychopath.

She wanted to be strong but she just could not help it, she began to cry and cursed the day, the hour and the minute when she first met Paul who led her to believe that he loved her and cared about her when in reality, she was nothing more than a camouflage to cover up his terrorist ways. Was it possible that the gentle man who slept beside her for ten years ordered the bombing of the CU flight and at the same time warned the FAA?

The messages that the two brothers were exchanging disturbed her more than she wanted to admit, as some of the Spanish language correspondence talked about others, outside the Lugo family and using MAHA001 was mentioned repeatedly in several Spanish language emails that Paul sent to an email address that was simply called MON.SAL@n.mail.PR. The individual, those emails were forwarded to, never responded to Paul's emails.

Question after question piled up in her mind concerning the terrorist organization that the Lugo family was involved with. She concluded that Paul was the leader of the *Red December* Puerto Rican terrorist organization who wanted Puerto Rico to be free from the control of the United States and to become an independent country. Just how many members does the group claim? How could she find out? Maggie realized that only the Homeland Security and the FBI had that kind of access and not a local police department.

She debated long and hard what to do with the thumb drive since she had no one to turn to, no one she could truly trust because of KC's untimely departure from life. Maggie could not trust Tony because he spoke Spanish to someone he called Monsignor. Was the mysterious Monsignor a real priest, or was that a code name for someone involved with what is being called the "Anderson Case."

A decision had to be made, although she reminded herself what would happen once another line of investigation began, or perhaps continue as Homeland Security already wanted to take her into custody once, and she was certain that they would come to see her sooner or later.

Before she went to sleep on her first night at home after her hospital stay, she decided to keep the thumb drive a secret for the time being, and wait and see what would develop in the near future. The dreamless sleep crashed down on her tired body and mind, for the first time in months, Maggie fell into a dreamless and refreshing sleep.

CHAPTER TWENTY-SIX

MAGGIE COULD NOT believe her eyes when she glanced at the clock on her nightstand. She was unable to recall the last time that she actually slept that sound, without any nightmares, vision or even just interruption. It was already after ten in the morning. She stretched after getting out of bed, took a shower and got dressed. She looked in the bathroom mirror and she smiled. She looked rested, no circles under her eyes and it was not just the visual part that seemed more relaxed, but actually, for the first time in a very long time that she actually felt physically well, too.

In the kitchen she prepared a plain omelet, two pieces of toast, made an espresso coffee and poured herself a small glass of orange juice. She took her food into the dining room and turned on CNN on the small television set in there to watch the latest events in the world. Maggie seldom ever watched the news, as she always felt depressed watching the Darfur tragedy, the Palestinian suicide bombers in Israel, the general misery of the world that she wanted change but she could not. *Sure, one person could make the difference but where to start?* She always wondered.

There was nothing new reported on the CU airline crash other than that all passengers and the people on the ground were accounted for, dead or alive, and that the notification of their relatives continued. What also continued was the FAA investigation of the crash, and by the time of reporting, the FBI was giving FAA a helping hand with the challenging task of identifying the cause of that crash.

The reporter mentioned, and she was not quoting anyone by name, that all leads were being thoroughly investigated, which will take some time, according to the officials.

Maggie barely finished with her breakfast and washing the dishes when she received a phone call from the Medical Examiner's office. They informed her that Captain Vargas signed a form in lieu of Mrs. Anderson in regards to the release of Paul Anderson's body to the Hatfield Funeral Home in Los Angeles. The caller, who identified himself as Thomas, called her to confirm if it was all right to do so. She gave her consent and hung up the phone.

As she was about to log on her computer, she heard the doorbell. She looked at the small monitor that showed the person who was pushing the doorbell. It was a tall, blondish haired woman who kept her long hair in a ponytail. She looked into the small camera and held up ID and badge that showed that she came from the Police Department, the very same district where KC and Tony worked. "Mrs. Anderson, may I come in to talk to you?" She asked.

After a brief moment of hesitation, Maggie turned off the security alarm and unlocked the door. Once the woman entered, Maggie re-set the alarm. "My name is Dr. Stacey Hernandez, but please just call me Stacey. I am the friend, or was the friend of KC."

"Have a seat and please call me Maggie," she told the woman and ushered her into the living room. Both of them sat down, facing each other in a few moments of awkward silence. "What is that I can do for you?" Maggie asked.

"It's more like what I can do for you," Stacey said, opened her red briefcase and pulled out two files. "First, I cannot tell you how upset and sadden I am about KC's murder, because that is what it was, a premeditated, cold blooded murder of a great and caring person." Stacey took a deep breath. "I have known KC for over twelve years. Unfortunately our lives become busier than ever so we were unable to get together as often as we used to do. She and I kept in touch via emails, and phone calls, not to mention that we quite frequently worked together on various cases."

"I agree with you one hundred percent, KC was an exceptional person. I didn't have the good fortune to know her as long as you did, but during that short time while I knew her, she and I became close friends. I knew that I could trust her one hundred percent, no questions asked." Maggie replied.

"She came to see me on the day of her murder and asked me to do a comparison of two bullets, one was removed from your husband's chest and one from a gun that belonged to Antonio Morales." Stacey began her explanation. She immediately noticed that when she mentioned the name of Tony, Maggie fidgeted in the armchair where she was sitting. "Do you know Tony?" Stacey asked before she continued. Maggie nodded. "How well do you know him?"

Stacey inquired further. Maggie thought about it for a moment, but she decided to tell the truth.

"Intimately," she told her visitor. It was Stacey's turn to sit back further. She looked around in the living room.

"I should have asked this earlier, are you alone now?" Stacey inquired.

"Yes, we are alone and we can talk freely," Maggie assured her. "Please, do not hesitate to talk about Tony. Lately I have had certain thoughts and I am sensing a level of dishonesty on his part. I would rather know the truth now or regret ignorance later."

"Very well," Stacey agreed and opened one of the folders with an enlarged copy of the same bullet comparison results that she gave to KC before she was murdered. "The bullet on the right was removed from Dr. Anderson's wound, and the bullet on the left belongs to a gun that is registered to Tony, it is a Glock, 9 millimeter, semi-automatic weapon, it is his service revolver. It is a perfect match."

Maggie couldn't believe what she was hearing. "You are telling me that Tony killed my husband?" She whispered.

"I am sorry, but there is no doubt about it," Stacey confirmed. "Each gun has its own characteristics and the bullet on the right without a doubt was fired from Detective Morales' gun."

Maggie felt shocked and very sad. She specifically told Tony that she did not tolerate lies and that she expected from him to always tell her only the truth. "Maggie," Stacey called her name seeing her stunned look. "Are you alright?"

Maggie nodded. "It's just one betrayal after another," she remarked. "You know, Stacey, there were emails on Tony's computer that my late husband wrote to his brother, in which he told him that he was going to end my life. I didn't try to find an excuse for what Tony had done, it is wrong no matter what angle you look at it, but it is possible that he killed Paul to save my life."

"Did KC send you a thumb drive?" Stacey asked.

"Yes, she did, with a note. She told me where she found those email correspondences," Maggie replied.

"I got a copy of that thumb drive too." Stacey informed her.

"I don't want to assume anything, but your last name is Hispanic, do you speak the language?" Maggie asked, than she added. "I know some people in college who had Hispanic background and they did not."

"Yes, I do, and I also read the Spanish language emails as well," Stacey told her.

"Do you know what MAHA001 means or what it is?" She asked.

Stacey shook her head. "No, not really."

"There was also an email address but I don't dare to send a message, who knows where that person is and who it is," Maggie said. "Maybe there is something else on Tony's computer." She suggested.

"There is a problem with that," Stacey said and put away her files. "Tony's gun and his laptop were in the car with KC when it exploded. They were completely destroyed in the fire that followed the explosion."

"Oh, no," Maggie whispered. "That is end of that hope."

"What are your plans?" Stacey asked.

Maggie took a deep breath. "My parents are arriving from New Mexico either tomorrow or a day after, depending how fast my dad is driving. They were at the campground when the CU airline's plane went done," she explained. Stacey nodded that she was aware of it. "Tony is going to be released from the hospital probably tomorrow and he is going to stay here until he fully recovers."

Her visitor was surprised. "You would allow an alleged killer into your home? Aren't you afraid that he may try to harm you?" She asked Maggie thought about for a brief moment. "You know that saying, *keep your friends close, and your enemies closer?* To be honest, I am not afraid of Tony. He actually saved my life when he had a chance to get rid of me, like pulling me from a car that was about to explode when the bomb went off just outside the safe house. I actually feel rather safe around him," Maggie confessed, but she added. "However, knowing what I know now, and what I heard from you, I will have to be more cautious."

Stacey leaned forward. "I think that you are a very special person to remain this strong after all that you lived through. I don't know you well, but any friend of KC's is my friend," she stretched her hands toward Maggie. "I want you to know that I am here for you, no matter what the problem is, no matter what kind of help you need."

"Thank you," Maggie replied solemnly with tears in her eyes. "I felt very lost yesterday when I got home. I felt very alone."

Stacey smiled. "You are no longer alone, I am only a phone call away." Maggie nodded.

"May I ask you something?" She inquired.

"Of course," Stacey agreed.

"You mentioned that you were a doctor, may I ask what is your field?" She asked.

"Well, I used to be a physician at the hospital until I realized that I was more interested the forensic part of medicine. I'm also a trained chemist, and I have a doctorate from that as well," Stacey told her.

"I am very pleased that you took time from your busy work to look me up," Maggie said. "I would like to repay you for your kindness."

"That is not for sale. I offered my friendship to you free of charge," Stacey laughed.

"Please, I want to show you something," Maggie said and motioned to Stacey to follow her into her studio.

"Oh, dear," Stacey whispered. "It is you? How stupid can I get? I never put your name together with one of my favorite painters, and it is you, in person." Stacey was genuinely surprised when she saw her finished paintings, still waiting to be framed.

"You can pick any of these," Maggie pointed to a few dozen paintings leaning against two of her studio walls.

It took several minutes for Stacey to select a cheerful and vibrant landscape, the type of painting that she preferred. "This perhaps," she showed the painting to Maggie who nodded with a smile.

"It's yours," she said and took out a FedEx box that was large enough to hold the painting. Before she put it in the box, she turned the painting over and without damaging the canvas; with a special pen she dedicated the painting to her new friend, Dr. Stacey Hernandez.

Stacey had to return to work and Maggie had lasagna to make, but they agreed that for the time being, they are not going to approach neither Captain Vargas, nor Tony about the gun, as it no longer existed, it was unrecognizable after the fire. However, Stacey promised Maggie that if anything suspicious is happening, or if she suspects any further wrong doing by Tony, that Maggie would call her right away.

Before Stacey left Maggie's home, she gave her a business card with both business and her cell phone numbers, in case she needed to contact her for any reason, or even if she just wanted to talk.

Once again, alone in the house, Maggie busied herself making a lasagna from scratch. She loved Italian food but not as much as Chinese. Her mother used to tease her that she must have been Chinese in her previous life. She smiled at the thought of her parents and felt joy knowing that it was only a matter of a day or two before she will be able to welcome them after their much delayed arrival.

She sipped coffee while she waited for the oven timer to go off, and read and re-read Paul correspondence's Spanish version of the emails, as well the English on her laptop. Why would Paul write in two languages when he clearly wrote to his brother in Spanish? There were no signs that he sent anyone complimentary copies, but what about BBC to someone so the original receiver would not know about him sending another copy to another person, *but to who*? Maggie wondered. She thought about the fact that she did not even know that Paul actually spoke Spanish and it was evident that there were many things that she did know about the man who claimed to love and cherish her, and whom she spent the last ten years of her life.

The timer interrupted her thoughts and she removed the baked lasagna from the oven and placed it on a cooling rack. After several minutes, when the food was not so hot, she placed a generous portion of the food into a plastic container and got ready to visit Tony the hospital.

When she arrived on his floor and approached the door, she was surprised to see that the uniformed guard was gone and Tony's bed was unoccupied. A nurse walked by and Maggie took the opportunity to ask her what happened to the patient in room 401. The nurse smiled. "Relax Mrs. Anderson, he just left for physical therapy on the sixth floor, he should be back in about an hour."

Maggie thanked her for the information and told the nurse that if it was okay, she was going to wait in Tony's room. The nurse told her that it was all right, and continued her way to the nurses' station. Maggie entered the room and she noticed that while Tony was gone an orderly changed his bed. She placed her food on the stand that was next to Tony's bed and sat down in the chair next to it.

Realizing that she forgot to bring napkins, Maggie began to look for a paper towel in the bathroom when she noticed the after-shave and the leather shaving kit holder on the side of the sink. It appeared that Tony was interrupted after he shaved and he didn't put his kit away, like she saw him doing while she was also a patient in the same room. She smiled after she smelled Tony's aftershave; she always liked his Stetson cologne, too. Her smile did not last long after unzipping the shaving kit and looking inside. Other than the electric razor, there was another small sized box and when she opened that one, what she saw took her breath away. There were several smaller syringes and two small containers inside. The label on the small containers read MAHA001 and MAHA002. She glanced at the door and her watch, she still had plenty of time before Tony was supposed to finish with his physical therapy but one never could tell how long exactly those really last, she had no time to waste.

Maggie quickly took one of the dozen small syringes and drew some of the liquid, almost a not noticeable amount into it, and then she carefully replaced everything as she find out and returned to Tony's room. Before she placed the syringe in her purse, she wrapped it into a wash towel for the safe side.

She watched some television and just as she suspected, Tony finished with his physical therapy sooner than the nurse suggested and he seemed genuinely glad to see her. He carefully hugged her and sat down at the edge of the bed. "You look beautiful," he said after kissing her. "And rested," he added.

"Oh, I had a great night. I actually slept very peacefully." Maggie confirmed.

"Did you have anymore visions or nightmares?" Tony asked and Maggie became uncertain if his question was out of real concern or wanted to know for other reasons, unknown to her.

"No, nothing," Maggie told him. "As a matter of fact, I haven't had any dreams, nightmares or visions since KC's murder."

"I am glad to hear that," Tony replied and kissed Maggie's hand. "I miss you," he said quietly.

"Are you still being released tomorrow?" Maggie asked while she opened the container and handed a fork to Tony.

"The doctor said if all goes well, they will release me tomorrow." He confirmed and began to eat. "Oh, my goodness, Maggie, this is delicious." Tony complimented her cooking.

"Thank you, and thank my mom, it's her recipe. By the way, speaking of mom, they are also arriving tomorrow, very likely in the late evening hours. I hope that it is all right with you," Maggie told him.

Tony put the fork down. "Why do you even have to ask me that? I will be delighted to meet them. You do know that I have plans for our future together, don't you?" Tony asked.

Maggie looked at him and he was watching her closely. "Do you? What kind of plan?" She asked and tried to smile.

Tony placed the plastic container on the stand next to his bed and reached for her hands. "I love you, Maggie. I hope that once all this madness passes, I can ask you to be my wife." Maggie felt both touched and troubled by his words.

"You would do anything for me?" She asked and pulled her hands away.

"Anything," Tony confirmed. "Anything, so you could remain safe, and that nothing would happen to you."

Maggie was very close to asking him that "anything" meant to kill her husband, too, but she remained silent. "Thank you Tony," she murmured.

"Maggie," Tony said when she got up from the chair, stopping her. "Do you love me?" He asked.

Maggie leaned forward and kissed him. "Yes, Tony, I do." She said hesitantly, feeling bad because she felt that she was actually lying. She got ready to leave. "Call me when you were released."

"If the thought of my stay at your place is troubling you, I can just go to my apartment, no problem at all." He commented. Maggie shook her head.

"No, it's no trouble at all. My parents would be pleased to meet you, too." Maggie assured Tony and kissed him goodbye. "I'll see you tomorrow."

As she was driving home, Maggie passed by *The Gallery* where her paintings were usually exhibited. On a spare of the moment decision, she turned around and drove up to *The Gallery* where amazingly enough, she managed to find a parking place right front of it. She walked in and inhaled the air, she loved the smell of paintings and she slowly made her way to the area where a modern artist exhibited his paintings. It wasn't her style but she liked them for what they were, innovating, modern, just something different. "Oh, my goodness, if it is not the best painter in Los Angeles," she heard Sarah Stern's, the gallery owner's voice. She rushed to her and hugged her tight.

"Hi, Sarah, it's good to see you," Maggie said and kissed her friend on her cheeks.

"You have been in the news for all the wrong reasons," Sarah said and pushed her away so she could measure her up. "I heard about Paul, I am so sorry. And you, are you alright, are you okay?" She asked.

Maggie assured her that everything was fine and under control which was far from the truth, but she didn't want to upset her friend she had not seen lately. "I wanted to talk to you about the exhibit we want to put together for later this year, but my parents are coming in tomorrow and all these crazy things that are happening. We will talk, I promise." Maggie told her.

"I have a new gallery director. He appeared out of nowhere and he just began to work here a couple of weeks ago." She leaned to Maggie and whispered. "Heads up, he is simply a gorgeous man and very single. Stay right here," she asked her and rushed off toward her office in the back.

Maggie continued her interrupted walk looking at the paintings on the wall when she heard whispers behind her. She turned around and saw Sarah having her arm locked into a tall man's arm. Sarah was not kidding, the man was like a highly paid model with broad shoulders. His blond curly hair reached his neck but it was well kept and his eyes were as green as emeralds. He stretched his hand out for a handshake and Maggie had to remind herself that he was not a God that needed to be worshipped, indeed he was just a good looking, athletic man. She placed her hand in his and they shook hands. "Maggie, let me introduce you to Hector Lord," she turned to Hector. "Hector, this is one of my oldest and dearest friend who is just about the most popular landscape and portrait artist in the world, Margaret Davis-Anderson," Sarah said and she couldn't help smiling when she noticed that Hector's hand was still holding Maggie's and that both of them were staring and smiling at each other. "By the way, Hector, that is the hand that does all those paintings I mentioned," she said and laughed. Maggie nervously pulled her hand back and the memory of her first meeting with Tony flashed through her mind.

"It's a pleasure to meet you Margaret," Hector told her.

"Same here and please call me Maggie, everybody does." She asked. He shook his head.

"Well then, I don't want to be like everybody else, so I will be the only one who will call you Margaret," he told her and lifted her hand to his lips.

Maggie felt her face flush when his lips touched her hand. "Well," Sarah remarked. "Your parents should have named you Casanova, instead you are the son of the Lord."

The smile on Maggie's face disappeared and she suddenly began to feel very uncomfortable. "If you excuse me, I should be heading home, tomorrow is promising to be a busy day." She leaned to Sarah and hugged each other for goodbye and then she nodded toward Hector. "I will call you Sarah when I am ready and we will talk about the exhibit." She promised her friend.

"Do you need a ride home?" Hector asked. She shook her head.

"No thanks, that car at the front is mine. See you later," Maggie said and left the gallery. She was still in earshot when she heard Hector's voice asking Sarah to tell him everything about her.

CHAPTER TWENTY-SEVEN

MAGGIE WAS PRE-OCCUPIED with thoughts after her visit to *The Gallery* and recalled her conversation with Tony, how he asked her if he loved her. It shouldn't have been a tough question to respond to, she either loved him or not. Tender moments and their lovemaking was still a very recent memory on her mind and she could not deny that she enjoyed, moreover, actually more than that, she loved being with Tony. Why is that her chance meeting with Hector Lord disturbed her inner peace? She wasn't sure, but she just couldn't help thinking about Hector's green eyes, as they tore into hers in a seductive glaze. "No, I have feelings for Tony," she said out loud.

In her kitchen she washed the plastic container after emptying the left over lasagna and it was then she recalled the syringe with the fluid she obtained from Tony's shaving kit case. From her wallet she removed Stacey's phone number and when she answered the phone, Maggie briefly explained what she had and how she got it. There was a momentarily silence at the other end of the line, she thought that perhaps Stacey hung up, but she spoke again and told Maggie that she was going to stop by her house a short time later.

Less than an hour passed by when Stacey showed up just as she promised and Maggie gave her the syringe wrapped into a wash towel. "I will test it tonight," Stacey promised and she looked at Maggie questioningly. "Was there anything written on the container?" She asked.

"Yes, one had MAHA001 and the other one had MAHA002 written on it, this one is from one that ended in 011," Maggie explained.

"I better go and start on it. I will call you as soon as I find out what it is, be safe," she said and gave a friendly hug to Maggie.

Maggie spent the rest of the evening getting the two guest rooms ready, she planned to have her parents stay in the larger one as it had its own bathroom, and the smaller, yet still fairly good size for Tony. After a quick shower she went to bed, watched some television and fell asleep watching the Tonight Show.

The telephone rang at three in the morning and when she answered, she did not know who would call her in the middle of the night. "I am sorry to wake you," she heard Stacey's voice. "I am outside your door, I really need to talk to you right away."

"Give me a second and I'll be right there," Maggie replied and put on her bathrobe, then rushed through the house to the front door. On the small screen she confirmed that it was Stacey so she unlocked the door for her.

Stacey was visibly upset and she threw her small purse on the couch and sat down while not taking her eyes off from Maggie. "What's going on?" Maggie asked noticing Stacey's strange stare. "Please, talk to me," she urged her.

"Honestly, I don't even know where to start," Stacey said and wiped her tired face as if it had water on it. "I think it would be the best if you tell me exactly when you had your first vision?" She asked.

"What?" Maggie asked. "Why is that important?"

"I'll explain later, but you have to give the information first as I don't know all the details," she told Maggie.

Maggie leaned back in her favorite armchair and crossed her arms as she recalled the first time she saw the vision of the white man and white dog. "I had a heart procedure," she began. "They had to sedate me and they could not bring me back for several hours. Normally, they would be able to wake you up in a few minutes. During that time, while I was unconscious, I had the vision. I was told by the white man in my vision that I was *The Gifted One*, it was a mission that God had given me."

"Where was the procedure performed and who was present when you woke up?" Stacey asked.

"It was done in the Good Samaritan Hospital, here in LA, and when I came through, I looked right into my husband, Paul's seemingly worried eyes," she replied.

"What happened later?" Stacey inquired.

"I had a vision that there will be an explosion at Paul's company and it did happen, unfortunately there were some casualties," said Maggie. "The second vision I had was the CU Airline crash and I had the distinct feeling at that time that my parents may also become victims of that crash, luckily they only suffered minor injuries despite that I begged them to leave the RV park where the plane crashed."

"How many visions did you have?" Stacey asked.

"Four, well five, sort of," Maggie said and then she explained. "The third vision came after the explosion when I suffered a concussion. The fourth vision was when KC interrogated Francisco Lugo and she almost got killed. In the original vision she was grabbed by Francisco and almost taken out of the building in a chock hold when the SWAT team shot Francisco. I told KC about that vision so she took precautions, but when I took a nap, I was still in the hospital; I had the same vision with a different ending. I did not have a chance to call KC but I kept praying and whispering her name and that she should put her jacket back on as she had a gun inside her jacket pocket."

"What about when her car exploded?" Stacey wanted to know. "Did you have another vision?"

Maggie shook her head. "No, I just felt it in my heart."

"What do you mean, felt it in your heart?"

"When it happened, my heart began to beat very fast and something in my brain was screaming at me that KC just died," Maggie told her.

"Who was with you when you had your second and third vision?" Stacey asked again.

"The second time it happened right here, at home with Paul sleeping along side me," Maggie told Stacey. "The third time it happened in the hospital, after Captain Vargas had visited me."

Stacey thought about what she just heard and took a deep breath before she told Maggie what she found out. "Before I began, I want to ask you one more thing. Maggie, do you really believe that you are God's *Gifted One?*"

"I honestly don't know what to think but I'd rather not have this "gift" which is more like a curse, so far," she answered.

"When I first tested the substance you gave me, I came across something so unusual and so powerful that I contacted a former colleague of mine at UCLA who teaches toxicology. His name Dr. James Stafford and he was kind enough to drop everything and we did further testing. What you gave me was a hallucinogen drug, one that none of us has ever worked with. It was a combination of diphenhydramine, atropira and three other genetically altered drugs, not mushrooms, or other drugs that normally administered to schizophrenic patents. We also concluded, and this is going to be very hard for you to hear," she stopped for a brief moment, and then she continued. "We believe that MAHA001 and MAHA002, were named after you, MA as Margaret or Maggie, HA for hallucinogen and the numbers just serial numbers. Since we had no sample from the 002 container, we assumed that it would have been even more potent and perhaps even deadly when it got into someone's system."

Maggie's shock was clearly visible on her face and Stacey fully understood that it was very difficult not only to believe, but also to comprehend what she just told her newly found friend. "Are you saying, that someone gave me shots and I had visions as a reaction to that?" She asked, trying to understand the complexity of what she was told.

"It is more complicated than you think and neither James nor I were fully competent to understand how the drugs worked on a larger scale. However, James being one of the most experienced scientist of the toxicology field in the US, believed that the drug stimulated, more commonly said, fed on the information that was already stored in the patient's brain. For example, you knew that Paul was very busy at his new company, so your brain processed that information and relayed it to the drugs that affected part of the brain where all the paranoid impulses were stored." Stacey explained.

"So what you are saying is; Paul had to administer the shot while I was in the hospital, having the heart procedure done?" Maggie asked.

"It is very likely that he injected the hallucinogen agent into your already flowing IV and that is why you were unable to regain consciousness under the normal recovery time," Stacey told her.

"What about seeing the airline crash?" Maggie thought back on her second vision.

"Once again, it had to be Paul," Stacey suggested. "You were expecting your parents to come for visit, right?" Maggie nodded. "Did you look at airline reservations for them perhaps?"

Maggie thought about it and she looked up Stacey's face. "Oh, my God," she covered her mouth in shock. "That's right. Paul and I even discussed which airlines would be the best and we even written down flight numbers and such. Eventually, even without having that vision, my parents decided to take their RV for the trip." Both of them were quiet for a brief time when Maggie recalled yet another vision, the location of the children's bodies at the Arboretum, so she asked Stacey for a possible explanation for that.

"The hallucinogen agent does not have to be injected, it could be put in drinks, juices, coffee and even tea, you do drink all of those and they were readily available to you in your refrigerator. By consuming the hallucinogen agent orally would have been a later reaction, in other words, it would take longer for the body to react versus injecting it. In reference to how did you know about where the bodies were located, it must have been something you heard, Paul said or you read in the newspaper. Have you ever visited the Arboretum?" Stacey asked.

Maggie nodded. "I did a lot of sketching there before I began to paint landscapes and I even painted that cottage, oh, about two years ago."

"The explanation for your vision about what is going to happen to KC is somewhat more difficult. As I mentioned, James told me that a hallucinogen agents works with information already stored in different areas of the brain.

What if you had that vision because of your concerns for KC's well being?" Stacey wondered.

"Paul was already dead, do you think that," she took a brief break before she continued as she had a difficult time saying what she wanted to tell Stacey. "Do you think that Tony injected that into my IV?" She said finally, and then she added. "He was not in the best shape himself and he could barely get out of the bed."

"Did you have many visitors?" Stacey asked.

Maggie shook her head. "No, not really. Of course we had a lot visits from nurses, doctors and therapists, and then there was KC, a priest that Tony mentioned stopped by while I was unconscious," she said and as soon as she said that, she questioningly looked at Stacey who just raised her shoulder.

"That is fairly common in hospitals that a chaplain stops by," she commented. "So you haven't seen his face, right?" Maggie nodded.

"Oh, yes, Captain Vargas also visited us," Maggie added.

Stacey picked up her head when she heard the name. "Captain Vargas? Just how many times did he visit you and Tony?"

"Every day," Maggie informed her. "Tony even asked him to bring me home after I was released from the hospital."

Stacey was puzzled and surprised at the same time. "Maggie, I noticed your laptop on your coffee table, may I use it please?" She asked.

"Of course," Maggie replied and handed the laptop over to Stacey. "Why don't we go to the dining room and while you boot it up, I could make some coffee." She suggested.

"That would be great, thanks." Stacey replied and followed Maggie into the dining room and began to work on the computer. She logged into the police department's data base and being a forensic specialist for most of the Los Angeles police force, although her work location was in the same building where KC worked, she had special access to just about everything concerning criminal data, such as their entire backgrounds, fingerprints, as well as data pertaining to police officers. She glanced toward the kitchen and cued up Captain Geraldo Vargas and waited for Maggie to join her. She appeared shortly with the freshly brewed coffee and some Oreo cookies.

"Okay, here we go," Stacey said and began to read. "Captain Geraldo Vargas was assigned into his present position four years ago. He was transferred from New York City, from the Bronx to be exact. There is nothing alarming in his career, according to his records, he received several citations for his outstanding service in the community, especially in the crime ridden Puerto Rican neighborhood where he brought back peace and order only within one year at that division."

"Where was he born?" Maggie asked. Stacey brought back the website to the desktop and looked it up.

"He was born in New York City to Puerto Rican parents, hmmm," she murmured. Maggie hesitated and then asked Stacey to look up Tony's background. "Here you go, Antonio Morales, age 36, never been married," Stacey smiled when she looked up at Maggie but her face reflected nothing less than concern. She continued. "Born in San Juan, Puerto Rico, enrolled in criminal justice studies at the University of Puerto Rico where after two years, he switched to theology and at age 26 he became an ordained Catholic Priest. He remained in San Juan under the leadership of Monsignor Salerno at the San Xavier Catholic Church in San Juan. After four years of priesthood, he left the church to return to college where he finished his criminal justice studies and graduated four years ago. He joined the San Juan Police Department got his college degree at the University of San Juan from criminal justice. He requested a transfer here, to Los Angeles and he arrived a few months ago, eventually taking over Detective Matthews' job, and became the partner of KC. Now this is cute," Stacey said and smiled.

"What is cute?" Maggie asked.

"Under miscellaneous personal data, they ask if he had any nicknames and he said, he was previously called "El Padre". Stacey read to her.

When Maggie heard the word "*El Padre*" she spilled her coffee. "What is wrong?" Stacey asked.

"On that thumb drive, in some of the Spanish language emails, Paul is referring to the alarming presence of "*El Padre*". Paul wrote that they have to watch out because he distanced himself from their real cause." Maggie reminded Stacey, who minimized her webpage and looked up the email on the thumb drive that Maggie was talking about. She was right.

"I am on your side, but it could be just a coincidence, maybe he just called him "El Padre" because he joined the police force after being a priest," Stacey suggested.

"He never mentioned a single word about that part of his life. As a matter of fact, he told me that he was born right here in LA, even KC told me that. How come she didn't know that he was from Puerto Rico?" Maggie said her thoughts out loud.

Stacey shrugged. "I honestly don't know. Maybe she trusted him," she suggested.

"My life is turning into a pile of lies and deceits," Maggie whispered and wiped the tears off from her face.

"What are you going to do now? Will you still allow him to stay here?" Stacey asked Maggie as she was about log off from the computer.

"Wait," Maggie yelled excitedly. "What did you say, what does Tony's resume say about a Monsignor?" She asked. Stacey looked again and she repeated the priest name as Monsignor Salinas. "There was an email address in one of the emails, it was MON.SAL@ n.mail.pr, Tony's former superior. I wonder what was the connection between Paul and the Monsignor?"

"Now that is a question for another day," Stacey said and logged off from the computer. "Listen, you need to get some rest, it's almost morning. You have a big day tomorrow with your parents arriving and perhaps Tony coming to your home." She told Maggie as she headed toward the front door.

"Are you going to stop by later, like in the evening?" Maggie said and her question sounded more like a request than anything else. Stacey smiled.

"Of course," she gave a hug to Maggie before leaving. "I still have some research to do. Call me if you need anything else."

CHAPTER TWENTY-EIGHT

MAGGIE WAS LYING in bed for another hour before sleep finally closed her eyes. It was difficult for her to comprehend all what she heard and what she had learned. Now that she knew the truth of what may have happened during the past months, everything seemed even more confusing to her. All those lies, all those deceits by those whom she thought she loved, all those whom she trusted. She was not a *Gifted One* after all. Maggie realized that for some reason she became a cruel target of either an experiment or just simply being drugged to believe that she had the power to foresee disasters or perhaps prevent them. Even that was questionable. Maggie thought that why would anyone want to prevent something that was purposely planned? Perhaps there is where the mystery lies? Perhaps, just perhaps there was the division within the terrorist group, perhaps one tried to accomplish objectives thru terrorists' acts and another wanted a peaceful solution.

She woke up almost at noon. Her sleep was dreamless and peaceful and she could not believe how rested and energetic she felt. Her head and thinking was never so clear, as if her body tuned itself up. She showered, got dressed and had some cereal that she did not feel hungry enough to eat. Maggie held her phone in her hand for a long period of time, she tried to decide if she should call Tony or not, and if she did, what would she say to him? She put the phone down and booted up her laptop as she curled up on the couch.

The phone rang around one thirty in the afternoon and she was tempted to answer it, but instead, she let the answering machine respond. "Hi Maggie," she heard Tony's voice. "Darling, I am afraid I have some bad news. The doctor refused to release me because the early morning blood test showed the signs of highly elevated white blood cells. Dr. Jenkins said that he thought that there was an infection around the incision on my chest, so I will be here another couple of more day. I am not happy, but I can't do very much about it, they started to give me antibiotics in my IV. I hope that this voice mail will catch you in time before coming for a visit. I hope to see you later. I love you, Maggie."

"Whatever," Maggie murmured and typed in the name Monsignor Salinas in the Yahoo search engine, finding several entries. She clicked on images and when she saw the picture of Monsignor Salinas, the laptop almost fell out of her hands. Salinas looked like the mirror image of Paul, an older version of him. She began to read the information. *"Cardinal Rodolfo Salinas was born in San Juan, Puerto Rico, February 11, 1958 to Inez Santos and Juan Lugo. His teenage, unmarried parents were unable to provide proper care for their infant son and placed him with foster parents, Benicio and Roslyn Salinas who a year later adopted the little boy. The Salinas family was devout Catholic and it did not come as a surprise to them that after graduation, Rodolfo announced his desire to become a priest. After eight years of required theological studies, Rodolfo Salinas became an ordained Catholic Priest and received his first parish in the city of Aibonito, located at the highest elevation of the island of Puerto Rico. His involvement with helping the poor and the misfortunate, brought him into the attention of the Vatican and soon after he quickly rose in the ranks of the church. By the time Father Salinas was forty-two years old, he was a Monsignor."* Maggie's reading was interrupted by another phone call that according to the caller ID came from the Hatfield Funeral Home. A polite and somber sounding man informed her that her late husband's ashes were available to either be picked up or have a memorial service planned at the funeral home itself.

Maggie thanked the person who probably wanted to get paid for the services rendered, and she promised him that she would stop by and pick up the urn either on the following day or a day after. She returned her attention to the Internet information on Monsignor Salinas as there were more interesting things to read. *"Monsignor Salinas rising to a possible higher office, as some suggested was very much possible sometime in the future was abruptly halted when an article appeared in a major Puerto Rican newspaper, that Salinas fathered a child while he attended his theological education. The alleged family came forward when their son refused to acknowledge his real family, Guadalupe and Jesus Morales, because, according to the newspaper, Monsignor Salinas brainwashed their son, Antonio.*

While he attended college, Antonio changed his curriculum and enrolled theological studies to become a priest. It was at that time that Guadalupe made a confession to her husband, Jesus, that while in college, she was raped by Salinas and the product of that crime was a child who was born to the newlywed couple. Jesus approached by then high ranked church official, who of course denied the desperate mother's claim and refused Jesus' request to talk to his son who eventually become a parish priest at the same church that was under Salina's jurisdiction.

A short time later, the desperate parents approached a relative of theirs who was a journalist and he ran the story in his newspaper. Soon, dozens of other women came forward and accused the Cardinal with rape throughout his years serving as a parish priest. Monsignor Salinas denied all allegations as fabrications and he claimed Father Morales choose himself not to be in contact with his family, and that he was going to sue the Morales family as well as the newspaper for defamation of character.

The trial however never took place after Guadalupe and Jesus Morales were found brutally murdered in their home during an apparent burglary attempt. Their relative's article regarding their death raised a strong suspicion and the journalist hired a well-known attorney to look into Monsignor Salinas' private doings. The attorney's investigators discovered that Salinas himself found his birth parents and became close to his twin brothers, Paulo and Eduardo Lugo, who were heavily involved in a nationalist movement. Their influence was evident in the sermons Cardinal Salinas performed, as they were filled of hatred toward those who wouldn't allow Puerto Rico to be independent from any other country, particularly the United States. His sermons were so full of venom that the attendance in his church steadily declined to the point that the Vatican could no longer look the other way.

The attorney, who was the journalist relative of the Morales family hired, collected over two dozen sworn affidavits from women who claimed to be the victims of Monsignor Salinas. He had a dangerous appetite for rape and other sadistic misconducts, so the attorney forwarded a letter regarding Salinas' conducts, along with the affidavits to the Vatican. He also expressed suspicion of the Cardinal's direct or indirect involvement with the murder of the Morales family. His actions, although it did not produce a court hearing, had a profound effect and Monsignor Salinas was called to the Vatican to answer the allegations, which he vehemently denied. Apparently the Vatican believed the lawyer and the journalist so much so, that Monsignor Salinas was unceremoniously excommunicated from the church with an effective immediately date.

It was suspected that after his separation from the church, he became closely involved in the Red December *terrorist organization's activities, especially after the disappearance of his brother, Paulo Lugo. Although it was never proven, his organization was involved with several deadly attacks against US properties and companies in Puerto Rico. Former Monsignor Salinas whereabouts at this point is unknown."*

Maggie looked at the painting above the fireplace mantel. She painted that beautiful landscape, one of her very first after her return from Puerto Rico and shortly before her marriage to Paul. At that time she did not suspect that someday she would become a well known painter, and that Paul turned out to be not only a respected Nobel Prize winner physicist, but nothing more than a common criminal, a wolf in the skin of a sheep.

It was getting late in the afternoon when she heard the sound of a vehicle stopping outside her house. She looked at the security screen and her heart began to fill with joy seeing her parents getting out of the SUV that they were renting. She opened the door and rushed out to welcome them. Maggie had never been happier to see her parents, and they seemed relatively well, but most importantly, they were alive.

They did not have much to carry in as most of their clothes were destroyed inside their RV that burned out completely after being hit by part of the broken up airplane. Her mother hugged her as they walked into the house. It was not their first visit but because they liked the large house, they always complimented her for the decorations and how spic-and-span the place looked.

A short time later, when they settled in, they gathered up in the living room. Maggie offered them food and drink, but all they wanted to hear is what happened to her and in her surroundings. It took Maggie over a half an hour to fill them in with all the details, and by the time she was finished, her parents' faces expressed deep concern and shock of what they just heard. "I am alright," Maggie assured them. "I never thought that I was special and I truly hated those visions because they were frightening."

"Honey, it just so hard to believe what you said about Paul," her father said. "He was nothing but nice, kind and caring to us. I always thought about him more like a son than a son-in-law and now as it turned out, he actually wanted to kill you? You understand how difficult it is for me, for us, to believe that?" He shook his head.

"Now you know how I must feel. I was married to a monster and I didn't notice anything. And now I have a problem with Tony. I am not sure yet how I am going to handle the situation with him, but it will come to me when I see him." As if it was on cue, the phone rang and Maggie checked the caller ID, it was Tony. She picked up the phone to answer. "Hi, Tony," she said calmly. Her parents turned Maggie's way but she waved at them that it was okay. "How are you feeling?"

"I missed you, I thought that you are coming to visit," Tony complained gently. "Is everything alright with you?" He asked.

"I am very sorry that I didn't make it to the hospital. I got busy in the morning and then my parents finally arrived," she announced.

"I understand," he told her. "That's great that they got here safe and sound."

"How are you feeling?" Maggie asked after a moment of awkward silence.

"I guess the antibiotic is kicking in, my fever is down and I managed to eat some yummy green Jell-O," he tried to joke. All of a sudden Maggie did not know what to say. "Is everything alright?" Tony asked again. "You are awfully quiet, lost for words." He commented.

"I am sorry, maybe I am just a little bit tired, I was up late last night," Maggie told him, which was the truth. "How about if I let you get some rest and I will see tomorrow for certain."

"I wanted to ask you if Captain Vargas talked to you yet?" Tony asked.

"About what?" She inquired.

"KC's memorial service is tomorrow afternoon. I wish I can make it but I don't think that Dr. Jenkins wants me to mingle with people yet." He told her.

"No, he hasn't called me yet, but I am sure that he will," she answered.

"I love you, Maggie," Tony said quietly before saying goodbye.

"Me, too," Maggie replied, incapable to say those words to him.

The moment she hung up the phone it rang again. "Hello," she replied.

"It's Captain Vargas," said the caller. "I am sorry that I didn't call you any sooner, but KC's memorial service will be held at four o'clock tomorrow afternoon. At her parents' request, she will be buried in Kentucky," he informed her.

"Thank you, Captain Vargas. I just got off the phone with Tony and he told me about it too, but it's good to know that you think of me. I am going to be there for certain," she told him.

"Excellent, see you tomorrow then," he said and ended the call.

Maggie made some of her mother's favorite Oolong tea, some hot chocolate for her father and served them in the living room. They were telling her about their trip before and after they got to Albuquerque, when the doorbell rang. "It's a regular Grand Central Station here," her father remarked.

Maggie confirmed that the visitor was a friend and opened the door for Stacey.

She entered and handed her a bag with some German pastries she picked up on her way to Maggie's house. "Their cheesecake is fabulous, if you are not on the diet," she remarked after handing Maggie the bag.

"My parents finally arrived," Maggie informed her.

"Great," Stacey said and introduced herself to Robert and Melanie. "It's good to meet you. Maggie is a wonderful lady and she is a great artist." She told them as she took as seat in the armchair.

"Is there anything new?" Maggie asked.

"Nothing worth mentioning just yet," Stacey said. "I sent the test results to the FBI for further analysis, it will be a while before we hear back from them, they always have a backlog on non-priority work."

"I read some interesting information regarding Monsignor Salinas," Maggie told her. "Remember the connection we wondered about he and Paul?"

"Yes, I remember," Stacey recalled.

"Well, apparently they were brothers," Maggie told her and reached for the laptop on the coffee table. "Wait until you see his picture."

Stacey was surprised to see the photo of the Monsignor and the photo Maggie showed her of her late husband, Paul. Her parents were equally surprised how much the two men looked alike. "Where is he now?" Stacey asked.

"Disappeared, according to the Internet," Maggie replied.

"So he can be anywhere, including here," Stacey suggested. "That is serious food for thoughts."

Maggie brought some small plates from the kitchen and they all had a piece of German cheesecake and all agreed that it was almost as good as the usual New York cheesecakes. "Are you coming for KC's memorial service?" Stacey asked. Maggie nodded. "How is Tony doing?" Stacey wanted to know.

Maggie told her about the infection that set in and that she did not go see Tony that day. She added that Tony may suspect something, but she also mentioned that she was not sure how she was going to handle the situation. One thing was for certain; she no longer wanted him in her home.

"That would be the best for all concerned," Stacey said and Maggie's parents agreed. "By the way, did you have any dreams, nightmares or visions?" She asked.

"No, nothing like that," Maggie told her. "As a matter of fact, I slept like a baby."

"I think that whatever they injected is wearing off," Stacey concluded. "It has been two days since you came home and about five since you had your latest vision."

"It's good not to have those visions of despair," Maggie commented.

"You don't feel bad not been *The Gifted One*?" Stacey asked. Maggie shook her head. "That's good, because it seems to me, you are special already without any of those additional talents." Stacey complimented her.

"I like you," Melanie, Maggie's mother said and laughed. "Anybody who recognizes our daughter for what she is about is a good person."

It was getting late and Maggie's parents had a long day driving behind them. They excused themselves and retired for the evening. Stacey stayed for a little while longer and after reminiscing about KC, Stacey also left for her home.

Maggie kept thinking about Tony and what she was going to say to him on the following day that promised to be a day of sorrow for many reasons.

CHAPTER TWENTY-NINE

MAGGIE'S PARENTS INSISTED on joining her at KC's memorial service, by chance at the Hatfield Funeral Home where she was supposed to pick up Paul's ashes. Before joining the mourners, she talked to the funeral director and wanted to pay for Paul's cremation, but the man told her discretely that they will bill her and that she could pick up the urn on her way out. She thanked the man and joined her parents inside a large, nicely and soothingly decorated room where they were surprised to see that the place was almost filled with KC's colleagues and even uniformed officers.

Stacey noticed that Maggie and her parents were standing in the entrance, so she made her way to walk them where she saved seats for them. The casket was closed for obvious reasons, but a beautiful picture with a smiling KC was placed on the nicely carved brown colored easel. Maggie walked up to the casket and placed a white rose on top of it. She kissed the casket and whispered. "Rest in peace KC, you were a good friend to me."

She desperately tried not to cry but she failed miserably. With her mother on one side and her father on the other, they both reached for her hand and held it throughout the service. Captain Vargas, speaking for the departments where KC used to work, he emphasized her dedication to her work and that he could always rely on KC's willingness to go not only an extra mile but a marathon. A couple of detectives talked about her sharpness and kindness at the same time, and retired Detective Matthews, KC's next to last partner told everyone that if he ever had a daughter, he wanted her to be like KC. Stacey also stepped up to the microphone and talked about their friendship without mentioning anything concrete about their great many collaborations, but she did tell the crowd that KC was the best friend she ever had, someone who would lay down her life for her fellow man. She looked at Maggie and smiled.

After the forty-five minute memorial service, they picked up Paul's ashes in a white ceramic urn. The funeral director politely asked her what her intentions were for her late husband's ashes. He explained that some people keep the ashes at home, some want to scatter them at the deceased favorite place, or if she wanted to place it in a mausoleum. A brief second later Maggie made the decision and asked the man what place would he suggest. He asked her to wait for just one moment and indeed he returned almost right away with a business card for the Home of Peace Memorial Park & Mausoleum. Maggie thanked him for their services and they left the funeral home.

She told her parents that if they did not mind, she would rather take care of Paul ashes right away, as she didn't want to be in the same house with him, meaning his ashes. They could not agree more. An hour later, Maggie handed over Paul's ashes into the capable hands of the cemetery's official. She made the selection of the location and she told them that she would return in couple of days to visit and settle the incidentals.

Before they went to her favorite Chinese restaurant for dinner, where she and KC had their last lunch together, her parents urged her to drive to the hospital to deal with the "Tony" issue first and foremost. The security guard recognized her and opened the door for her to enter. "There is my girl," Tony said and he immediately smiled seeing her in the doorway.

"Hello, Tony," she said, allowing herself a brief smile. She glanced at the other bed in the room that she once occupied and which was empty. "How are you doing, did they get rid of the infection?" She asked.

"I am doing much better," Tony said and got up from the chair where he was sitting to embrace her. She did not hug him back which immediately triggered an alarm in him. He sat back down and showed the other chair to Maggie, who took it. "How was the memorial service?" Tony asked.

"Other than very sad, there was a full house, everybody complimented her for what she truly was. Ironically, it was the same funeral home who handled the cremation of Paul," she told him. He did not reply. "I took his ashes to the cemetery to place him in a mausoleum, I suppose that doesn't make me a nice and loving widow. He didn't even have a memorial service and he was not even announced in the newspapers, other than that he was murdered."

"I am sorry," Tony murmured.

"Sorry for what, Tony?" Maggie asked him in a quiet, calm voice.

"That you have to lose a husband and a friend almost at the same time," he replied and reached for her hand but she pulled it away.

"Tony, I need to ask you something," Maggie said. "You told me that you would not lie to me, so I hold you to your words."

"Of course," he promised.

"Did you kill Paul?" Maggie blurted out. The expression on Tony's face was clear and although she wanted to hear it coming from his lips, she already knew the answer.

"Before I answer your question, I need to ask you a question first," Tony told her. She nodded to proceed. "What if you knew that someone you love deeply is in deadly danger? Wouldn't you try to protect that person?" He asked.

"Tony, I would try to warn that person before I used deadly force," she replied.

The concern to her reaction was evident in Tony's eyes, but he had to come clean with the woman he loved. "I found out from an email correspondence that Paul was planning to kill you. I did not know when, I just knew that time was running out."

"I need to hear that you say that you took Paul's life," Maggie said stubbornly.

Tony got up and stepped in front of her. "Are you wearing a wire or have a tape recorder in your purse?" He asked. She got up and opened her blouse, showing her front and back to him, then she opened her purse and emptied it on the bed.

"It's just me Tony, I need to know." She said calmly and put everything away.

"I shot Paul on his way home from the restaurant. I was extremely concerned for your well being," Tony confessed his crime without any remorse. "I wanted to make sure that KC knew that I did it out of concern for you. If I felt that it was an unjust action, I would not have given her my gun, which I knew that she would take to the lab. I would not have given her access to my computer where I saved all the emails that your husband sent to his brother." He said trying to justify Paul's killing.

Maggie looked at him when he pulled a chair in front of her. It was she who reached for his hands at that time. He turned her hands over and kissed them, and then he pressed his face to them. "Tony, is there anything else you want to tell me? This is the time, I repeat, this is the time that would make or break us," she told him.

"I beg you not to talk like that," he said when Maggie pulled her hands back. "I love you like I never loved anyone in my life. When you walked into that room at Matthews' retirement party, you took my breath away and I knew, I knew," he emphasized those two words. "That you are the person I want to be with, the very person I want to spend the rest of my life with."

"Tony, what is MAHA 001 and MAHA 002?" Maggie asked straight out and the shock on Tony's face was vivid and priceless. It was a total, undeniable shock for a question that he certainly did not expect.

"How do you know about those?" Tony asked quietly.

"Was I injected with those so I would have visions, or hallucinations?" Maggie asked without mercy.

Tony stared in front of him before he lifted his head. Maggie noticed that tears were shining in his eyes. "I fought so hard not to do that to you, even before I ever met you. I fought against using it on an innocent person because it was clearly a sinful thing, but Paul and Eduardo had it no other way. Paul was convinced that you could be useful for the *Red December* organization. He said that because you visualize your paintings and portrait, you could be influenced by those injections to see upcoming disasters that *Red December* was about to commit."

"But that doesn't make any sense," Maggie said not understanding the philosophy behind that reasoning. "Didn't they think that I would contact the authorities?"

"It is a reverse philosophy," Tony tried to explain. "If you contact the authorities, they counted on people such as Riggs at the FAA, who would think that it was just another phony psychic and they will ignore the warning. He even blew up his own company because he found out that Christopher Collins was working for the CIA."

"Did you inject me with MAHA001 or 002?" Maggie asked, not taking her eyes off from Tony. He did not blink; he placed his hands over his heart.

"God strike me down if I ever have done anything in any way to harm you," he told her and she had a feeling that he was telling the truth about that.

"I saw those small containers in your shaving kit," Maggie remarked.

Tony got up and went to the bathroom and brought out the kit, the containers and syringes were gone. "I don't know who put them there, I had not even seen them, I only knew that they existed, and now they are gone." He said, not understanding their disappearance himself.

"Who came to visit you this morning or afternoon?" Maggie asked.

"Captain Vargas and the priest," he told her.

Maggie heard enough. Her heart was breaking but she had made the decision that she knew that may haunt her for a long time to come. She got up and picked up her purse. "*Padre, te escuché hablar español a Monseñor Salinas en el teléfono. Usted mantuvo un gran secreto de mí, el secreto que utilizó para ser sacerdote, que monseñor Salinas como su mentor mientras servía como un sacerdote, pero la mayoría de todos, le han fallado a decirme que eran en realidad el sobrino de Pablo.* (Father, I heard you talking Spanish to Monsignor Salinas on the phone. You kept a great secret from me, the secret that you used to be a priest, and that Monsignor Salinas was your mentor while serving as a priest. But most of all, you have failed to tell me that you were actually Paul's nephew.)"

Hearing Maggie speaking Spanish made Tony's eyes widen and he collapsed on the bed. *"Sé que el antiguo Monsignore Salinas es su padre natural. Le han matado a sus verdaderos padres no podían testificar que fueron producto de su madre, la violación que ha cometido.* (I know that the former Cardinal Salinas is your natural father. He killed your birth parents so they could not testify that you are a product of your mother's rape, that he committed.)"

Maggie walked to the door; she stopped and turned around to look at Tony's devastated face. *"¿Dígame Capellán de El, estuvo eso en los planes de seducirme, también?* (Tell me El Padre, was that in the plans to seduce me, too?)" Tony was visibly shaking as he whispered.

"No, it wasn't planned at all. You came as a blessing into my miserable life," his voice was a man's who knew that he just lost the love of his life, his reason for living.

Maggie was chocking on her tears but she fought them back, she didn't want Tony to see how devastated she felt herself. She took a deep breath before she spoke. *"Tony, yo nunca, jamás quiero verle otra vez.* (Tony, I never, ever want to see you again)."

Her parents did not have to ask her anything, it all showed her face. Once outside the building, Maggie broke down in tears and buried herself in the arms of her loving parents.

CHAPTER THIRTY

SOMETIME DURING THE night Maggie heard a noise but it stopped almost immediately and she went back to a restless sleep. Once again she was not dreaming or had any visions, she just cried herself to sleep from the disappointment she felt about her failed relationship with Tony, whom she thought was capable of giving her what she needed, love, pleasure and a steady happy home. She fell in love with Tony the moment they met, just as he claimed he felt about her, but after leaving his hospital room, Maggie was no longer sure what to believe.

What woke her she wasn't sure, but the noises most definitely were coming from her parents' room. She got dressed quickly and knocked on the door but received no response. "Mom, dad, are you okay?" She asked and once again there was no reply. She turned the doorknob. Her blood froze in her veins seeing her parents all tied up with masking tape across their mouths. She saw pure terror in her parents' eyes and she wanted to rush to free them when the door closed behind her and someone grabbed her by the hair and forced her down on her knees.

The man tied her hands behind her back, and then he grabbed her by the arm and dragged her out of her parents' room into the living room where he pushed her down on the couch. "How did you get in?" She asked the question that was no longer relevant, the intruder was in and no police man or anyone from the security company was trying to break down her front door. She glanced at the large living room window facing the street but it was a little bit hard to see thru the thick lace curtain coming down from the ceiling to the floor.

"So finally I got you all to myself," the former Monsignor Salinas said with a cynical smile on his face. "You have no idea what trouble you put me through and how many family members I have lost along the way." He said calmly and studied her face.

Maggie's heart was beating so fast that she thought that it was going to jump out of her chest. She did not talk to the man who was the mirror image of Paul; he was undeniably Paul's older brother. "Thanks to you, Tony killed my brother, the smartest man I have ever known, who completely understood how important our mission was to free Puerto Rico from under American oppression." He shook his head. "Who could of thought that my son was actually capable to love someone as much as he loved you," he said almost angrily. "Although, once a priest always a priest." He chuckled. "He couldn't handle the pressure that he killed your husband, he just had to give access to his computer to your friend. Because of you, I had to risk my own life to go into the garage of a police station to get rid of her." He actually laughed when he confessed killing KC. He leaned forward, toward Maggie. "You should have seen it, puff, bing, bang, flames, chaos," he gestured with his arms.

"How could you kill innocent people?" Maggie said quietly. "For Christ sake, you were a priest yourself."

"Well, there are good angels in heaven and bad angels in hell. I suppose eventually I will join the band of bad angels, but not just yet," he said and he pulled out a familiar box from his jacket pocket. Maggie shook her head and watched as the former Cardinal took the MAHA002 container and drew almost the entire contents up into a larger syringe. "My dear Margaret, it is payback time. Enjoy your trip," he said and got up to go around the coffee table. Maggie tried to get up but he grabbed her and pushed her down, kneeling on her stomach to prevent her from moving.

The needle almost pierced Maggie's skin when the door came crushing down as the SWAT team rushed in and behind them entered Captain Vargas. All guns were pointing at Salinas as he held the syringe in his right hand, ready to inject the deadly dosage into Maggie's vein. "Put it down," Vargas ordered Salinas. "It is over."

"Far from it," Salinas said defiantly. "You may kill me but our cause will live on. Puerto Rico will be a proud country of her own."

"Put the syringe down," Captain Vargas ordered Salinas on a louder voice.

"Make me," Salinas said and moved his hand with the needle back to Maggie's arm. It only took one single shot and the former Monsignor Salinas rolled off dead from Maggie. She took a deep breath when Vargas removed the bondage from her hands. She rushed into her parents' room and began to remove the nylon handcuffs and the tape from their mouths with Vargas' help while the SWAT team searched the rest of the house, finding nobody and nothing suspicious.

When the SWAT team left, they lifted the damaged door and covered the entrance with it, Captain Vargas re-entered the living room where Maggie sat between her parents on the sofa.

"How did you know?" She asked Captain Vargas after thanking him for saving their lives. Maggie had no doubt that after Salinas killed her, he would have taken her parents' lives as well.

"I got a call from Tony in the middle of the night. He was very distraught and I had great difficulty understanding what he was saying. He told me that you knew everything and that you had broken up with him. He said that he had to confess what he did, he told me that he killed your husband to save your life and he also told us, and he emphasized that it was extremely important that I come to your house immediately because his father, the former Monsignor Salinas will make an attempt to take your and your family's life. And then," he said but he didn't continue. He nervously looked up at Maggie.

"What happened?" Maggie asked squeezing her mother's hand.

"Evidently the uniformed officer dozed off outside his door and Tony removed the cop's service revolver. He …" he swallowed hard before he continued. "Tony shot himself in the head. He is dead, I am very sorry." Vargas finally told her about Tony. Maggie stared at Vargas when all of a sudden everything around her began to spin. She felt her heart speed up and then everything went blank. She whispered one word before losing consciousness. "Tony."

CHAPTER THIRTY-ONE

THE BREEZE SHE felt was warm and calming as she walked across the field covered with colorful flowers. She felt something touching her hand and when she looked down, she noticed a large dog, like the one she had seen in her visions, but this time he had his natural golden color, and he ran besides her, circling her with his tail wagging. She was talking to the dog but she heard no sounds, yet, Maggie knew that the dog understood her.

She followed the dog as he began to run ahead of her. As they reached the end of the meadow, a house appeared in front of her. The building had no particular style, it wasn't baroque, or modern, it was just a pleasant looking place that she wanted to see the inside of it too. Something drew her in there, as if an invisible force pushed her forward and moved her hand to press down the old-fashioned door handle.

"Hello," she said and that time she was able to hear her own voice. "Is anybody here?" She asked. There was no response, so she slowly made her way around the small but tidy kitchen that reminded her of her own, in a smaller scale. She slowly walked into the still pleasant size replica of her living room at home, and then moved down the narrow hallway to find another room, the exact replica of her own big bedroom, once again a smaller version of it.

"Do you like it?" She heard someone asking in the tingling voice that sounded like chimes, but in a human like way. She turned around and saw a beautiful long blonde haired woman standing in the doorway.

"Yes, I do," Maggie replied with a smile. "Where am I?"

"You are at peace," the woman replied.

"Are you an angel?" Maggie wondered out loud.

The woman looked at her and was about to reply, but instead she picked up her head as if she was listening to someone, then she turned around and with the blink of an eye, she was gone. Maggie looked around and she noticed that one by one, the furniture pieces began to disappear as she stood stunned in the middle of the room. Once the furniture disappeared, the walls were gone, too, as if they vaporized in thin air.

Maggie found herself in the middle the field again but the first thing she noticed, the color of the plants began to fade and everything was turning a pure white color. "Oh, no," she said out loud. "Not again."

The white man with the dog, white again, sat on a large white chair in the middle of the field, only steps away from her. There were no white bars in front of him, as if he trusted her somewhat better. She turned around, toward the woods that she walked through earlier and which had beautiful green trees and shrubs; they were also changed into a pure white color. "Why am I here again?" She asked from the white man with the long white beard.

"It is not your time yet to join us," the white man said.

"You told me that I was God's *Gifted One*, it wasn't so. You probably know what happened," Maggie said and looked at the white man who was staring down at her.

"You have not begun to follow your Lord yet," he replied.

Maggie knew a man named Lord, Hector Lord, the new gallery director at her friend Sarah's place, where she held her exhibits. She looked at the white man and she could not believe her eyes. It was just not possible, or was it? The man who was pure white from his head to his toes was smiling at her and then he began to fade into thin air along with the white dog who was also watching her and wagging his tail.

CHAPTER THIRTY-TWO

"MAGGIE, HONEY, CAN you hear me?" She heard her mother's concerned voice. She opened her eyes and saw her parents by her bedside, her father was there along with Dr. McFarland, her cardiologist who treated her once before.

"You gave us a quite a scare," he said after checking her heart.

Maggie glanced at the heart monitor by the wall and her heartbeat couldn't have been better. "What happened?" She asked.

"Well, I suppose you worked yourself up to have a mild heart attack. Luckily you were taking your Flecainide and Metoprolol on a regular basis so you are going to be all right, no new procedure is necessary. You do have to promise me to take it easy," Dr. McFarland said.

"Thank you, I will," Maggie promised.

"I am going to keep you overnight, and if your condition doesn't change, I'll let you go home tomorrow," Dr. McFarland promised and left her room.

"There are some people here who would like to see you," her mother informed her.

"Okay," Maggie agreed. Her mother opened the door and Stacey walked in with a large bouquet of flowers.

"I talked to your doctor and he said that you are doing great," Stacey said and bent down to kiss her on the cheek.

"It's good to see you Stacey," Maggie said and squeezed her new friend's hand.

"Don't scare me like that again," Stacey waved her finger at her. "I can't afford losing another friend." Maggie shook her head. "Okay, now that was said, I have to get back to work, but before I do that, I found someone walking the hallway looking for your room. Do you want to see him?" She asked with nutty smile on her face.

"Who is it?" Maggie asked curiously.

"Lord knows, but he is simply gorgeous," she remarked.

"Okay," Maggie agreed.

A few minutes after Stacey left and her parents were still in the hallway, she heard a knock on the door. "It's open," she said.

The door open and his appearance made Maggie's face blush. "Hello, Margaret," he said and approached her bed. He pulled his arm from behind his back and a dozen pure white roses appeared in front of her.

"I was hoping that you would come to see me," she whispered.

ALTERNATE ENDING # 1

DR. STACEY MOYNIHAN stood by the stainless steel table at the sadly often-used pathology lab and stared at the body in front of her. She acknowledged many times that when she did autopsies, the bodies lost their identities that she was ever so determined to keep alive to find the cause of their deaths, that were mostly homicides. The fact remained that it was a steady flow of murder victims that reached her spotlessly clean work facility at the LA County Coroners Office and there was no end in sight.

The person on the table was not a murder victim, yet she wanted to know exactly what happened to the woman who left life much too early, in her opinion as well as in others. She knew her only for a year or so, but they shared a mutual memory of a friend, KC, a well liked and admired police detective who was senselessly killed by a car bomb.

Stacey gently touched the woman's face and sighed as she reached for the scalpel. She hesitated with the incision as she thought about the circumstances how they met and why. She shook her head, as she could not believe it, that after what Maggie Davis-Lord went through, her life ended so unexpectedly not to violence, rather, a normally painful but also a most delightful event, the birth of a child.

She recalled the phone call that she received from Maggie's OB/GYN as her friend went into labor. Maggie, for some reason wanted Stacey to be there, it was not something that they discussed earlier, but just the same, she dropped what she doing and rushed to the hospital where Maggie was about to give birth.

Although she did not scrub in, she put on surgical garbs and joined Maggie's husband, Hector Lord at the head of Maggie's bed in the delivery room. She took her hand on the side where she had an IV going into her vein, Hector held her other hand and occasionally he gently touched Maggie's forehead to dry off the perspiration.

Stacey never had a child of her own but she witnessed childbirth many times, not to mention that she delivered a few babies herself during her hospital residency, so she knew the routine by heart. Maggie whispered a quiet *thank you* to her when she took her place by her side and Hector smiled at her gratefully for being there, too.

Maggie also said something to Stacey and it got her worry because she knew from Maggie's past that she could see things ahead before they happened, and although they turned out to be drug induced visions, she never did shake the thought that perhaps there was something natural in Maggie's talent to be able to not only predict but to paint the fore coming events.

"If something happens to me," she said to Stacey in a clearly audible voice that was even heard by the obstetrician, Dr. Karen Welsh. "I want you to make sure that my son is named Salvator Lord."

"You can tell that to the doctor after delivery," Stacey suggested. Maggie slowly shook her head.

"I won't be around that long," she said in a weaken voice. Stacey looked at Hector Lord's face and he was smiling down at his wife. She also noticed that Maggie had a smile on her face as well. *What is going on?* Stacey thought.

Maggie did as she asked, she pushed with all her might, which was every energy cell that was still working in her body, and then a beautiful sound was heard. Her son Salvator relayed to the world that he arrived. Stacey picked up her head when the alarm of the vital signs machine went off. Maggie's blood pressure was dropping and from the frantic actions of her obstetrician was a clear sign that something was terribly wrong.

As she was holding onto Maggie's hand, she checked her pulse and became panicky and yelled at Dr. Welsh, inquiring what was going on. Dr. Welsh ordered the nurses to bring more supplies and within minutes the door opened and more blood arrived. Stacey could not help but to notice the large amount of blood that was soaking the floor. It was then that she knew that Maggie Davis-Lord was dying.

"Oh, no, God, please don't take her," she whispered and looked at Maggie's husband. It occurred to her that Hector's eyes were calm and that he was smiling, an odd thing to do when it was clear that Maggie had perhaps only minutes, or perhaps only seconds to live.

"Don't be afraid my love," Hector said to Maggie. Stacey could not take her eyes off from Hector. His calmness was out of the ordinary and it was very soothing and comforting. "I'll be with you all of the way and always." Stacey broke her stance from Hector and glanced at Maggie. She was smiling too and then, she turned her attention to Stacey.

"When I am gone, please take Salvator to my parents," she asked in an extremely weak voice. Stacey nodded and then she felt Maggie's hand relax.

"No, please don't," she pleaded with her as she looked at Hector. Their eyes met and Hector smiled at her. She could not understand or interpret his smile. Stacey blinked and when a second later she looked again, Maggie was dead and Hector was gone. Where did he go and how did he get out the door so fast when there were nurses everywhere?

"Did anyone see Hector?" She asked from Dr. Welsh who just called the time of death. She shook her head and she looked around too.

"Did anybody seen him leave?" She asked but there were negative responses from everybody. "Now that is strange," Dr. Welsh remarked. "Didn't he want to say goodbye to Maggie?"

Stacey, not only as a doctor but also as a human being was puzzled by the chain of events, such as how Maggie knew that she was going to die and yet her husband, whose name was "Lord" remained calm as if he knew too and as if… Stacey shook her head because what she thought was simply impossible.

Before leaving the delivery room where silence rescinded with the exception of the baby's cry, she asked Dr. Welsh to send over Maggie's remains to the Coroner's Office. She nodded that she would and Stacey departed. She glanced at Maggie's parents waiting in the lobby but she decided to let Dr. Welsh do her job and relay the bad news about Maggie and the good news about their grandson, who was named Salvator, without an *e* on the end of his name.

She left the hospital and drove to the art gallery where Maggie Davis-Lord, formerly Maggie Davis-Anderson, had her latest art exhibit a few weeks before her baby's birth. Sarah Stern, the gallery's director was talking to a client but she joined Stacey a few minutes later.

"How is my *Gifted One* doing?" Sarah asked semi jokingly but she immediately realized that Stacey had tears in her eyes. It was certainly not a good sign. Stacey talked to her for a while comforted her and sat with her after breaking the news about Maggie.

"Just how long did you know Hector?" She asked Sarah.

"Not long," she replied. "He came in one day, looking for a job. He did not have a resume but he made me believe that he knew all old masters as well as modern artists, so I hired him on the spot. He seemed to be very special, he was very good at talking to people." She added.

"He is gone too," Stacey remarked.

"What do you mean gone too?" Sarah echoed her visitor's words. Stacey closed her eyes and took a deep breath.

"I am going to say some things that perhaps don't make sense. What if she was indeed selected by a higher power unknown to us, to be *The Gifted One* to deliver something very special? If I may remind you, I am a scientist, a doctor and miracles do not often happen in my line of work if ever, but what I experienced, heard and felt just had to be miracles." She said.

"Tell me an example," Sarah asked.

"Well, it was the calmness in that situation and between Maggie and Hector. It had a certain beauty how they looked at each other. As if both knew that although she would die, she was still going to be all right. Does that make any sense?" Stacey tried to explain. "When I looked at Hector, the goodness and kindness was written all over his face and then, he said something to Maggie in the last moments of her life. He said, *don't be afraid my love, I'll be with you all of the way and always.*" She stopped and looked at Sarah. "May I use your computer?" Sarah nodded.

Stacey cued up the Police Department and later the FBI database that she had privileged access and did a quick search for a person name Hector Lord. None of them who were on the database matched the description of the Hector Lord she met and briefly knew. "As if he never existed," she murmured. Sarah touched her arm. Stacey turned to the woman.

"What if," Sarah began. "What if he was HIM and he came for her but not before HE gave the world a new savior."

Sarah shook her head. "It's way too much of a miracle."

"Just think about it," Sarah insisted. "You speak Latin, and I learned some too in college, but what does Salvator means in Latin?" Stacey stared at her and shook her head. "It means *"Savior"* isn't it?"

It was than that the two women wept.

ALTERNATE ENDING # 2

"PUSH, MAGGIE, JUST one more big push," she heard the doctor's encouraging words. She felt that her entire body was on fire as the pain ripped through her, and then she felt relief when her baby finally arrived into the world. Maggie looked up at her husband, Hector and could not understand the reason why he had tears in his eyes. Were they tears of happiness or was there something wrong? He bent over her and gently tapped her forehead and face that was covered with perspiration, the sign of her hard labor while giving birth.

She turned her head and noticed frantic activity in the delivery room. Another doctor whom she recognized as Dr. McFarland, her cardiologist was rushing in. Her OB/GYN was busy doing something in her private area but Dr. McFarland and even her husband was staring at the instruments above her head. She knew that it was monitoring her blood pressure and her heart monitor, probably other things as well.

Hector was telling her that they had a beautiful baby girl and as soon as he said that, she had to ask. "Is she all right? I haven't heard her crying yet," she mumbled. She began to feel incredibly weak and before she closed her eyes, she heard Hector's voice.

"She is going to be just fine," he said quietly and the last thing Maggie saw before she fell into a deep sleep were the teardrops that rolled down on Hector's sad, yet smiling face.

Maggie was not certain how long she slept but when she opened her eyes, she felt refreshed and healthier as she had ever felt. She glanced up from her easel where she was painting the scenery and looked over to the baby carriage where her daughter that Hector named *Angel* was peacefully sleeping with a baby smile on her beautiful face.

It was incredibly peaceful around her and the birds in the forest to her right entertained her with their chirping and mate calling. She smiled as she truly enjoyed those sounds and they were not disturbing the baby either. The air was clean and the temperature couldn't have been anymore perfect. Although she was sitting in the middle of a meadow with her easel set up as usual, she could feel, more like sense that someone was approaching.

She did not fear the person because in her heart she knew that it was the place where there was no violence of any kind, where only eternal tranquility existed. She did not have to turn around to recognize the voice, she had heard it before more than once, but it was the first time that she actually heard the dog bark. Maggie looked over at the baby with concern that the dog's barking woke her child and indeed, Angel's eyes were open. She had a gorgeous smile on her face. The dog sniffed the baby and happily wagged his tail.

"I am pleased to see that you settled in nicely," said the man with the deep voice. Maggie smiled at him and nodded.

"Oh, yes, everything I need is all right here," she said and motioned around her.

"What are you working on?" Asked the white man with the long white beard and the long white hair and stepped next to Maggie.

"It's my first portrait," Maggie replied.

"Indeed," the white man said. "You are a very talented painter."

Maggie thanked him and sensing that he was leaving. She told him to stop by again sometime. He promised that he would. Maggie went back to painting. It was a self-portrait in her image all right, her white face, her white hair and her white skin.

ALTERNATE ENDING # 3

MAGGIE SAT IN front of her canvas and stared at the beautiful landscape that she was painting and which was about to be finished. She glanced toward the large window from where the sun brightened up her lovely studio. Maggie loved their new home, located just outside Malibu. It was spacious and it even had a separate entrance for her studio. There was a smaller house in the back of the yard; which is where her parents moved when they decided that they did not want to be separated from her ever again.

The house was quiet; her two beautiful and playful new Shelties were lying by her feet while she painted. The door opened and he entered carrying freshly brewed coffee, just the way she liked it, her only cup for the day. She looked at him with so much love that he couldn't help it but to smile. She was the love of his life and he would have laid his life down for her if it was necessary, but those days were gone when her life was in danger.

She couldn't explain where the year and half since all those horrible things happened had gone, but time passed so fast as if it was a rush of cool air. He placed the tray on a small table that was in a hand's reach from where she was sitting and knelt down in front of her. "How are you feeling?" He asked and placed his hands on her growing stomach.

"I am fine, we are fine," Maggie replied with a smile on her face. "Did you feel that?" She asked. He looked up at her and she bent down to kiss him.

"He moved just as I touched you," Hector replied.

"He already knows that you love him," Maggie said and touched her husband's shoulder length blonde hair.

"Thank you for marrying me," Hector said. Maggie laughed, as she always did when he said that to her. "You are my God sent."

You have no idea, Maggie thought and lovingly smiled at him. "I love you Hector," she replied. "I am a very lucky woman to have you as my husband."

"I am truly a fortunate man," Hector said and kissed her. Just then he glanced down on the painting that Maggie was working on. Strangely, the entire canvas had a black background and the characters in the painting were pure white. He was surprised because he thought that Maggie was already over those visions where he saw God's left hand angel who carried messages to the selected few. "It has been a while since you saw him, can you recall his face?" Hector asked with concern.

Maggie smiled and turned her head to the left of the canvas where on a heavy chair sat a pure white man with a pure white dog by his feet. She looked up at her husband who followed her eyes but saw nothing at the space where she mysteriously focused her attention. "I'll leave you to it." Hector said and headed toward the door where he turned around one more time. "Don't stay up to late." He told her.

When the door closed, the white man with the long white hair and long white beard smiled and said. "Maggie, my dear, we have to stop meeting like this." His dog's barking followed his words. Maggie sighed and went about her painting.

Edwards Brothers Malloy
Thorofare, NJ USA
February 15, 2017